PENGUIN BOOKS

LAUGHABLE LOVES

Milan Kundera was born in Czechoslovakia. He worked as a labourer, then as a jazz musician and finally ended up devoting himself to literature. For several years he was a professor at the Prague Institute for Advanced Cinematographic Studies, where his students were the creators of the Czech New Wave in film.

After the Russian invasion in 1968, he lost his post and saw all his books removed from the public libraries in his country. In 1975 he settled in France, and in 1979 the Czech government, responding to the publication of *The Book of Laughter and Forgetting* (1970; Penguin, 1982), revoked his Czech citizenship.

The Joke, his first novel, and this collection of stories, *Laughable Loves*, appeared in print in Prague before 1968. His other novels have not been allowed publication in his homeland. *Life is Elsewhere* won the Prix Médicis for the best foreign novel published in France in 1973, and *The Farewell Party* (1976) won a similar prize, the Premio Mondello, for the best foreign novel published in Italy in 1978. In 1981 he was awarded the American Prize 'Commonwealth Award' for his work and a year later the Prix Europa-Littérature. In 1984 he won the Jerusalem Prize, awarded every two years to 'the writer who has contributed most to the world's understanding of the freedom of the individual in society'. His most recent novel, *The Unbearable Lightness of Being*, received the *Los Angeles Times* Prize for 1984 and was made into a highly acclaimed film. He has also published a collection of essays entitled *The Art of the Novel* (1987).

Kundera now lives in Paris as a French citizen. Since 1980 he has been a Professor at the Ecole des hautes études en sciences sociales. He writes in both Czech and French.

MILAN KUNDERA

——

LAUGHABLE LOVES

TRANSLATED FROM THE CZECH BY
SUZANNE RAPPAPORT

INTRODUCTION BY PHILIP ROTH

PENGUIN BOOKS

PENGUIN BOOKS

Published by the Penguin Group
27 Wrights Lane, London W8 5TZ, England
Viking Penguin Inc., 40 West 23rd Street, New York, New York 10010, USA
Penguin Books Australia Ltd, Ringwood, Victoria, Australia
Penguin Books Canada Ltd, 2801 John Street, Markham, Ontario, Canada L3R 1B4
Penguin Books (NZ) Ltd, 182–190 Wairau Road, Auckland 10, New Zealand

Penguin Books Ltd, Registered Offices: Harmondsworth, Middlesex, England

First published in Czechoslovakia under the title *Smesné lásky* by
Ceskoslovensky Spisovatel 1969
First published in the United States of America by Alfred A. Knopf, Inc., 1974
Published in Penguin Books 1975
15 17 19 20 18 16

Philip Roth's Introduction (in a slightly different form), 'The Hitchhiking Game,' 'Let the Old
Dead Make Room for the Young Dead,' and 'The Golden Apple of Eternal Desire' were printed in
the April 1974 issue of *Esquire* magazine; 'Edward and God' was printed in *The American Poetry
Review*

Made and printed in Great Britain by
Richard Clay Ltd, Bungay, Suffolk
Set in Electra

CONTENTS

INTRODUCING MILAN KUNDERA
by Philip Roth

1

The book that made Milan Kundera famous, and in- famous, in Czechoslovakia was a political novel entitled, un- jokingly, *The Joke*. A direct and realistic book, openly reflec- tive about the issues it raises—proceeding by means of philo- sophical thoughtfulness and accurate observation of a fairly broad spectrum of "politicized" citizens, it is something like a cross between Dos Passos and Camus—*The Joke* is largely con- cerned with the absurdities that wreck the life of a skeptical young Czech party intellectual during the bitter post-war years of Stalinist purges, trials, and other dogmatic enthusiasms. *The Joke* was published in Prague in 1967, at the time when the pressure from writers and intellectuals like Kundera against official government repression was building rapidly toward the spirited national uprising that would become known (at first somewhat romantically—then altogether accurately) as "the Prague Spring." "An attempt," Kundera called the doomed re- form movement that lasted little more than a season, "to create a socialism without an omnipotent secret police; with freedom of the spoken and written word; with a public opin- ion of which notice is taken and on which policy is based; with a modern culture freely developing; and with citizens who have lost their fear."

In January 1968, Alexander Dubček's government—the political offspring of the reform movement—came to power and immediately set out to dismantle the totalitarian machin- ery that had been integral to Communist party rule since the

"Revolution of 1948." According to the inspired slogan of the Dubček government, very soon now in Czechoslovakia there would be "socialism with a human face." Instead, soon enough, Soviet tanks appeared in Prague's Old Town Square, and overnight—the night of August 20, 1968—some 200,000 Russian and other Warsaw Pact soldiers had occupied Czechoslovakia.

Six years later an eighty thousand-man Russian army is still there, largely in the countryside now, hidden from the sight of the demoralized Czechs but close enough to the capital to lend whatever authority is needed to the repressive edicts and punitive decrees of the regime that the Russians have placed back in power. Alexander Dubček is currently employed as an inspector in a trolley factory in Slovakia. The author of *The Joke*, and of the stories that follow, also lives in the provinces, in Brno, the city where he was born forty-five years ago. Along with the other leading intellectuals whose speeches and writings helped to make the Prague Spring (and who continue to refuse to "confess" to their "mistakes" so as to receive official absolution) he is excluded from membership in the post-occupation writers' union (an undistinguished government-approved group bearing little resemblance to the old and outspoken writers' union that was dissolved by the government when it refused to comply with Soviet "normalization") and he has been fired from his teaching position at the Prague Film School; he is forbidden to travel to the West, his literary works have been removed from the nation's libraries and bookstores, his plays have been banned from the theaters, and as a result of a series of government decrees establishing confiscatory taxes aimed specifically at ten dissident writers, he now receives less than ten per cent of the royalties that his books earn in Europe, where he is a writer of reputation. Recently his new novel, *Life Is Elsewhere*, received the Médicis Literary Award as the best foreign novel published in France in 1973; the book cannot, however, be published in the country, and in the language, in which it was written.

2

The Czech novelist and journalist, Ludvík Vaculík, certainly no less of a political criminal to the current Czech rulers than Kundera, has remarked in an interview (given to a Swiss journalist visiting Prague, and printed subsequently in several Western magazines) that he considers it "unfortunate . . . when foreign critics judge the quality of Czech literary work exclusively by the degree to which it 'settles accounts with illusions about socialism' or by the acerbity with which it stands up to the regime here. I cannot use the foreign book market to stand up to the regime, nor do I want to." Likewise the Czech poet and immunologist Miroslav Holub let me know, when we were introduced in Prague a year ago, that he did not care to receive attention from foreign literary visitors simply because he was considered by them to be "a poor Czech." I had just expressed admiration for his Penguin collection of poems, which I'd read at the suggestion of the English critic and editor of the Penguin European Poets series, A. Alvarez. Still, Dr. Holub momentarily bristled, as though it could well be that I actually had more sympathy for the predicament in which he and other Czech writers found themselves, than for his verse. Only a few months after our first meeting, Holub went on Prague radio and made what was described by the government announcer as "a self-critical confession of the political standpoint he took . . . in the crisis years of 1968 and 1969 . . ." Reading a transcript of Holub's confession of error—a windy, clichéd document in no way like the sharp and elegant poetry—I wondered if this sternly intelligent and very theoretical poet-scientist, with whom I'd developed something of a friendship during my weeks in Prague, might have been moved to denounce himself on the radio like this, not necessarily to curry favor with the authorities, or because he had finally to yield for personal reasons to government threat and intimidation, or even because he had changed his mind about '68, but rather, perhaps, to discourage once and for all sympathetic judgments about himself or his work that might be thought to arise in response to the conspicuously grave circumstances in which he writes poetry and studies blood.

I would think that like Holub and Vaculík, Milan Kundera too would prefer to find a readership in the West that was not drawn to his fiction because he is a writer who is oppressed by a Communist regime, especially since Kundera's political novel, *The Joke*, happens to represent only an aspect of his wide-ranging intelligence and talent. To date, Kundera has published, aside from *The Joke*, two plays; three books of poems (one on the subject of women in love, another on a Czech resistance hero of World War Two); a study of the modern Czech novelist Vladislav Vancura, entitled *The Art of the Novel*; and several volumes of short stories which, like these stories, focus largely on the private world of erotic possibilities, rather than on politics and the state. Currently Kundera, whose father was a pianist and rector of the state music conservatory at Brno, is at work on study of the Czech composer, Leoš Janáček, whose strong interest in Moravian folk music Kundera shares. (An early book on Janáček was written in 1924, by Max Brod, Franz Kafka's friend and biographer.)

But having written *The Joke*, Kundera, for all his wide-ranging interests, now finds himself an enemy of the state and nothing more—in a position, ironically enough, very much like the protagonist of *The Joke*, whose error it is as a young Communist student to send a teasing post card to his girl friend, making fun of her naive political earnestness; she happens to be away from him for a few weeks, taking a summer course in the strategies of the revolutionary movement, and seems to Ludvík Jahn not to be missing him quite enough. So, playful lover that he is, he dashes off a message to his ardent young Stalinist:

> *Optimism is the opium of the people!*
> *The healthy atmosphere stinks!*
> *Long live Trotsky!*
>
> *Ludvík*

Well, in Eastern Europe a man should be more careful of what he writes, even to his girl friend. For his three joking sentences, Jahn is found guilty by a student tribunal of being an enemy of the state, is expelled from the university and the party, and consigned to an army penal corps where for seven years he works in the coal mines. "But, Comrades," says Jahn, "it was only a joke." Nonetheless, he is swallowed up by a state somewhat lacking a sense of humor about itself, and subsequently, having misplaced his own sense of humor somewhere in the mines, he is swallowed up and further humiliated by his plans for revenge.

The Joke is, of course, not so benign in intent as Jahn's postcard; I would suppose that Kundera must himself have known, somewhere along the line, that one day the authorities might confirm the imaginative truthfulness of his book by bringing their own dogmatic seriousness down upon him for writing as he did about the plight of Ludvík Jahn. "Socialist realism," after all, is the approved artistic mode in his country, and as one Prague critic informed me when I asked for a definition, "socialist realism consists of writing in praise of the government and the party so that even *they* understand it." Oddly (just another joke, really) Kundera's book actually conforms more to Stalin's own prescription for art: "socialist content in national form." Since two of the most esteemed books ever written in the nation in question happen to be *The Trial* by Franz Kafka and *The Good Soldier Schweik* by Jaroslav Hašek, Kundera's own novel about a loyal citizen upon whom a terrible joke is played by the powers that be, would seem to be entirely in keeping with the spirit of Stalin's injunction. If only Stalin were alive so that Kundera could point out to him this continuity in "national form" and historical preoccupation.

At any rate: that he has received from reality such verification of what was, after all, only a literary invention, must furnish some consolation to a writer so attuned to harsh irony, and so intrigued by the startling consequences that can flow from playing around.

3
_____

Erotic play and power are the subjects frequently at the center of the stories that Kundera calls, collectively, *Laughable Loves*. To be sure, sexuality as a weapon (in this case, the weapon of him who is otherwise wholly assailable) is to the point of *The Joke* as well: to revenge himself upon the political friend who had turned on him back in his remote student days, Ludvík Jahn, released from the coal mines at last, coldly conceives a plan to seduce the man's wife. In this decision to put his virility in the service of his rage, there is in Kundera's hero a kinship to characters in the fiction of Mailer and Mishima—the vengeful husband, for example, in Mishima's *Forbidden Colors*, who engages a beautiful young homosexual to arouse the passion and then break the hearts of the women who have betrayed and rejected him; or the Greenwich Village bullfight instructor, in Mailer's "Time of Her Time," whose furious copulations seem to be aimed at producing pleasure for his partner in the form of punishment. What distinguishes Kundera's cocksman from Mailer's or Mishima's is the ease with which his erotic power play is thwarted, and in fact turns into yet another joke at *his* expense. He is so much more vulnerable, of course, in good part because he has been so crippled by ostracism from the party and imprisonment in the penal corps (compare the limitless social freedom of Mailer's Americans, O'Shaughnessy and Rojack) but also because Kundera, unlike either Mailer or Mishima, seems even in a book as bleak and cheerless as *The Joke*, to be fundamentally amused by the uses to which a man will think to put his sexual member, or the uses to which his member will put him; this amusement, mixed though it is with sympathy and sorrow, leads Kundera away from anything even faintly resembling a mystical belief or ideological investment in the power of potency or orgasm.

In *Laughable Loves*, what I've called Kundera's "amusement" with erotic enterprises and lustful strategies emerges as the mild satire of a story like "The Golden Apple of Eternal Desire," wherein Don Juanism is viewed as a sport played by a man against a team of women, oftentimes without body contact—or, in the wry, rather worldly irony of the Dr. Havel stories, "Symposium" and "Dr. Havel After Ten Years," where Don Juanism is depicted as a way of life, in which women of all social stations eagerly and willingly participate. as "sexual objects," particularly so with Havel, eminent physician and ageing Casanova, who in his prime is matter-of-factly told by a professional colleague, ". . . you're like death, you take everything." Or Kundera's amusement emerges as a kind of detached Chekhovian tenderness in the story about the balding, thirtyish, would-have-been erotocist, who sets about to seduce an aging woman whose body he expects to find disgusting, a seduction undertaken to revenge himself upon his own stubborn phallic daydreams. Narrated alternately from the point of view of the thirty-five-year-old seducer and the fifty-year-old seduced, and with a striking air of candor that borders somehow on impropriety—as though a discreet acquaintance were suddenly letting us in on sexual secrets both seamy and true—this story, "Let the Old Dead Make Room for the Young Dead," seems to me "Chekhovian" not merely because of its tone, or its concern with the painful and touching consequences of time passing and old selves dying, but because it is so very good.

In "The Hitchhiking Game," "Nobody Will Laugh," and "Edward and God," Kundera turns to those jokes he is so fond of contemplating, the ones that begin in whimsy, or perversity, and end in trouble. In "The Hitchhiking Game," for example, a young couple off for a vacation together decide on the way to their destination to play at being strangers, the girl pretending to be a hitchhiker, and her boy friend just another man passing in his car. The ensuing confusion of identities, and the heightened erotocism this provokes in the lovers, with its scary sado-masochistic edge, is not so catastrophic to either of them as his joke turns out to be for Ludvík Jahn; still, simply by fooling around and indulging their curiosity, the lovers find they have managed to deepen responsibility as well as passion—as if children playing doctor out in the garage were to look up from one another's privates to discover they were administrating a national health program, or being summoned to perform surgery in the Mount Sinai operating room. What is so often laughable, in the stories of Kundera's Czechoslovakia, is how grimly serious just about everything turns out to be, jokes and games and pleasure included; what's laughable is how terribly little there is to laugh at with any joy.

My own favorite story is "Edward and God," which, like *The Joke*, deals with a young Czech whose playfulness (with women, of course) and admitted taste for cynicism and blasphemy expose him to the harsh judgments of a dogmatic society, or rather, expose him to those authorities who righteously promulgate and protect the dogmas, but do so stupidly, and without even genuine conviction or understanding. What is particularly appealing here is that the young schoolteacher Edward, an erotic Machiavelli who feigns religious piety to seduce a pietistic knockout and so falls afoul of the atheistic school board that employs him, gets no more than he gives, and is more of a thoughtful Lucky Jim, really, than a Ludvík Jahn. His difficulties are not come by so innocently, nor are the consequences so brutal or humiliating as they are in *The Joke*. Indeed, the ugly school directress with a secret sexual need who sets out to reeducate Edward the believer, winds up, in what is for Kundera a rare moment of thoroughgoing farce, naked and on her knees before him, reciting the Lord's Prayer at Edward's ministerial command, an "image of degradation," that luckily (for his political future) and just in the nick of time, sets the machinery of tumescence in motion. "As the directress said, 'And lead us not into temptation,' he quickly threw off all his clothes. When she said 'Amen,' he violently lifted her off the floor and dragged her onto the couch." So, where there is something of an aggrieved tone and polemical intent in *The Joke*—a sense communicated, at least to a Westerner, that the novel is also a *statement*, made in behalf of an abused nation, made in defiance of a heartless regime—"Edward and God" is more like a rumination, in anecdotal form, upon a social predicament that rouses the author to comic analysis and philosophical speculation, even to farce, rather than to angry exposé.

Not that one should minimize the cost to Edward (and probably to the author as well) of maintaining a detached "amused" intellectual cunning in the midst of a social order rigidly devoted to simple-minded pieties having little to do with the realities of need and desire (other than the need and desire for pieties). "Yet even if [Edward] was inwardly laughing, and thus making an effort to mock them secretly (and so exonerate his accomodation), it didn't alter the case. For even malicious imitation remains imitation, and the shadow that mocks remains a shadow, subordinate, derivative, and wretched, and nothing more." Or, as Kundera comments wearily at the conclusion of Edward's story, "Ah, ladies and gentlemen, a man lives a sad life when he cannot take anything or anyone seriously" As the tone suggests, "Edward and God" does not derive from manifesto or protest literature, but connects in spirit as well as form to those humorous stories one hears by the hundreds in Prague these days, stories such as a powerless or oppressed people are often adept at telling about themselves, and in which they seem to take an aesthetic pleasure— what pleasure is there, otherwise?—from the very absurdities and paradoxes that characterize their hardship and cause them pain.

PHILIP ROTH

The Hitchhiking Game

1

The needle on the gas gauge suddenly dipped toward empty and the young driver of the sports car declared that it was maddening how much gas the car ate up. "See that we don't run out of gas again," protested the girl (about twenty-two), and reminded the driver of several places where this had already happened to them. The young man replied that he wasn't worried, because whatever he went through with her had the charm of adventure for him. The girl objected; whenever they had run out of gas on the highway it had, she said, always been an adventure only for her. The young man had hidden and she had had to make ill use of her charms by thumbing a ride and letting herself be driven to the nearest gas station, then thumbing a ride back with a can of gas. The young man asked the girl whether the drivers who had given her a ride had been unpleasant, since she spoke as if her task had been a hardship. She replied (with awkward flirtatiousness) that sometimes they had been *very* pleasant but that it hadn't done her any good as she had been burdened with the can and had had to leave them before she could get anything going. "Pig," said the young man. The girl protested that she wasn't a pig, but that he really was. God knows how many girls stopped him on the highway, when he was driving the car alone! Still driving, the young man put his arm around the girl's shoulders and kissed her gently on the forehead. He knew that she loved him and that she was jealous. Jealousy isn't a pleasant quality, but if it isn't overdone (and if it's combined with modesty), apart from its inconvenience there's even something touching about it. At least that's what the young man thought. Because he was only twenty-eight, it seemed to him that he was old and knew everything that a man could know about women. In the girl sitting beside him he valued precisely what, until now, he had met with least in women: purity.

The needle was already on empty, when to the right the young man caught sight of a sign, announcing that the sta- tion was a quarter of a mile ahead. The girl hardly had time to say how relieved she was before the young man was signaling left and driving into a space in front of the pumps. However, he had to stop a little way off, because beside the pumps was a huge gasoline truck with a large metal tank and a bulky hose, which was refilling the pumps. "We'll have to wait," said the young man to the girl and got out of the car. "How long will it take?" he shouted to the man in overalls. "Only a moment," replied the attendant, and the young man said: "I've heard that one before." He wanted to go back and sit in the car, but he saw that the girl had gotten out the other side. "I'll take a little walk in the meantime," she said. "Where to?" the young man asked on purpose, wanting to see the girl's embarrassment. He had known her for a year now but she would still get shy in front of him. He enjoyed her moments of shyness, partly because they distinguished her from the women he'd met before, partly because he was aware of the law of universal transience, which made even his girl's shyness a precious thing to him.

2
_____

The girl really didn't like it when during the trip (the young man would drive for several hours without stopping) she had to ask him to stop for a moment somewhere near a clump of trees. She always got angry when, with feigned surprise, he asked her why he should stop. She knew that her shyness was ridiculous and old-fashioned. Many times at work she had noticed that they laughed at her on account of it and deliberately provoked her. She always got shy in advance at the thought of how she was going to get shy. She often longed to feel free and easy about her body, the way most of the women around her did. She had even invented a special course in self-persuasion: she would repeat to herself that at birth every human being received one out of the millions of available bodies, as one would receive an allotted room out of the millions of rooms in an enormous hotel. Consequently, the body was fortuitous and impersonal, it was only a ready-made, borrowed thing. She would repeat this to herself in different ways, but she could never manage to feel it. This mind-body dualism was alien to her. She was too much one with her body; that is why she always felt such anxiety about it.

She experienced this same anxiety even in her relations with the young man, whom she had known for a year and with whom she was happy, perhaps because he never separated her body from her soul and she could live with him *wholly*. In this unity there was happiness, but right behind the happiness lurked suspicion, and the girl was full of that. For instance, it often occurred to her that the other women (those who weren't anxious) were more attractive and more seductive and that the young man, who did not conceal the fact that he knew this kind of woman well, would someday leave her for a woman like that. (True, the young man declared that he'd had enough of them to last his whole life, but she knew that he was still much younger than he thought.) She wanted him to be completely hers and she to be completely his, but it often seemed to her that the more she tried to give him everything, the more she denied him something: the very thing that a light and superficial love or a flirtation gives to a person. It worried her that she was not able to combine seriousness with lightheartedness.

But now she wasn't worrying and any such thoughts were far from her mind. She felt good. It was the first day of their vacation (of their two-week vacation, about which she had been dreaming for a whole year), the sky was blue (the whole year she had been worrying about whether the sky would really be blue), and he was beside her. At his, "Where to?" she blushed, and left the car without a word. She walked around the gas station, which was situated beside the highway in total isolation, surrounded by fields. About a hundred yards away (in the direction in which they were traveling), a wood began. She set off for it, vanished behind a little bush, and gave herself up to her good mood. (In solitude it was possible for her to get the greatest enjoyment from the presence of the man she loved. If his presence had been continuous, it would have kept on disappearing. Only when alone was she able to *hold on* to it.)

When she came out of the wood onto the highway, the gas station was visible. The large gasoline truck was already pulling out and the sports car moved forward toward the red turret of the pump. The girl walked on along the highway and only at times looked back to see if the sports car was coming. At last she caught sight of it. She stopped and began to wave at it like a hitchhiker waving at a stranger's car. The sports car slowed down and stopped close to the girl. The young man leaned toward the window, rolled it down, smiled, and asked, "Where are you headed, miss?" "Are you going to Bystritsa?" asked the girl, smiling flirtatiously at him. "Yes, please get in," said the young man, opening the door. The girl got in and the car took off.

3

The young man was always glad when his girl friend was gay. This didn't happen too often; she had a quite tiresome job in an unpleasant environment, many hours of overtime without compensatory leisure and, at home, a sick mother. So she often felt tired. She didn't have either particularly good nerves or self-confidence and easily fell into a state of anxiety and fear. For this reason he welcomed every manifestation of her gaiety with the tender solicitude of a foster parent. He smiled at her and said: "I'm lucky today. I've been driving for five years, but I've never given a ride to such a pretty hitchhiker."

The girl was grateful to the young man for every bit of flattery; she wanted to linger for a moment in its warmth and so she said, "You're very good at lying."

"Do I look like a liar?"

"You look like you enjoy lying to women," said the girl, and into her words there crept unawares a touch of the old anxiety, because she really did believe that her young man enjoyed lying to women.

The girl's jealousy often irritated the young man, but this time he could easily overlook it for, after all, her words didn't apply to him but to the unknown driver. And so he just casually inquired, "Does it bother you?"

"If I were going with you, then it would bother me," said the girl and her words contained a subtle, instructive message for the young man; but the end of her sentence applied only to the unknown driver, "but I don't know you, so it doesn't bother me."

"Things about her own man always bother a woman more than things about a stranger" (this was now the young man's subtle, instructive message to the girl), "so seeing that we are strangers, we could get on well together."

The girl purposely didn't want to understand the implied meaning of his message, and so she now addressed the unknown driver exclusively:

"What does it matter, since we'll part company in a little while?"

"Why?" asked the young man.

"Well, I'm getting out at Bystritsa."

"And what if I get out with you?"

At these words the girl looked up at him and found that he looked exactly as she imagined him in her most agonizing hours of jealousy. She was alarmed at how he was flattering her and flirting with her (an unknown hitchhiker), and *how becoming it was to him*. Therefore she responded with defiant provocativeness, "What would *you* do with me, I wonder?"

"I wouldn't have to think too hard about what to do with such a beautiful woman," said the young man gallantly and at this moment he was once again speaking far more to his own girl than to the figure of the hitchhiker.

But this flattering sentence made the girl feel as if she had caught him at something, as if she had wheedled a confession out of him with a fraudulent trick. She felt toward him a brief flash of intense hatred and said, "Aren't you rather too sure of yourself?"

The young man looked at the girl. Her defiant face appeared to him to be completely convulsed. He felt sorry for her and longed for her usual, familiar expression (which he used to call childish and simple). He leaned toward her, put his arm around her shoulders, and softly spoke the name with which he usually addressed her and with which he now wanted to stop the game.

But the girl released herself and said: "You're going a bit too fast!"

At this rebuff the young man said: "Excuse me, miss," and looked silently in front of him at the highway.

4

The girl's pitiful jealousy, however, left her as quickly as it had come over her. After all, she was sensible and knew perfectly well that all this was merely a game. Now it even struck her as a little ridiculous that she had repulsed her man out of jealous rage. It wouldn't be pleasant for her if he found out why she had done it. Fortunately women have the miraculous ability to change the meaning of their actions after the event. Using this ability, she decided that she had repulsed him not out of anger but so that she could go on with the game, which, with its whimsicality, so well suited the first day of their vacation.

So again she was the hitchhiker, who had just repulsed the overenterprising driver, but only so as to slow down his conquest and make it more exciting. She half turned toward the young man and said caressingly:

"I didn't mean to offend you, mister!"

"Excuse me, I won't touch you again," said the young man.

He was furious with the girl for not listening to him and refusing to be herself when that was what he wanted. And since the girl insisted on continuing in her role, he transferred his anger to the unknown hitchhiker whom she was portraying. And all at once he discovered the character of his own part: he stopped making the gallant remarks with which he had wanted to flatter his girl in a roundabout way, and began to play the tough guy who treats women to the coarser aspects of his masculinity: willfulness, sarcasm, self-assurance.

This role was a complete contradiction of the young man's habitually solicitous approach to the girl. True, before he had met her, he had in fact behaved roughly rather than gently toward women. But he had never resembled a heartless tough guy, because he had never demonstrated either a particularly strong will or ruthlessness. However, if he did not resemble such a man, nonetheless he had *longed* to at one time. Of course it was a quite naive desire, but there it was. Childish desires withstand all the snares of the adult mind and often survive into ripe old age. And this childish desire quickly took advantage of the opportunity to embody itself in the proffered role.

The young man's sarcastic reserve suited the girl very well—it freed her from herself. For she herself was, above all, the epitome of jealousy. The moment she stopped seeing the gallantly seductive young man beside her and saw only his inaccessible face, her jealousy subsided. The girl could forget herself and give herself up to her role.

Her role? What was her role? It was a role out of trashy literature. The hitchhiker stopped the car not to get a ride, but to seduce the man who was driving the car. She was an artful seductress, cleverly knowing how to use her charms. The girl slipped into this silly, romantic part with an ease that astonished her and held her spellbound.

5

There was nothing the young man missed in his life more than lightheartedness. The main road of his life was drawn with implacable precision. His job didn't use up merely eight hours a day, it also infiltrated the remaining time with the compulsory boredom of meetings and home study, and, by means of the attentiveness of his countless male and female colleagues, it infiltrated the wretchedly little time he had left for his private life as well. This private life never remained secret and sometimes even became the subject of gossip and public discussion. Even two weeks' vacation didn't give him a feeling of liberation and adventure; the gray shadow of precise planning lay even here. The scarcity of summer accommodations in our country compelled him to book a room in the Tatras six months in advance, and since for that he needed a recommendation from his office, its omnipresent brain thus did not cease knowing about him even for an instant.

He had become reconciled to all this, yet all the same from time to time the terrible thought of the straight road would overcome him—a road along which he was being pursued, where he was visible to everyone, and from which he could not turn aside. At this moment that thought returned to him. Through an odd and brief conjunction of ideas the figurative road became identified with the real highway along which he was driving—and this led him suddenly to do a crazy thing.

"Where did you say you wanted to go?" he asked the girl.

"To Banska Bystritsa," she replied.

"And what are you going to do there?"

"I have a date there."

"Who with?"

"With a certain gentleman."

The car was just coming to a large crossroads. The driver slowed down so he could read the road signs, then turned off to the right.

"What will happen if you don't arrive for that date?"

"It would be your fault and you would have to take care of me."

"You obviously didn't notice that I turned off in the direction of Nove Zamky."

"Is that true? You've gone crazy!"

"Don't be afraid, I'll take care of you," said the young man.

So they drove and chatted thus—the driver and the hitchhiker who did not know each other.

The game all at once went into a higher gear. The sports car was moving away not only from the imaginary goal of Banska Bystritsa, but also from the real goal, toward which it had been heading in the morning: the Tatras and the room that had been booked. Fiction was suddenly making an assault upon real life. The young man was moving away from himself and from the implacable straight road, from which he had never strayed until now.

"But you said you were going to the Low Tatras!" The girl was surprised.

"I am going, miss, wherever I feel like going. I'm a free man and I do what I want and what it pleases me to do."

6

When they drove into Nove Zamky it was already getting dark.

The young man had never been here before and it took him a while to orient himself. Several times he stopped the car and asked the passersby directions to the hotel. Several streets had been dug up, so that the drive to the hotel, even though it was quite close by (as all those who had been asked asserted), necessitated so many detours and roundabout routes that it was almost a quarter of an hour before they finally stopped in front of it. The hotel looked unprepossessing, but it was the only one in town and the young man didn't feel like driving on. So he said to the girl, "Wait here," and got out of the car.

Out of the car he was, of course, himself again. And it was upsetting for him to find himself in the evening somewhere completely different from his intended destination—the more so because no one had forced him to do it and as a matter of fact he hadn't even really wanted to. He blamed himself for this piece of folly, but then became reconciled to it. The room in the Tatras could wait until tomorrow and it wouldn't do any harm if they celebrated the first day of their vacation with something unexpected.

He walked through the restaurant—smoky, noisy, and crowded—and asked for the reception desk. They sent him to the back of the lobby near the staircase, where behind a glass panel a superannuated blonde was sitting beneath a board full of keys. With difficulty, he obtained the key to the only room left.

The girl, when she found herself alone, also threw off her role. She didn't feel ill-humored, though, at finding herself in an unexpected town. She was so devoted to the young man that she never had doubts about anything he did, and confidently entrusted every moment of her life to him. On the other hand the idea once again popped into her mind that perhaps—just as she was now doing—other women had waited for her man in his car, those women whom he met on business trips. But surprisingly enough this idea didn't upset her at all now. In fact, she smiled at the thought of how nice it was that today she was this other woman, this irresponsible, indecent other woman, one of those women of whom she was so jealous. It seemed to her that she was cutting them all out, that she had learned how to use their weapons; how to give the young man what until now she had not known how to give him: lightheartedness, shamelessness, and dissoluteness. A curious feeling of satisfaction filled her, because she alone had the ability to be all women and in this way (she alone) could completely captivate her lover and hold his interest.

The young man opened the car door and led the girl into the restaurant. Amid the din, the dirt, and the smoke he found a single, unoccupied table in a corner.

7

"So how are you going to take care of me now?" asked the girl provocatively.

"What would you like for an aperitif?"

The girl wasn't too fond of alcohol, still she drank a

little wine and liked vermouth fairly well. Now, however, she purposely said: "Vodka."

"Fine," said the young man. "I hope you won't get drunk on me."

"And if I do?" said the girl.

The young man did not reply but called over a waiter and ordered two vodkas and two steak dinners. In a moment the waiter brought a tray with two small glasses and placed it in front of them.

The man raised his glass, "To you!"

"Can't you think of a wittier toast?"

Something was beginning to irritate him about the girl's game. Now sitting face to face with her, he realized that it wasn't just the *words* which were turning her into a stranger, but that her *whole persona* had changed, the movements of her body and her facial expression, and that she unpalatably and faithfully resembled that type of woman whom he knew so well and for whom he felt some aversion.

And so (holding his glass in his raised hand), he corrected his toast: "O.K., then I won't drink to you, but to your kind, in which are combined so successfully the better qualities of the animal and the worse aspects of the human being."

"By 'kind' do you mean all women?" asked the girl.

"No, I mean only those who are like you."

"Anyway it doesn't seem very witty to me to compare a woman with an animal."

"O.K.," the young man was still holding his glass aloft, "then I won't drink to your kind, but to your soul. Agreed? To your soul, which lights up when it descends from your head into your belly, and which goes out when it rises back up to your head."

15

The girl raised her glass. "O.K., to my soul, which descends into my belly."

"I'll correct myself once more," said the young man. "To your belly, into which your soul descends."

"To my belly," said the girl, and her belly (now that they had named it specifically), as it were, responded to the call; she felt every inch of it.

Then the waiter brought their steaks and the young man ordered them another vodka and some soda water (this time they drank to the girl's breasts), and the conversation continued in this peculiar, frivolous tone. It irritated the young man more and more how *well able* the girl was to become the lascivious miss. If she was able to do it so well, he thought, it meant that she really *was* like that. After all, no alien soul had entered into her from somewhere in space. What she was acting now was she herself; perhaps it was that part of her being which had formerly been locked up and which the pretext of the game had let out of its cage. Perhaps the girl supposed that by means of the game she was *disowning* herself, but wasn't it the other way around? Wasn't she becoming herself only through the game? Wasn't she freeing herself through the game? No, opposite him was not sitting a strange woman in his girl's body; it was his girl, herself, no one else. He looked at her and felt growing aversion toward her.

However, it was not only aversion. The more the girl withdrew from him *psychically*, the more he longed for her *physically*. The alien quality of her soul drew attention to her body, yes, as a matter of fact it turned her body into a body for *him* as if until now it had existed for the young man hidden within clouds of compassion, tenderness, concern, love, and emotion, as if it had been lost in these clouds (yes, as if this body had been lost!). It seemed to the young man that today he was seeing his girl's body for the first time.

After her third vodka and soda the girl got up and said flirtatiously, "Excuse me."

The young man said, "May I ask you where you are going, miss?"

"To piss, if you'll permit me," said the girl and walked off between the tables back toward the plush screen.

8

She was pleased with the way she had astounded the young man with this word, which—in spite of all its innocence —he had never heard from her. Nothing seemed to her truer to the character of the woman she was playing than this flirtatious emphasis placed on the word in question. Yes, she was pleased, she was in the best of moods. The game captivated her. It allowed her to feel what she had not felt till now: a *feeling* of *happy-go-lucky irresponsibility*.

She, who was always uneasy in advance about her every next step, suddenly felt completely relaxed. The alien life in which she had become involved was a life without shame, without biographical specifications, without past or future, without obligations. It was a life that was extraordinarily free. The girl, as a hitchhiker, could do anything, *everything was permitted her*. She could say, do, and feel whatever she liked.

She walked through the room and was aware that people were watching her from all the tables. It was a new sensation, one she didn't recognize: *indecent joy caused by her body.* Until now she had never been able to get rid of the fourteen-year-old girl within herself who was ashamed of her breasts and had the disagreeable feeling that she was indecent, because they stuck out from her body and were visible. Even though she was proud of being pretty and having a good figure, this feeling of pride was always immediately curtailed by shame. She rightly suspected that feminine beauty functioned above all as sexual provocation and she found this distasteful. She longed for her body to relate only to the man she loved. When men stared at her breasts in the street it seemed to her that they were invading a piece of her most secret privacy which should belong only to herself and her lover. But now she was the hitchhiker, the woman without a destiny. In this role she was relieved of the tender bonds of her love and began to be intensely aware of her body. And her body became more aroused the more alien the eyes watching it.

She was walking past the last table when an intoxicated man, wanting to show off his worldliness, addressed her in French: *"Combien, mademoiselle?"*

The girl understood. She thrust out her breasts and fully experienced every movement of her hips, then disappeared behind the screen.

9

It was a curious game. This curiousness was evidenced, for example, in the fact that the young man, even though he himself was playing the unknown driver remarkably well, did not for a moment stop seeing his girl in the hitchhiker. And it was precisely this that was tormenting. He saw his girl seducing a strange man, and had the bitter privilege of being present, of seeing at close quarters how she looked and of hearing what she said when she was cheating on him (when she had cheated on him, when she would cheat on him). He had the paradoxical honor of being himself the pretext for her unfaithfulness.

This was all the worse because he worshipped rather than loved her. It had always seemed to him that her inward nature was *real* only within the bounds of fidelity and purity, and that beyond these bounds it simply didn't exist. Beyond these bounds she would cease to be herself, as water ceases to be water beyond the boiling point. When he now saw her crossing this horrifying boundary with nonchalant elegance, he was filled with anger.

The girl came back from the rest room and complained: "A guy over there asked me: *Combien, mademoiselle?*"

"You shouldn't be surprised," said the young man, "after all, you look like a whore."

"Do you know that it doesn't bother me in the least?"

"Then you should go with the gentleman!"

"But I have you."

"You can go with him after me. Go and work out something with him."

"I don't find him attractive."

"But in principle you have nothing against it, having several men in one night."

"Why not, if they're good-looking."

"Do you prefer them one after the other or at the same time?"

"Either way," said the girl.

The conversation was proceeding to still greater extremes of rudeness; it shocked the girl slightly but she couldn't protest. Even in a game there lurks a lack of freedom; even a game is a trap for the players. If this had not been a game and they had really been two strangers, the hitchhiker could long ago have taken offense and left. But there's no escape from a game. A team cannot flee from the playing field before the end of the match, chess pieces cannot desert the chessboard: the boundaries of the playing field are fixed. The girl knew that she had to accept whatever form the game might take, just because it was a game. She knew that the more extreme the game became, the more it would be a game and the more obediently she would have to play it. And it was futile to evoke good sense and warn her dazed soul that she must keep her distance from the game and not take it seriously. Just because it was only a game her soul was not afraid, did not oppose the game, and narcotically sank deeper into it.

The young man called the waiter and paid. Then he got up and said to the girl, "We're going."

"Where to?" The girl feigned surprise.

"Don't ask, just come on," said the young man.

"What sort of way is that to talk to me?"

"The way I talk to whores," said the young man.

10

They went up the badly lit staircase. On the landing below the second floor a group of intoxicated men was standing near the rest room. The young man caught hold of the girl from behind so that he was holding her breast with his hand. The men by the rest room saw this and began to call out. The girl wanted to break away, but the young man yelled at her: "Keep still!" The men greeted this with general ribaldry and addressed several dirty remarks to the girl. The young man and the girl reached the second floor. He opened the door of their room and switched on the light.

It was a narrow room with two beds, a small table, a chair, and a washbasin. The young man locked the door and turned to the girl. She was standing facing him in a defiant pose with insolent sensuality in her eyes. He looked at her and tried to discover behind her lascivious expression the familiar features which he loved tenderly. It was as if he were looking at two images through the same lens, at two images superimposed one upon the other with the one showing through the other. These two images showing through each other were telling him that *everything* was in the girl, that her soul was terrifyingly amorphous, that it held faithfulness and unfaithfulness, treachery and innocence, flirtatiousness and chastity. This disorderly jumble seemed disgusting to him, like the variety to be found in a pile of garbage. Both images continued to show through each other and the young man understood that the girl differed only on the surface from other women, but deep down was the same as they: full of all possible thoughts, feelings, and vices, which justified all his secret misgivings and fits of jealousy. The impression that certain outlines delineated her as an individual was only a delusion to which the other person, the one who was looking, was subject—namely himself. It seemed to him that the girl he loved was a creation of his desire, his thoughts, and his faith and that the *real* girl now standing in front of him was hopelessly alien, hopelessly *ambiguous*. He hated her.

"What are you waiting for? Strip," he said.

The girl flirtatiously bent her head and said, "Is it necessary?"

The tone in which she said this seemed to him very

familiar; it seemed to him that once long ago some other woman had said this to him, only he no longer knew which one. He longed to humiliate her. Not the hitchhiker, but his own girl. The game merged with life. The game of humiliating the hitchhiker became only a pretext for humiliating his girl. The young man had forgotten that he was playing a game. He simply hated the woman standing in front of him. He stared at her and took a fifty-crown bill from his wallet. He offered it to the girl. "Is that enough?"

The girl took the fifty crowns and said: "You don't think I'm worth much."

The young man said: "You aren't worth more."

The girl nestled up against the young man. "You can't get around me like that! You must try a different approach, you must work a little!"

She put her arms around him and moved her mouth toward his. He put his fingers on her mouth and gently pushed her away. He said: "I only kiss women I love."

"And you don't love me?"

"No."

"Whom do you love?"

"What's that got to do with you? Strip!"

11

She had never undressed like this before. The shyness, the feeling of inner panic, the dizziness, all that she had always felt when undressing in front of the young man (and she couldn't hide in the darkness), all this was gone. She was standing in front of him self-confident, insolent, bathed in light, and astonished at where she had all of a sudden discovered the gestures, heretofore unknown to her, of a slow, provocative striptease. She took in his glances, slipping off each piece of clothing with a caressing movement and enjoying each individual stage of this exposure.

But then suddenly she was standing in front of him completely naked and at this moment it flashed through her head that now the whole game would end, that, since she had stripped off her clothes, she had also stripped away her dissimulation, and that being naked meant that she was now herself and the young man ought to come up to her now and make a gesture with which he would wipe out everything and after which would follow only their most intimate lovemaking. So she stood naked in front of the young man and at this moment stopped playing the game. She felt embarrassed and on her face appeared the smile, which really belonged to her—a shy and confused smile.

But the young man didn't come to her and didn't end the game. He didn't notice the familiar smile. He saw before him only the beautiful, alien body of his own girl, whom he hated. Hatred cleansed his sensuality of any sentimental coating. She wanted to come to him, but he said: "Stay where you are, I want to have a good look at you." Now he longed only to treat her as a whore. But the young man had never had a whore and the ideas he had about them came from literature and hearsay. So he turned to these ideas and the first thing he recalled was the image of a woman in black underwear (and black stockings) dancing on the shiny top of a piano. In the little hotel room there was no piano, there was only a small table covered with a linen cloth leaning against the wall. He ordered the girl to climb up on it. The girl made a pleading gesture, but the young man said, "You've been paid."

When she saw the look of unshakable obsession in the

young man's eyes, she tried to go on with the game, even though she no longer could and no longer knew how. With tears in her eyes she climbed onto the table. The top was scarcely three feet square and one leg was a little bit shorter than the others so that standing on it the girl felt unsteady.

But the young man was pleased with the naked figure, now towering above him, and the girl's shy insecurity merely inflamed his imperiousness. He wanted to see her body in all positions and from all sides, as he imagined other men had seen it and would see it. He was vulgar and lascivious. He used words that she had never heard from him in her life. She wanted to refuse, she wanted to be released from the game. She called him by his first name, but he immediately yelled at her that she had no right to address him so intimately. And so eventually in confusion and on the verge of tears, she obeyed, she bent forward and squatted according to the young man's wishes, saluted, and then wiggled her hips as she did the Twist for him. During a slightly more violent movement, when the cloth slipped beneath her feet and she nearly fell, the young man caught her and dragged her to the bed.

He had intercourse with her. She was glad that at least now finally the unfortunate game would end and they would again be the two people they had been before and would love each other. She wanted to press her mouth against his. But the young man pushed her head away and repeated that he only kissed women he loved. She burst into loud sobs. But she wasn't even allowed to cry, because the young man's furious passion gradually won over her body, which then silenced the complaint of her soul. On the bed there were soon two bodies in perfect harmony, two sensual bodies, alien to each other. This was exactly what the girl had most dreaded all her life and had scrupulously avoided till now: love-making without emotion or love. She knew that she had crossed the forbidden boundary, but she proceeded across it without objections and as a full participant—only somewhere, far off in a corner of her consciousness, did she feel horror at the thought that she had never known such pleasure, never so much pleasure as at this moment—beyond that boundary.

12

Then it was all over. The young man got up off the girl and, reaching out for the long cord hanging over the bed, switched off the light. He didn't want to see the girl's face. He knew that the game was over, but didn't feel like returning to their customary relationship. He feared this return. He lay beside the girl in the dark in such a way that their bodies would not touch.

After a moment he heard her sobbing quietly. The girl's hand diffidently, childishly touched his. It touched, withdrew, then touched again, and then a pleading, sobbing voice broke the silence, calling him by his name and saying, "I am me, I am me . . ."

The young man was silent, he didn't move, and he was aware of the sad emptiness of the girl's assertion, in which the unknown was defined in terms of the same unknown quantity.

And the girl soon passed from sobbing to loud crying and went on endlessly repeating this pitiful tautology: "I am me, I am me, I am me . . ."

The young man began to call compassion to his aid (he had to call it from afar, because it was nowhere near at hand), so as to be able to calm the girl. There were still thirteen days' vacation before them.

Let the
Old Dead
Make Room
for the
Young Dead

1

He was returning home along the street of a small Czech town, where he had been living for several years. He was reconciled to his not too exciting life, his backbiting neighbors, and the monotonous rowdiness which surrounded him at work, and he was walking so totally without seeing (as one walks along a path traversed a hundred times) that he almost passed her by. But she had already recognized him from a distance, and coming toward him she gave him that gentle smile of hers. Only at the last moment, when they had almost passed each other, that smile rang a bell in his memory and snapped him out of his drowsy state.

"I wouldn't have recognized you!" he apologized, but it was a stupid apology, because it brought them precipitately to a painful subject, about which it would have been advisable to keep silent; they had not seen each other for fifteen years and during this time they had both aged. "Have I changed so much?" she asked and he replied that she hadn't, and even if this was a lie it wasn't an out-and-out lie, because that gentle smile (expressing demurely and restrainedly a capacity for some sort of eternal enthusiasm) emerged from the distance of many years quite unchanged, and it confused him. It evoked for him so distinctly the former appearance of this woman that he had to make a definite effort to disregard it and to see her as she was now: she was almost an old woman.

He asked her where she was going and what was on her agenda, and she replied that she had nothing else to do but wait for the train which would take her back to Prague that evening. He evinced pleasure at their unexpected meeting, and because they agreed (with good reason) that the two local cafes were overcrowded and dirty, he invited her to his bachelor apartment, which wasn't very far away. He had both coffee and tea there, and, more important, it was clean and peaceful.

2

Right from the start it had been a bad day. Twenty-five years ago she had lived here with her husband for a short time as a new bride, then they had moved to Prague, where he'd died ten years back. He was buried, thanks to an eccentric wish in his last will and testament, in the local cemetery. At that time she had paid in advance for a ten-year lease on the grave, but a few days before, she had become afraid that the time limit had expired and that she had forgotten to renew the lease. Her first impulse had been to write to the cemetery administration, but then she had realized how futile it was to correspond with the authorities and she had come out here.

She knew the path to her husband's grave from memory, and yet today she felt all at once as if she were in this cemetery for the first time. She couldn't find the grave and it seemed to her that she had gone astray. It took her a while to understand. There, where the gray sandstone monument with the name of her husband in gold lettering used to be, precisely on that spot (she confidently recognized the two neighboring graves) now stood a black marble headstone with a quite different name in gilt.

Upset, she went to the cemetery administration. There they told her that upon expiration of the leases, the graves were canceled. She reproached them for not having advised her that she should renew the lease, and they replied that there was little room in the cemetery and that the *old dead ought to make room for the young dead.* This exasperated her and she told them, holding back her tears, that they knew absolutely nothing of humaneness or respect for man, but she soon understood that the conversation was useless. Just as she could not have prevented her husband's death, so also she was defenseless against his second death, this death "of an old dead man," which no longer permitted him to exist even as a dead man.

She went off into town and anxiety quickly began to get mixed in with her sorrow. She tried to imagine how she would explain to her son the disappearance of his father's grave and how she would justify her neglect. At last fatigue overtook her. She didn't know how to pass the long hours until time for the departure of her train. She no longer knew anyone here, and nothing encouraged her to take even a senti- mental stroll, because over the years the town had changed too much and the once familiar places looked quite strange to her now. That is why she gratefully accepted the invitation of the (half-forgotten) old acquaintance, whom she'd met by chance. She could wash her hands in his bathroom and then sit in his soft armchair (her legs ached), look around his room, and listen to the boiling water bubbling away behind the screen which separated the kitchen nook from the room.

3

Not long ago he had turned thirty-five, and exactly at that time he had noticed that the hair on the top of his head was thinning very visibly. The bald spot still wasn't there yet, but its appearance was quite conceivable (the scalp was show- ing beneath the hair) and, more important, it was certain to appear and in the not too distant future. Certainly it was ridiculous to make thinning hair a matter of life or death, but he realized that baldness would change his face and that his hitherto youthful appearance (undeniably his best) was on its way out.

And now these considerations made him think about how the balance sheet of this person (with hair), who was just about to take his leave, actually stood, what he had actually experienced and enjoyed. What astounded him was the knowledge that he had experienced rather little. When he thought about this he felt embarrassed, yes, he was ashamed, because to live here on earth so long and to experience so little—that was ignominious.

What did he actually mean when he said to himself that he had not experienced much? Did he mean by this travel, work, public service, sport, women? Of course he meant all of these things; yet, above all, women. Because if his life was deficient in other spheres this certainly upset him, but he didn't have to lay the blame for it on himself; anyhow, not for work that was uninteresting and without prospects; not for curtailing his travels because he didn't have money or reliable party references; finally, not even for the fact that when he was twenty he had injured his knee and had had to give up sports, which he had enjoyed. On the other hand, the realm of women was for him a sphere of relative freedom and that being so, he couldn't make any excuses about it. Here he could have demonstrated his wealth; women became for him the one legitimate criterion of life's *density*.

But as ill luck would have it, things had gone somewhat badly for him with women. Until he was twenty-five (though he was a good-looking guy), shyness would tie him up in knots; then he fell in love, got married, and after seven years had persuaded himself that it was possible to find infinite erotic possibilities in one woman. Then he got divorced and the one-woman apologetics (and the illusion of infinity) melted away, and in its place came an agreeable taste for and boldness in the pursuit of women (a pursuit of their varied finiteness). Unfortunately, his bad financial situation frustrated his new-found desires (he had to pay his former wife alimony for their child, whom he was allowed to see once or twice a year), and the conditions in the small town were such that the curiosity of the neighbors was as enormous as the choice of women was scant.

And time was already passing very quickly and all at once he was standing in the bathroom in front of the oval mirror located above the washbasin. In his right hand he held over his head a round mirror and was transfixed examining the bald spot that had begun to appear. This sight suddenly (without preparation) brought home to him the banal truth that what he'd missed couldn't be made good. He found himself in a state of chronic ill humor and was even assailed by thoughts of suicide. Naturally (and it is necessary to emphasize this, in order that we should not see him as a hysterical or stupid person), he appreciated the comic aspect of these thoughts, and he knew that he would never carry them out (he laughed inwardly at his own suicide note: *I couldn't put up with my bald spot. Farewell!*), but it is enough that these thoughts, however platonic they may have been, assailed him at all. Let us try to understand: the thoughts made themselves felt within him perhaps like the overwhelming desire to give up the race makes itself felt within a marathon runner, when in the middle of the track he discovers that shamefully (and moreover through his own fault, his own blunders) he is losing. And he is then apt to consider the race lost and doesn't feel like running any further.

And now he bent down over the small table and placed

one cup of coffee on it in front of the couch (where he later sat down), the other in front of the armchair, in which his visitor was sitting. He said to himself that there was a curious malice in the fact that he had met this woman, with whom he'd once been head over heels in love and whom in those days he'd let escape (through his own fault, his own blunders), precisely when he found himself in this state of mind and at a time when it was no longer possible to rectify anything.

4

She would hardly have guessed that she appeared to him as that woman who had escaped him; still, she was aware all the time of the night they'd spent together. She remembered how he had looked then. (He was twenty, didn't know how to dress; he used to blush and his boyishness amused her.) And she remembered herself. (She had been thirty-five, and a certain desire for beauty drove her into the arms of other men, but at the same time drove her away from them. She always imagined that her life should have resembled a *beautiful ball* and she feared that her unfaithfulness to her husband might turn into an ugly habit.)

Yes, she had decreed beauty for herself, as people decree moral injunctions for themselves. If she had noticed any ugliness in her own life, she would perhaps have fallen into despair. And because she was now aware that after fifteen years she must seem old to her host (with all the ugliness that this brings with it), she wanted quickly to unfold an imaginary fan in front of her own face, and to this end she deluged him with hasty questions: she asked him how he had come to this town; she asked him about his job. She complimented him on the coziness of his bachelor apartment, and praised the view from the window over the rooftops of the town (she said that it was in no way a special view, but that there was a certain airiness and freedom about it). She named the painters of several framed reproductions of Impressionist pictures (this was not difficult, in the apartments of poor Czech intellectuals you will unfailingly find these cheap prints). Then she got up from the table with her unfinished cup of coffee in her hand and bent over a small writing desk, upon which were a few photographs in a stand (it didn't escape her that among them there was no photo of a young woman), and she asked whether the face of the old woman in one of them belonged to his mother. (He confirmed this).

Then he asked her what she'd meant when she'd told him earlier that she had come here to settle "some affairs." She really dreaded speaking about the cemetery (here on the fifth floor she not only felt high above the roofs, but also pleasantly high above her own life). When he insisted, though, she finally confessed (but very briefly, because the immodesty of hasty frankness had always been foreign to her) that she had lived here many years before, that her husband was buried here (she was silent about the cancellation of the grave), and that she and her son had been coming here for the last ten years without fail on All Souls' Day.

5

"Every year?" This statement saddened him and once again he thought that a spiteful trick was being played on him. If only he'd met her six years ago when he'd moved here, perhaps it would have been possible to save everything. She wouldn't have been so marked by her age, her appearance wouldn't have been so different from the image he had of the woman he had loved fifteen years before. It would have been within his power to surmount the difference and perceive both images (the past and the present) as one. But now they stood hopelessly far apart.

She drank her coffee and talked. He tried hard to determine precisely the extent of the transformation by means of which she was eluding him *for the second time*. Her face was wrinkled (in vain did the layer of powder try to deny this). Her neck was withered (in vain did the high collar try to hide this). Her cheeks sagged. Her hair (but it was almost beautiful!) had grown gray. However, her hands drew his attention most of all (unfortunately, it was not possible to touch them up with powder or paint): blue bunches of veins stood out on them, so that all at once they were the hands of a man.

In him, pity was mixed with anger and he felt like drowning their too-long-put-off meeting in alcohol; he asked her if she fancied some cognac (he had an opened bottle in the cabinet behind the screen). She replied that she didn't and he remembered that even years before she had drunk almost not at all, perhaps so that alcohol wouldn't make her behave contrary to the demands of good taste and decorum. And when he saw the delicate movement of her hand with which she refused the offer of cognac, he realized that this charm, this magic, this grace, which had enraptured him, was still the same in her, though hidden beneath the mask of old age, and was in itself still attractive, though doubly cut off from him.

When it crossed his mind that she was *cut off by old age*, he felt immense pity for her, and this pity brought her nearer to him (this woman who had once been so dazzling, before whom he used to be tonguetied), and he wanted to have a long conversation with her and to talk the way a man would talk with his girl friend when he really felt down. He started to talk (and it did indeed turn into a long talk) and eventually he got to the pessimistic thoughts, which had visited him of late. Naturally he was silent about the bald spot that was beginning to appear (it was just like her silence about the canceled grave). On the other hand, the vision of the bald spot was transubstantiated into quasi-philosophical maxims to the effect that time passes more quickly than man is able to live, and that life is terrible, because everything in it is necessarily doomed to extinction. He voiced these and similar maxims, to which he awaited a sympathetic response; but he didn't get it.

"I don't like that kind of talk," she said almost vehemently. "All that you've been saying is awfully superficial."

6

She didn't like conversations about growing old or dying, because they contained images of physical ugliness, which went against the grain with her. Several times, almost in a fluster, she repeated to her host that his opinion was *superficial*. After all, she said, man is more than just a body which wastes away, a man's work is substantial and that is what he leaves behind for others. Her advocacy of this opinion wasn't new; it had first come to her aid when, twenty-five years earlier, she had fallen in love with her former husband, who was nineteen years older than she. She had never ceased to respect him wholeheartedly (in spite of all her infidelities, about which he either didn't know or didn't want to know) and she took pains to convince herself that her husband's intellect and importance would fully outweigh the heavy load of his years.

"What kind of work, I ask you! What kind of work do we leave behind!" protested her host with a bitter smile.

She didn't want to refer to her dead husband, though she firmly believed in the lasting value of everything that he had accomplished. She therefore only said that every man accomplishes something, which in itself may be most modest, but that in this and only in this is his value. Then she went on to talk about herself, how she worked in a house of culture in a suburb of Prague, how she organized lectures and poetry readings. She spoke (with an excitement that seemed out of proportion to him) about "the grateful faces" of the public, and straight after that she expatiated upon how beautiful it was to have a son and to see her own features (her son looked like her) changing into the face of a man, how it was beautiful to give him everything that a mother can give a son and then to fade quietly into the background of his life.

It was not by chance that she had begun to talk about her son, because all day her son had been in her thoughts, a reproachful reminder of the morning's failure at the cemetery. It was strange; she had never let any man impose his will on her, but her own son subjugated her, and she didn't know how. The failure at the cemetery had upset her so much today, above all because she felt guilty before him and feared his reproaches. Of course she had long suspected that her son so jealously watched over the way she honored his father's memory (after all it was he who insisted every All Souls' Day that they should not fail to visit the cemetery), not so much out of love for his dead father, as from a desire to usurp his mother, to assign her to a widow's proper confines. For it was like this, even if he never voiced it and she tried hard (without success) not to know it, the idea that his mother could still have a sex life disgusted him. Everything in her that remained sexual (at least in the realm of possibility and chance) disgusted him, and because the idea of sex is connected with the idea of youthfulness, he was disgusted by everything that was still youthful in her. He was no longer a child and his mother's youthfulness (combined with the aggressiveness of her motherly care) disagreeably thwarted his relationship with girls, who had begun to interest him. He wanted to have an old mother. Only from such a mother would he tolerate love and only of such a mother could he be fond. And although at times she realized that in this way he was pushing her toward the grave, she had finally submitted to him, succumbed to his pressure, and even idealized her capitulation, persuading herself that the beauty of her life consisted precisely in quietly fading out in the shadow of another life. In the name of this idealization (without which the wrinkles on her face would after all have made her far more uneasy), she now conducted with such unexpected warmth this dispute with her host.

But he suddenly leaned across the little table which stood between them, stroked her hand, and said, "Forgive me for my chatter. You know, I always was an idiot."

7

Their dispute didn't irritate him; on the contrary, his visitor yet again confirmed her identity for him. In her protest against his pessimistic talk (wasn't this above all a protest against ugliness and bad taste?), he recognized her as the person he had once known, so her former appearance and their old story filled his thoughts all the more. Now he wished only that nothing destroy the intimate mood, so favorable to their conversation (for that reason he stroked her hand and called himself an idiot), and he wanted to tell her about the thing that seemed most important to him at this moment: their adventure together. For he was convinced that he had experienced something very special with her, which she didn't suspect and which he alone could, if he made the effort, put into words.

He no longer even remembered how they had met. Apparently, she sometimes came in contact with his student friends, but he remembered perfectly the out-of-the-way Prague cafe where they had been alone together for the first time. He had been sitting opposite her in a plush booth, depressed and silent, but at the same time thoroughly elated by her delicate hints that she was favorably disposed toward him. He had tried hard to visualize (without daring to hope for the fulfillment of these fancies) how she would look if he kissed her, undressed her, and made love to her—but he just couldn't bring it off. Yes, there was something odd about it: he had tried a thousand times to imagine her in bed, but in vain. Her face kept on looking at him with its calm, gentle smile and he couldn't (even with the most dogged efforts of his imagination) distort it with the grimace of physical ecstasy. *She absolutely defied his imagination.*

And that was the situation, which had never since been repeated in his life. At that time he had stood face to face with the unimaginable. Obviously he was experiencing that very short period (a *heavenly* period) when fancy is not yet satiated by experience, has not become routine, knows little, and knows how to do little, so that the unimaginable still exists; and should the unimaginable become reality (without the mediation of the imaginable, without that narrow bridge of fancies), a man will be seized by panic and vertigo. Such vertigo did actually overtake him, when after several further meetings, in the course of which he hadn't resolved anything, she began to ask him in detail and with meaningful curiosity about his student room in the dormitory, so that she soon forced him to invite her there.

He shared the little room in the dorm with another student, who for a glass of rum had promised not to return till after midnight. It bore little resemblance to his bachelor apartment of today: two metal cots, two chairs, a cupboard, a glaring, unshaded lightbulb, and frightful disorder. He tidied up the room and at seven o'clock (it went with her refinement that she was habitually on time) she knocked on the door. It was September and only gradually did it begin to get dark. They sat down on the edge of a cot and kissed. Then it got even darker and he didn't want to switch on the light, because he was glad that he couldn't be seen, and hoped that the darkness would relieve the state of embarrassment in which he would find himself having to undress in front of her. (If he knew tolerably well how to unbutton women's blouses, he himself would undress in front of them with bashful haste.) This time, however, he didn't for a long time dare to undo her first button (it seemed to him that in the matter of beginning to undress there must exist some tasteful and elegant procedure, which only men who were *experts* knew, and he was afraid of betraying his ignorance), so that in the end she herself stood up and, asking with a smile, "Shouldn't I take off this armor? . . ." began to undress. It was dark, however, and he saw only the shadows of her movements. He hastily undressed too and gained some confidence only when they began (thanks to her patience) to make love. He looked into her face, but in the dusk her expression entirely eluded him, and he couldn't even make out her features. He regretted that it was dark, but it seemed impossible for him to get up and move away from her at that moment to turn on the switch by the door, so vainly he went on straining his eyes! But he didn't recognize her. It seemed to him that he was making love with someone else—with someone spurious or else someone quite unreal and unindividuated.

Then she got on top of him (at that time he saw only her raised shadow), and moving her hips, she said something in a muffled tone, in a whisper, and it wasn't clear whether she was talking to him or to herself. He couldn't make out the words and asked her what she had said. She went on whispering, and even when he clasped her to him again, he couldn't understand what she was saying.

8

She listened to her host and became increasingly absorbed in the details, which she had long ago forgotten: for instance, in those days she used to wear a pale blue summer suit, in which, they said, she looked like an inviolable angel (yes, she recalled that suit). She used to wear a large ivory comb stuck in her hair, which they said gave her a majestically old-fashioned look; at the cafe she always used to order tea with rum (her only alcoholic vice), and all this pleasantly carried her away from the cemetery, away from her sore feet, and away from the reproachful eyes of her son. Look, it flashed across her mind, regardless of what I am like today, if a bit of my youth lives on in this man, I haven't lived in vain. This immediately struck her as a new corroboration of her conviction that the worth of a man lies in his ability to extend beyond himself, to go outside himself, to exist in and for other people.

She listened, and didn't resist him when from time to time he stroked her hand. The stroking merged with the soothing tone of the conversation and had a disarming indefiniteness about it (for whom was it intended? For the woman *about whom* he was speaking or for the woman *to whom* he was speaking?); after all, she liked the man who was caressing her; she even said to herself that she liked him better than the youth of fifteen years ago, whose boyishness, if she remembered correctly, had been rather a nuisance.

When he got to the place in his account where her moving shadow had risen above him and he had vainly endeavored to understand her whispering, for a moment he fell silent and she (foolishly, as if he would know these words and would want to remind her of them after so many years like some forgotten mystery) asked softly: "And what did I say then?"

9

"I don't know," he replied. He didn't know. At that time she had eluded not only his fancies, but also his perceptions; she had eluded his sight and hearing. When he had switched on the light in the dormitory room, she was already dressed. Everything about her was once again sleek, dazzling, perfect, and he vainly sought a connection between her face in the light and the face which a moment before he had been guessing at in the darkness. They hadn't parted yet, but he was already trying to remember her. He tried to imagine how her (unseen) face and (unseen) body had looked when they'd made love a little while before—but without success. She still defied his imagination.

He made up his mind that next time he must make love to her with the light on. Only there wasn't a next time. From that day on she adroitly and tactfully avoided him. He had failed hopelessly, yet it wasn't clear why. They'd certainly made love beautifully, but he also knew how impossible he had been *beforehand*, and he was ashamed of this. He now felt condemned by her avoidance and no longer dared to pursue her.

"Tell me, why did you avoid me then?"

"I beg you," she said in the gentlest of voices, "it's so long ago, that I don't know . . ." And when he pressed her further she protested, "You shouldn't always return to the past. It's enough that we have to devote so much time to it against our will." She said this only to ward off his insistence (and perhaps the last sentence, spoken with a light sigh, referred to her morning visit to the cemetery). But he perceived her statement differently: as an intense and purposeful clarification for him of the fact (this obvious thing) that there were not two women (a past and a present), but only one and the same woman, and that she, who had eluded him fifteen years earlier, was here now, was within reach of his hand.

"You're right, the present is more important," he said in a meaningful tone and looked intently at her face. She was smiling with her mouth half-open and he glimpsed a row of white teeth. At that instant a recollection flashed through his head: that time in his dorm room she had put his fingers into her mouth, bitten them hard until it had hurt. Meanwhile he had been feeling the whole inside of her mouth and still knew that on one side at the top the back upper teeth were all missing (this had not discouraged him at the time; on the con-

44

trary, such a trivial imperfection went with her age, which attracted and excited him). But now, looking into the crack between her teeth and the corner of her mouth, he saw that her teeth were strikingly white and none were missing, and this made him shudder. Both images got loose again, but he didn't want to admit it. He wanted to reunite them by force and violence, and so said, "Don't you really feel like having some cognac?" When with a charming smile and a mildly raised eyebrow she shook her head, he went behind the screen, took out the bottle, put it to his lips, and took a swig. Then it occurred to him that she would be able to detect his secret action from his breath, and so he picked up two small glasses and the bottle and carried them into the room. Once more she shook her head. "At least symbolically," he said and filled both glasses. He clinked her glass. "To speaking about you only in the present tense!" He downed his drink, she moistened her lips. He took a seat on the arm of her chair and seized her hand.

10

She hadn't suspected when she went to his bachelor apartment, that it could come to *this* sort of intimacy, and at first she felt dismay, as if it had come before she had been able to prepare herself (that *perpetual preparedness*, familiar to the mature woman, she had lost long ago). (We should perhaps find in this dismay something akin to the dismay of a very young girl who has been kissed for the first time, for if the young girl is *not yet* and she was *no longer* prepared, then this "no longer" and "not yet" are mysteriously related, as the peculiarities of old age and childhood are related.) Then he moved her from the armchair to the couch, clasped her to him, and stroked her whole body, and in his arms she felt amorphously soft (yes, soft, because her body had long ago lost the sensuality that had once ruled it, that sensuality which had readily endowed her muscles with the rhythm of contractions and with the relaxation and activity of a hundred delicate movements).

The moment of dismay, however, soon melted away in his embrace and she, though far removed from the beautiful mature woman she had once been, now almost immediately rediscovered her former character. She regained a feeling of herself, she regained her knowledge, and once again found the confidence of an erotically adept woman; and because this was a confidence long untasted she felt it now more intensely than ever before. Her body, which a short while before had been trapped, alarmed, passive, and soft, revived and responded now with its own caresses and she felt the nicety and expertise of these caresses and it gratified her. These caresses, the way she put her face to his body, the delicate movements with which her body answered his embrace, she found all this not like something she was merely affecting, something that she knew how to do and which she was now performing with cold complaisance, but like something *essential*, of which she was elatedly and enthusiastically a part, as if this were her homeland (ah, land of beauty!), from which she had been exiled, and to which she now returned in triumph.

Her son was now infinitely far away. When her host had grabbed her, in a corner of her mind she caught sight of the boy warning her of the danger, but then he quickly disappeared. Now there remained only she and the man, who was stroking and embracing her. But when he placed his lips on her lips and wanted to open her mouth with his tongue, everything was suddenly reversed: she woke up. She firmly clenched her teeth (she imagined the bitter unfamiliarity of the substance, which would press against the roof of her mouth, and how her mouth would be full), and she didn't give herself to him; then she gently pushed him away and said: "No. Really, please, I'd rather not."

When he kept on insisting, she held him by the wrists of both hands and repeated her refusal. Then she said (it was hard for her to speak, but she knew that she must speak if she wanted him to obey her) that it was too late for them to make love. She reminded him of her age, if they did make love he would be disgusted with her and she would feel wretched about this, because what he had told her about the two of them was for her immensely beautiful and important. Her body was mortal and wasted, but she now knew that of it there still remained something incorporeal, something like the glow which shines even after a star has burned out. What did it matter that she was growing old if her youth remained preserved—intact—within someone. "You've erected a memorial to me within yourself. We cannot allow it to be destroyed. Please understand me," she warded him off. "Don't let it happen. No, don't let it happen!"

11

He assured her that she was still beautiful, that in fact nothing had changed, that a human being always remains the same, but he knew that he was deceiving her and that she was right. After all, he was well aware of his physical supersensitivity, his increasing fastidiousness about the external defects of a woman's body, which in recent years had driven him to ever younger and therefore, as he bitterly realized, also ever emptier and stupider women. Yes, there was no doubt about it; if he got her to make love it would end in disgust, and this disgust would then splatter with mud not only the present, but also the image of the beloved woman of long ago, an image cherished like a jewel in his memory.

He knew all this, but only intellectually, and the intellect meant nothing in the face of this desire, which knew only one thing: the woman whom he had thought of as unattainable and elusive for a whole fifteen years—was here. At last he could see her in broad daylight, at last he might discern from her body of today what her body had been like then, from her face of today what her face had been like then. At last he might discern her (unimaginable) love-making, first the movements and then the orgasm.

He put his arms around her shoulders and looked into her eyes: "Don't fight me. It's absurd to fight me."

12

But she shook her head, because she knew that it wasn't absurd for her to refuse him. She knew men and their approach to the female body. She was aware that in love even the most passionate idealism will not rid the body's surface of its terrible, basic importance. It is true that she still had a nice figure, which had preserved its original proportions, and especially in her clothes she looked quite youthful. But she knew that when she undressed she would expose the wrinkles in her neck, the long scar from a stomach operation ten years before, and her gray hair. She wasn't ashamed of the gray hair on her head, but that which she had in the center of her body she wore like a secret badge of dishonor.

And just as the consciousness of her present physical appearance, which she had forgotten a short while before, returned to her, so there arose from the street below (until now, this room had seemed to her safely high above her life) the anxieties of the morning. They were filling the room, they were alighting on the prints behind glass, on the armchair, on the table, on the empty coffee cup—and her son's face dominated their procession. When she caught sight of it, she blushed and fled somewhere deep inside herself. Foolishly, she had been on the point of wishing to escape from the path he had assigned to her and which she had trodden up to now with a smile and words of enthusiasm. She had been on the point of wishing (at least for a moment) to escape, and now she must obediently return and admit that it was the only path suitable for her. Her son's face was so derisive that, in shame, she felt herself growing smaller and smaller before him until, humiliated, she turned into the mere scar on her stomach.

Her host held her by the shoulders and once again repeated: "It's absurd for you to fight me," and she shook her head, but quite mechanically, because what she was seeing was not her host but her own youthful features in the face of her son-enemy, whom she hated the more the smaller and the more humiliated she felt. She heard him reproaching her about the canceled grave, and now, from the chaos of her memory, illogically there leaped out the sentence, which she enragedly threw into his face: *The old dead must make room for the young dead, my boy!*

13

He didn't have the slightest doubt that this would actually end in disgust. After all, he couldn't even give her a look (a searching and penetrating look) without feeling a certain disgust. But the curious thing was that it didn't make any difference to him. The very opposite, it excited him and goaded him on as if he were wishing for this disgust. The desire to read, finally, from her body what he had for so long not been permitted to know, was mixed with the desire to debase this reading immediately.

Where did this come from? Whether he realized it or not, a unique opportunity was presenting itself. To him, his visitor stood for everything that he had not had, that had eluded him, that he had overlooked, that by its absence amounted to what was so intolerable to him—his present age, his thinning hair, his dismally meager balance sheet. And he, whether he realized it or only vaguely suspected it, could now strip all these pleasures that had been denied him of their significance and color (for it was precisely their colorfulness that made his life so sadly dull). He could reveal that they were worthless, that they were only appearances doomed to destruction, that they were only dust transforming itself. He could take revenge upon them, demean them.

"Don't fight me," he repeated, and made an effort to draw her close.

14

Before her eyes she still saw her son's derisive face, and when now her host drew her to him by force she said, "Please, leave me alone for a minute," and released herself from his embrace. She didn't want to interrupt what was racing through her head: the old dead must make room for the young dead and memorials were no good and her memorial, which this man beside her had honored for fifteen years in his thoughts, was no good, and her husband's memorial was no good, and yes, my boy, all memorials were no good, she said inwardly to her son. And with vengeful delight she watched his contorted face and heard him yell, "You never spoke like this, Mother!" Of course she knew that she'd never spoken like this, but this moment was full of a light, under which everything became quite different.

There was no reason why she should give preference to memorials over life. Her own memorial had a single meaning for her: that at this moment she could abuse it for the sake of her disparaged body. The man who was sitting beside her appealed to her. He was young and very likely (almost certainly) he was the last man who would appeal to her and whom, at the same time, she could have—and that alone was important. If he then became disgusted with her and destroyed her memorial in his thoughts, it made no difference because her memorial was outside her, just as his thoughts and memory were outside her, and everything that was outside her made no difference. "You never spoke like that, Mother!" She heard her son's cry, but she paid no attention to him. She was smiling.

"You're right, why should I fight you," she said quietly, and got up. Then she slowly began to unbutton her dress. Evening was still a long way off. This time the room was full of light.

Nobody
Will Laugh

1

"Pour me some more slivovits," said Klara, and I wasn't against it. It was by no means unusual for us to open a bottle and this time there was a genuine excuse for it. That day I had received a considerable sum for the last part of a study, which was being published in installments by a professional visual arts magazine.

Publishing the study hadn't been so easy—what I'd written was polemical and controversial. That's why my studies had previously been rejected by *Visual Arts Journal*, where the editors were old and cautious, and had then been published only in a minor rival periodical, where the editors were younger and not so conservative.

The mailman brought the payment to the university along with another letter; an unimportant letter; in the morning in the first flush of beatitude I had hardly read the letter. But now at home, when it was approaching midnight and the wine was nearly gone, I took it off the table to amuse us.

"Esteemed comrade and if you will permit the expression—my colleague!" I read aloud to Klara. "Please excuse me, a man whom you have never met, for writing to you. I am turning to you with a request that you should read the enclosed article. True, I do not know you, but I respect you as a man whose judgments, reflections, and conclusions astonish me by their agreement with the results of my own research; I am completely amazed by it. Thus, for example, even though I bow before your conclusions and your excellent comparative analysis, I wish to call attention emphatically to the thought that Czech art has always been close to the people. I voiced this opinion before reading your treatise. I could prove this quite easily, for among other things, I even have witnesses. However, this is only marginal, for your treatise . . ." There followed further praise of my excellence and then a request. Would I kindly write a review of his article, that is, a specialist's evaluation for *Visual Arts Journal*, where they had been underestimating and rejecting his article for more than six months. They had told him that my opinion would be decisive, so now I had become the writer's only hope, a single light in an otherwise total darkness.

We made fun of Mr. Zaturetsky, whose aristocratic name fascinated us. But it was just fun; fun that meant no harm, for the praise which he had lavished on me, along with the excellent slivovits, softened me. It softened me so that in those unforgettable moments I loved the whole world. However, out of the whole world, especially Klara, because she was sitting opposite me, while the rest of the world was hidden from me by the walls of my Vrshovits attic. And because at that moment I didn't have anything to reward the world with, I rewarded Klara; at least with promises.

Klara was a twenty-year-old girl from a good family. What am I saying, from a good family? From an excellent family! Her father had been a bank manager, and some time in the fifties, as a representative of the upper bourgeoisie, had been exiled to the village of Chelakovits, which was some distance from Prague. As a result, his daughter had a bad party record and worked as a seamstress in a large Prague dress factory. I can't bear prejudice. I don't believe that the extent of a father's property can leave its mark on his child's genes. I ask you, who today is really a plebeian and who is a patrician? Everything has been mixed up and has changed places so completely, that it's sometimes difficult to understand anything in terms of sociological concepts. I was far from feeling that I was sitting opposite a class enemy; on the contrary, I was sitting opposite a beautiful seamstress and trying to make her like me more by telling her lightheartedly about the advantages of a job I'd promised to get her through connections. I assured her that it was absurd for such a pretty girl to lose her beauty over a sewing machine, and I decided that she should become a model.

Klara didn't offer any resistance and we spent the night in happy understanding.

2

Man passes through the present with his eyes blindfolded. He is permitted merely to sense and guess at what he is actually experiencing. Only later when the cloth is untied can he glance at the past and find out *what* he has experienced and what meaning it has had.

That evening I thought I was drinking to my successes and didn't in the least suspect that it was the prelude to my undoing.

And because I didn't suspect anything I woke up the next day in a good mood, and while Klara was still breathing contentedly by my side, I took the article, which was attached to the letter, and skimmed through it with amused indifference.

It was called "Mikolash Alesh, Master of Czech Drawing," and it really wasn't worth even the half hour of inattention that I devoted to it. It was a collection of platitudes heaped together with no sense of continuity and without the least intention of advancing through them some original thought.

Quite clearly it was pure nonsense. The very same day Dr. Kalousek, the editor of *Visual Arts Journal* (in other respects an unusually hostile man), confirmed my opinion over the telephone; he called me at the university: "Say, did you get that treatise from the Zaturetsky guy? . . . Then take care of it. Five lecturers have already cut him to pieces, but he keeps on bugging us; he's got it into his head that you're the only genuine authority. Tell him in two sentences that it's crap, you know how to do that, you know how to be really venomous; and then we'll all have some peace."

But something inside me protested: why should *I* have to be Mr. Zaturetsky's executioner? Was *I* the one receiving an editor's salary for this? Besides, I remembered very well that they had refused my article at *Visual Arts Journal* out of overcautiousness; what's more, Mr. Zaturetsky's name was firmly connected in my mind with Klara, slivovits, and a beautiful evening. And finally, I shan't deny it, it's human—I could have counted on one finger the people who think me "a genuine authority": why should I lose this only one?

I closed the conversation with some clever vaguery, which Kalousek considered a promise and I, an excuse. I put down the receiver firmly convinced that I would never write the review for Mr. Zaturetsky.

Instead I took some writing paper out of the drawer and wrote a letter to Mr. Zaturetsky, in which I avoided any kind of judgment of his work, excusing myself by saying that my opinions on nineteenth century art were commonly considered devious and eccentric, and therefore my intercession —especially with the editors of *Visual Arts Journal*—would harm rather than benefit his cause. At the same time, I overwhelmed Mr. Zaturetsky with friendly loquacity, from which it was impossible not to detect approval on my part.

As soon as I had put the letter in the mailbox I forgot Mr. Zaturetsky. But Mr. Zaturetsky did not forget me.

3

One day when I was about to end my lecture—I lecture at college in the history of art—there was a knock at the door; it was our secretary, Mary, a kind elderly lady, who occasionally prepares coffee for me, and says that I'm out when there are undesirable female voices on the telephone. She put her head in the doorway and said that some gentleman was looking for me.

I'm not afraid of gentlemen and so I took leave of the students and went good-humoredly out into the corridor. A smallish man in a shabby black suit and a white shirt bowed to me. He very respectfully informed me that he was Zaturetsky.

I invited the visitor into an empty room, offered him an armchair, and began pleasantly discussing everything possible with him, for instance what a bad summer it was and what exhibitions were on in Prague. Mr. Zaturetsky politely agreed with all of my chatter, but he soon tried to apply every remark of mine to his article, which lay invisibly between us like an irresistible magnet.

"Nothing would make me happier than to write a review of your work," I said finally, "but as I explained to you in the letter, I am not considered an expert on the Czech nineteenth century, and, in addition, I'm on bad terms with the editors of *Visual Arts Journal*, who take me for a hardened modernist, so that a positive review from me could only harm you."

"Oh, you're too modest," said Mr. Zaturetsky, "how can you, who are such an expert, judge your own standing so blackly! In the editors' office they told me that everything depends on your review. If you support my article they'll publish it. You are my only recourse. It's the work of three years of study and three years of toil. Everything is now in your hands."

How carelessly and from what bad masonry does a man build his excuses! I didn't know how to reply to Mr. Zaturetsky. I involuntarily looked at his face and noticed there not only small, ancient, and innocent spectacles staring at me, but also a powerful, deep vertical wrinkle on his forehead. In a brief moment of clairvoyance a shiver shot down my spine. This wrinkle, concentrated and stubborn, betrayed not only the intellectual torment which its owner had gone through over Mikolash Alesh's drawings, but also unusually strong willpower. I lost my presence of mind and failed to find any clever excuse. I knew that I wouldn't write the review, but I also knew that I didn't have the strength to say so to this pathetic little man's face.

And then I began to smile and promise something vague. Mr. Zaturetsky thanked me and said that he would come again soon. We parted smiling.

In a couple of days he did come. I cleverly avoided him, but the next day I was told that he was searching for me again at the university. I realized that bad times were on the way; I went quickly to Mary so as to take appropriate steps.

"Mary dear, I beg you, if that man should come looking for me again, say that I've gone to do some research in Germany and I'll be back in a month. And you should know about this: I have, as you know, all my lectures on Tuesday and Wednesday. I'll shift them secretly to Thursday and

Friday. Only the students will know about this, don't tell anyone, and leave the schedule uncorrected. I'll have to disobey the rules."

4

Indeed Mr. Zaturetsky did soon come back to look me up and was miserable when the secretary informed him that I'd suddenly gone off to Germany. "But this is not possible. Mr. Klima has to write a review about me. How could he go away like this?" "I don't know," said Mary. "However, he'll be back in a month." "Another month . . . ," moaned Mr. Zaturetsky: "And you don't know his address in Germany?" "I don't," said Mary.

And then I had a month of peace, but the month passed more quickly than I expected and Mr. Zaturetsky stood once again in the office. "No, he still hasn't returned," said Mary, and when she met me later about something she asked me imploringly: "Your little man was here again, what in heaven's name should I tell him?" "Tell him, Mary, that I got jaundice and am in the hospital in Jena." "In the hospital!" cried Mr. Zaturetsky, when Mary told him the story a few days later. "It's not possible! Don't you know that Mr. Klima has to write a review about me!" "Mr. Zaturetsky," said the secretary reproachfully, "Mr. Klima is lying in a hospital somewhere abroad seriously ill, and you think only about your review." Mr. Zaturetsky backed down and went away, but two weeks later was once again in the office: "I sent a registered letter to Mr. Klima in Jena. It is a small town, there can only be one hospital there, and the letter came back to me!" "Your little man is driving me crazy," said Mary to me the next day. "You mustn't get angry with me, what could I say to him? I told him that you've come back. You must deal with him by yourself now."

I didn't get angry with Mary. She had done what she could. Besides, I was far from considering myself beaten. I knew that I was not to be caught. I lived under cover all the time. I lectured secretly on Thursday and Friday; and every Tuesday and Wednesday, crouching in the doorway of a house opposite the school, I would rejoice at the sight of Mr. Zaturetsky, who kept watch in front of the school waiting for me to come out. I longed to put on a bowler hat and stick on a beard. I felt like Sherlock Holmes or the Invisible Man, who strides stealthily; I felt like a little boy.

One day, however, Mr. Zaturetsky finally got tired of keeping watch and jumped on Mary. "Where exactly does Comrade Klima lecture?" "There's the schedule," said Mary, pointing to the wall, where the times of all the lectures were laid out in exemplary fashion on a large, checkered board.

"I see that," said Mr. Zaturetsky, refusing to be put off. "Only Comrade Klima never lectures here on either Tuesday or Wednesday. Is he reported sick?"

"No," said Mary hesitantly. And then the little man turned again on Mary. He reproached her for the confusion in the schedule. He inquired ironically how it was that she didn't know where every teacher was at a given time. He told her that he was going to complain about her. He shouted. He said that he was also going to complain about Comrade Assistant Klima, who wasn't lecturing, although he was supposed to be. He asked if the dean was in.

Unfortunately, the dean was in. Mr. Zaturetsky knocked on his door and went in. Ten minutes later he returned to Mary's office and demanded the address of my apartment.

"Twenty Skalnik Street in Litomyshl," said Mary. "In Prague, Mr. Klima only has a temporary address and he doesn't want it disclosed . . ." "I'm asking you to give me the address of Assistant Klima's Prague apartment," cried the little man in a trembling voice.

Somehow Mary lost her presence of mind. She gave him the address of my attic, my poor little refuge, my sweet den, in which I would be caught.

5

Yes, my permanent address is in Litomyshl; there I have my mother, my friends, and memories of my father; I flee from Prague, as often as I can, and write at home in my mother's small apartment. So it happened that I kept my mother's apartment as my permanent residence and in Prague I didn't manage to get myself a proper bachelor's apartment, as you're supposed to do, but lived in Vrshovits in lodgings, in a small, completely private attic, whose existence I concealed as much as possible. I didn't register anywhere so as to prevent unnecessary meetings between undesirable guests and my various transient female roommates or visitors, whose comings and goings, I confess, were sometimes most disorganized. For precisely these reasons I didn't enjoy the best reputation in the house. Also, during my stays in Litomyshl I had several times lent my cozy little room to friends, who amused themselves only too well there, and didn't allow anyone in the house to get a wink of sleep. All this scandalized some of the occupants, who conducted a quiet war against me. Sometimes they had the local committee express unfavorable opinions of me and they even handed in a complaint to the apartment office.

At that time it was inconvenient for Klara to get to work from such a distance as Chelakovits, and so she began to stay overnight at my place. At first she stayed timidly and as an exception, then she left one dress, then several dresses, and within a short time my two suits were stuffed into a corner of the wardrobe, and my little room was transformed into a woman's boudoir.

I really liked Klara; she was beautiful; it pleased me that people turned their heads when we went out together; she was at least thirteen years younger than me, which increased the students' respect for me; I had a thousand reasons for taking good care of her. But I didn't want it to be known that she was living with me. I was afraid of rumors and gossip about us in the house; I was afraid that someone would start attacking my good old landlord, who lived for the greater part of the year outside Prague, was discreet, and didn't concern himself about me; I was afraid that one day he would come to me, unhappy and with a heavy heart, and ask me to send the young lady away for the sake of his good name.

Klara had been strictly ordered not to open the door to anyone.

One day she was alone in the house. It was a sunny day and rather stuffy in the attic. She was lounging almost naked on my couch, occupying herself with an examination of the ceiling, when suddenly there was a pounding on the door.

There was nothing alarming in this. I didn't have a bell, so anyone who came had to knock. So Klara wasn't going to let herself be disturbed by the noise and didn't stop examining the ceiling. But the pounding didn't cease; on the contrary, it went on with imperturbable persistence. Klara was getting nervous. She began to imagine a man standing behind the door, a man who slowly and significantly turns up the lapels of his jacket, and who will later pounce on her demanding why she hadn't opened the door, what she was concealing, and whether she was registered. A feeling of guilt seized her; she lowered her eyes from the ceiling and tried to think where she had left her dress lying. But the pounding continued so stubbornly, that in the confusion she found nothing but my raincoat hanging in the hall. She put it on and opened the door.

Instead of an evil, querying face, she only saw a little man, who bowed: "Is Mr. Klima at home?" "No, he isn't." "That's a pity," said the little man and apologized for having disturbed her. "The thing is that Mr. Klima has to write a review about me. He promised me and it's very urgent. If you would permit it, I could at least leave him a message."

Klara gave him paper and pencil, and in the evening I read that the fate of the article about Mikolash Alesh was in my hands alone, and that Mr. Zaturetsky was waiting most respectfully for my review and would try to look me up again at the university.

6

The next day, Mary told me how Mr. Zaturetsky had threatened her, and how he had gone to complain about her; her voice trembled and she was on the verge of tears; I flew into a rage. I realized that the secretary, who until now had been laughing at my game of hide-and-seek (though I would bet anything that she did what she did out of kindness toward me, rather than simply from a sense of fun), was now feeling hurt and conceivably saw me as the cause of her troubles. When I also included the exposure of my attic, the ten-minute pounding on the door, and Klara's fright—my anger grew to a frenzy.

As I was walking back and forth in Mary's office, biting my lips, boiling with rage and thinking about revenge, the door opened and Mr. Zaturetsky appeared.

When he saw me a glimmer of happiness flashed over his face. He bowed and greeted me. He had come a little prematurely, he had come before I had managed to consider my revenge.

He asked if I had received his message yesterday.

I was silent. He repeated his question. "I received it," I replied.

"And will you, please, write the review?"

I saw him in front of me: sickly, obstinate, beseeching; I saw the vertical wrinkle—etched on his forehead, the line of a single passion—I examined this line and grasped that it was a straight line determined by two points, my review and his article; that beyond the vice of this maniacal straight line nothing existed in his life but saintly asceticism; and then a spiteful trick occurred to me.

"I hope that you understand that after yesterday I can't speak to you," I said.

"I don't understand you."

"Don't pretend. She told me everything. It's unnecessary for you to deny it."

"I don't understand you," repeated the little man once again; but this time more decidedly.

I assumed a genial, almost friendly tone. "Look here, Mr. Zaturetsky, I don't blame you. I chase women as well and

I understand you. In your position I would have tried to seduce a beautiful girl like that, if I'd found myself alone in an apartment with her and she'd been naked beneath a man's raincoat."

"This is an outrage!" The little man turned pale.

"No, it's the truth, Mr. Zaturetsky."

"Did the lady tell you this?"

"She has no secrets from me."

"Comrade Assistant, this is an outrage! I'm a married man. I have a wife! I have children!" The little man took a step forward, so that I had to step back.

"So much the worse for you, Mr. Zaturetsky."

"What do you mean, so much the worse?"

"I think being married must be a drawback to chasing women."

"Take it back!" said Mr. Zaturetsky menacingly.

"Well, all right," I conceded, "the matrimonial state need not always be an obstacle. Sometimes it can, on the contrary, excuse all sorts of things. But it makes no difference. I've already told you that I'm not angry with you and I understand you quite well. There's only one thing I don't understand. How can you still want a review from a man whose woman you've been trying to make?"

"Comrade Assistant! Dr. Kalousek, the editor of the magazine of the Academy of Sciences, *Visual Arts Journal*, is asking you for this review. And you must write the review!"

"The review or the woman. You can't ask for both."

"What kind of behavior is this, comrade!" screamed Mr. Zaturetsky in desperate anger.

The odd thing is that I suddenly felt that Mr. Zaturetsky had really wanted to seduce Klara. Seething with rage, I shouted, "You have the audacity to tell me off? You who should humbly apologize to me in front of my secretary."

I turned my back on Mr. Zaturetsky, and, confused, he staggered out.

"Well then," I sighed with relief like a general after the victorious conclusion of a hard campaign, and I said to Mary, "Perhaps he won't want a review by me any more."

Mary smiled and after a moment timidly asked, "Just why is it you don't want to write this review?"

"Because, Mary my dear, what he's written is the most awful crap."

"Then why don't you write in your review that it's crap?"

"Why should I write it? Why do I have to antagonize people?"—but hardly had I said this when I realized that Mr. Zaturetsky was my enemy all the same and that my struggle not to write the review was an aimless and absurd struggle—unfortunately, there was nothing I could do either to stop it or to back down.

Mary was looking at me with an indulgent smile, as women look upon the foolishness of children; then the door opened and there stood Mr. Zaturetsky with his arm raised. "It's not me! It's you who will have to apologize," he shouted in a trembling voice and disappeared again.

7

I don't remember exactly when, perhaps that same day or perhaps a few days later, we found an envelope in my mailbox without an address.

Inside there was a letter in a clumsy, almost primitive handwriting:

Dear Madame:
Present yourself at my house on Sunday regarding the
insult to my husband. I shall be at home all day. If
you don't present yourself, I shall be forced to take
measures.
Anna Zaturetsky, 14 Dalimilova Street, Prague 3.

Klara was scared and began saying something about
my guilt. I waved my hand, declaring that the purpose of
life is to give amusement, and if life is too lazy for this, there
is nothing left but to help it along a little. Man must con-
stantly saddle events, those swift mares without which he
would be dragging his feet in the dust like a weary foot-
slogger. When Klara said that she didn't want to saddle any
events, I assured her that she would never meet Mr. or Mrs.
Zaturetsky, and that the event into whose saddle I had
jumped, I'd take care of with one hand tied behind my back.

In the morning when we were leaving the house, the
porter stopped us. The porter wasn't an enemy. Prudently, I
had once bribed him with a fifty-crown bill, and I had lived
until this time in the agreeable conviction that he'd learned
not to know anything about me, and didn't add fuel to the fire,
which my enemies in the house kept alight.

"Some couple was here looking for you yesterday,"
he said.

"What sort of couple?"

"A little guy with a woman."

"What did the woman look like?"

"Two heads taller. Terribly energetic. A stern woman.
She was asking about all sorts of things." He turned to Klara.
"Chiefly about you. Who you are and what your name is."

"Good heavens, what did you say to her?" exclaimed
Klara.

"What could I say? How do I know who comes to see Mr. Klima? I told her that a different person comes every evening."

"Great!" I laughed and drew ten crowns from my pocket. "Just go on talking like that."

"Don't be afraid," I then said to Klara, "you won't go anywhere on Sunday and nobody will find you."

And Sunday came, and after Sunday, Monday, Tuesday, Wednesday; nothing happened. "You see," I said to Klara. But then came Thursday. I was lecturing to my students at the customary secret lecture about how feverishly and in what an atmosphere of unselfish camaraderie the young Fauvists had liberated color from its former impressionistic character, when Mary opened the door and whispered to me, "The wife of that Zaturetsky is here." "But I'm not here," I said, "just show her the schedule!" But Mary shook her head. "I showed her, but she peeped into your office and saw your raincoat on the stand. Just then Assistant Professor Zeleny came by and assured her that it was yours. So now she's sitting in the corridor waiting."

Had fate been able to pursue me more systematically, it is quite possible that I would have been a success. A blind alley is the place for my best inspirations. I said to my favorite student:

"Be so kind as to do me a small favor. Run to my office, put on my raincoat, and go out of the building in it. Some woman will try to prove that you are me, and your task will be not to admit it at any price."

The student went off and returned in about a quarter of an hour. He told me that the mission had been completed, the coast was clear, and the woman was out of the building.

This time then I had won. But then came Friday, and

in the afternoon Klara returned from work trembling almost like a leaf.

The polite gentleman who received customers in the tidy office of the dress factory had suddenly opened the door leading to the workroom, where my Klara and fifteen other seamstresses were sitting over their sewing machines, and cried:

"Does any one of you live at 5 Pushkin Street?"

Klara knew that it concerned her, because 5 Pushkin Street was my address. However, well-advised caution kept her quiet, for she knew that her living with me was a secret and that nobody knew anything about it.

"You see, that's what I've been telling her," said the polished gentleman when none of the seamstresses spoke up, and he went out again. Klara learned later that a strict female voice on the telephone had made him search through the directory of employees, and had talked for a quarter of an hour trying to convince him there must be a woman employee from 5 Pushkin Street in the factory.

The shadow of Mrs. Zaturetsky was cast over our idyllic room.

"But how could she have found out where you work? After all, here in the house nobody knows about you!" I yelled.

Yes, I was really convinced that nobody knew about us. I lived like an eccentric who thinks that he lives unobserved behind a high wall, while all the time one detail escapes him: the wall is made of transparent glass.

I had bribed the porter not to reveal that Klara lived with me, I had forced Klara into the most troublesome inconspicuousness and concealment and, meanwhile, the whole house knew about her. It was enough that once she had entered into an ill-advised conversation with a woman on the second floor—and they got to know where Klara was working.

Without suspecting it we had been living exposed for quite some time. What remained concealed from our persecutors was merely Klara's name and then one small detail: that she lived with me unregistered. These two were the final and only secrets behind which, for the time being, we eluded Mrs. Zaturetsky, who launched her attack so consistently and methodically that I was horror-struck.

I understood that it was going to be tough. The horse of my story was damnably saddled.

8

This was on Friday. And when Klara came back from work on Saturday, she was trembling again. Here is what had happened:

Mrs. Zaturetsky had set out with her husband for the factory. She had called beforehand and asked the manager to allow her and her husband to visit the workshop, to examine the faces of the seamstresses. It's true that this request astonished the comrade manager, but Mrs. Zaturetsky put on such an air that it was impossible to refuse. She said something vague about an insult, about a ruined existence, and about court. Mr. Zaturetsky stood beside her, frowned, and was silent.

They were shown into the workroom. The seamstresses raised their heads indifferently, and Klara recognized the little man; she turned pale and with conspicuous inconspicuousness quickly went on with her needlework.

"Here you are," exclaimed the manager with ironic

politeness to the stiff-looking pair. Mrs. Zaturetsky realized that she must take the initiative and she urged her husband: "Well look!" Mr. Zaturetsky assumed a scowl and looked around. "Is it one of them?" whispered Mrs. Zaturetsky.

Even with his glasses Mr. Zaturetsky couldn't see clearly enough to examine the large room, which in any case wasn't easy to survey, full as it was of piled-up junk and dresses hanging from long horizontal bars, with fidgety seamstresses, who didn't sit neatly with their faces toward the door, but in various positions; they were turning round, getting up and down, and involuntarily averting their faces. Therefore, Mr. Zaturetsky had to step forward and try not to skip anyone.

When the women understood that they were being examined by someone, and in addition by someone so unsightly and unattractive, they felt vaguely insulted, and sneers and grumbling began to be heard. One of them, a robust young girl, impertinently burst out:

"He's searching all over Prague for the shrew who made him pregnant!"

The noisy, ribald mockery of the women overwhelmed the couple; they stood downcast, and then became resolute with a peculiar sort of dignity.

"Ma'am," the impertinent girl yelled again at Mrs. Zaturetsky, "you look after your little son badly! I would never have let such a nice little boy out of the house."

"Look some more," she whispered to her husband, and sullenly and timidly he went forward step by step as if he were running the gauntlet, but firmly all the same—and he didn't miss a face.

All the time the manager was smiling noncommittally; he knew his women and he knew that you couldn't do anything with them; and so he pretended not to hear their clamor, and he asked Mr. Zaturetsky, "Now please tell me, what is this woman supposed to look like?"

Mr. Zaturetsky turned to the manager and spoke slowly and seriously: "She was beautiful . . . She was very beautiful . . ."

Meanwhile Klara crouched in a corner, setting herself off from all the playful women by her agitation, her bent head, and her dogged activity. Oh, how badly she feigned her inconspicuousness and insignificance! And Mr. Zaturetsky was only a little way away from her; in the next minute he must look into her face.

"That isn't much, when you only remember that she was beautiful," said the polite comrade manager to Mr. Zaturetsky. "There are many beautiful women. Was she short or tall?"

"Tall," said Mr. Zaturetsky.

"Was she brunette or blonde?" Mr. Zaturetsky thought a moment and said, "She was blonde."

This part of the story could serve as a parable on the power of beauty. When Mr. Zaturetsky had seen Klara for the first time at my place, he was so dazzled that he actually hadn't seen her. Beauty created before her some opaque screen. A screen of light, behind which she was hidden as if beneath a veil.

For Klara is neither tall nor blonde. Only the inner greatness of beauty lent her in Mr. Zaturetsky's eyes a semblance of great physical size. And the glow, which emanates from beauty, lent her hair the appearance of gold.

And so when the little man finally approached the corner where Klara, in a brown work smock, was huddled over a shirt, he didn't recognize her, because he had never seen her.

74

9

When Klara had finished an incoherent and barely intelligible account of this event I said, "You see, we're lucky."

But amid sobs Klara said to me, "What kind of luck? If they didn't find me today, they'll find me tomorrow."

"I should like to know how."

"They'll come here for me, to your place."

"I won't let anyone in."

"And what when they send the police?"

"Come now, I'll make a joke of it. After all, it was just a joke and fun."

"Today there's no time for jokes, today everything gets serious. They'll say that I wanted to blacken his reputation. When they take a look at him, how could they ever believe that he was capable of trying to seduce a woman?"

"You're right, Klara," I said, "they'll probably lock you up. But look, Karel Havlichek Borovsky was also in jail and think how far he got; you must have learned about him in school."

"Stop chattering," said Klara. "You know it looks bad for me. I'll have to go before the disciplinary committee and I'll have it on my record, and I'll never get out of the workshop. Anyway, I'd like to know what's happening about the modeling job you promised me. I can't sleep at your place any longer. I'll always be afraid that they're coming for me. Today I'm going back to Chelakovits." This was one conversation.

And that afternoon after a departmental meeting I had a second.

The chairman of the department, a gray-haired art historian and a wise man, invited me into his office.

"I hope you know that you haven't helped yourself with that study that has just come out," he said to me.

"Yes, I know," I replied.

"Many of our professors think that it applies to them and the dean thinks that it was an attack on his views."

"What can be done about it?" I said.

"Nothing," replied the professor, "but your three-year period as a lecturer has expired and candidates will compete to fill the position. It is customary for the committee to give the position to someone who has already taught in the school, but are you so sure that this custom will be upheld in your case? But this is not what I wanted to speak about. So far it has spoken in your favor that you lectured regularly, that you were popular with the students, and that you taught them something. But now you can't even rely on this. The dean has informed me that for the last three months you haven't lectured at all. And quite without excuse. Well, this in itself would be enough for immediate dismissal."

I explained to the professor that I hadn't missed a single lecture, that it had all been a joke, and I told him the whole story about Mr. Zaturetsky and Klara.

"Fine, I believe you," said the professor, "but what does it matter if I believe you? Today the whole school says that you don't lecture and don't do anything. It has already been discussed at the union meeting and yesterday they took the matter to the board of regents."

"But why didn't they speak to me about it first?"

"What should they speak to you about? Everything is clear to them. Now they are only looking back over your whole performance trying to find connections between your past and your present."

"What can they find bad in my past? You know yourself how much I like my work! I've never shirked! My conscience is clear."

"Every human life has many aspects," said the professor. "The past of each one of us can be just as easily arranged into the biography of a beloved statesman as into that of a criminal. Only look thoroughly at yourself. Nobody is denying that you like your work. But what if it served you above all as an opportunity for escape? You weren't often seen at meetings and when you did come, for the most part, you were silent. Nobody really knew what you thought. I myself remember that several times when a serious matter was being discussed you suddenly made a joke, which caused embarrassment. This embarrassment was of course immediately forgotten, but today, when it is retrieved from the past, it acquires a particular significance. Or remember how various women came looking for you at the university and how you refused to see them. Or else your last article, about which anyone who wishes can allege that it was written from suspicious premises. All these, of course, are isolated facts; but just look at them in the light of today's offense, and they suddenly unite into a totality of significant testimony about your character and attitude."

"But what sort of offense! Everything can be explained so easily! The facts are quite simple and clear!"

"Facts mean little compared to attitudes. To contradict rumor or sentiment is as futile as arguing against a believer's faith in the Immaculate Conception. You have simply become a victim of faith, Comrade Assistant."

"There's a lot of truth in what you say," I said, "but if a sentiment has arisen against me like an act of faith, I shall fight faith with reason. I shall explain before everyone the things that took place. If people are human they will have to laugh at it."

"As you like. But you'll learn either that people aren't human or that you don't know what humans are like. They will not laugh. If you place before them everything as it happened, it will then appear that not only did you fail to fulfill your obligations as they were indicated on the schedule— that you did not do what you should have done—but on top of this, you lectured secretly, that is, you did what you shouldn't have done. It will appear that you insulted a man who was asking for your help. It will appear that your private life is not in order, that you have some unregistered girl living with you, which will make a very unfavorable impression on the female chairman of the union. The issue will become confused and God knows what further rumors will arise. Whatever they are they will certainly be useful to those who have been provoked by your views, but were ashamed to be against you on account of them."

I knew that the professor wasn't trying to alarm or deceive me. In this matter, however, I considered him a crank and didn't want to give myself up to his skepticism. The scandal with Mr. Zaturetsky made me go cold all over, but it hadn't tired me out yet. For I had saddled this horse myself, so I couldn't let it tear the reins from my hands and carry me off wherever it wished. I was prepared to engage in a contest with it. And the horse did not avoid the contest. When I reached home, there in the mailbox was a summons to a meeting of the local committee, and I had no doubt as to what it was about.

10

I was not mistaken. The local committee, which was in session in what had been a store, was seated around a long table. The members assumed a gloomy expression when I came in. A grizzled man with glasses and a receding chin pointed to a chair. I said thank you, sat down, and this man took the floor. He informed me that the local committee had been watching me for some time, that it knew very well that I led an irregular private life; that this did not produce a good impression in my neighborhood; that the tenants from my apartment house had already complained about me once, when they couldn't sleep because of the uproar in my apartment; that all this was enough for the local committee to have formed a proper conception of me. And now, on top of all this, Comrade Madame Zaturetsky, the wife of a scientific worker, had turned to them for help. Six months ago I should have written a review about her husband's scientific work, and I hadn't done so, even though I well knew that the fate of the said work depended on my review.

"What the devil d'you mean by scientific work!" I interrupted the man with the little chin: "It's a patchwork of plagiarized thoughts."

"That is interesting, comrade." A fashionably dressed blonde of about thirty now joined in the discussion; on her face was permanently glued a beaming smile. "Permit me a question; what is your field?"

"I am an art theoretician."

"And Comrade Zaturetsky?"

"I don't know. Perhaps he's trying at something similar."

"You see," the blonde turned enthusiastically to the remaining members, "Comrade Klima sees a worker in the same field as a competitor and not as a comrade. This is the way that almost all our intellectuals think today."

"I shall continue," said the man with the receding chin. "Comrade Madame Zaturetsky told us that her husband visited your apartment and met some woman there. It is said that this woman accused Mr. Zaturetsky of wanting to molest her sexually. Comrade Madame Zaturetsky has in her hand documents which prove that her husband is not capable of such a thing. She wants to know the name of this woman who accused her husband, and to transfer the matter to the disciplinary section of the people's committee, because she claims this false accusation has damaged her husband's good name."

I tried again to cut this ridiculous affair short. "Look here, comrades," I said, "it isn't worth all the trouble. It's not a question of damaged reputation. The work is so weak that no one else could recommend it either. And if some misunderstanding occurred between this woman and Mr. Zaturetsky, it shouldn't really be necessary to summon a meeting."

"Fortunately, it is not you who will decide about our meetings, comrade," replied the man with the receding chin. "And when you now assert that Comrade Zaturetsky's work is bad, then we must look upon this as revenge. Comrade Madame Zaturetsky gave us a letter to read, which you wrote, after reading her husband's work."

"Yes. Only in that letter I didn't say a word about what the work was like."

"That is true. But you did write that you would be

glad to help him; in this letter it is clearly implied that you respect Comrade Zaturetsky's work. And now you declare that it's a patchwork. Why didn't you say it to his face?"

"Comrade Klima has two faces," said the blonde.

At this moment an elderly woman with a permanent wave joined the discussion (she had an expression of self-sacrificing goodwill in examining the lives of others); she passed at once to the heart of the matter. "We would need to know, comrade, who this woman was whom Mr. Zaturetsky met at your home."

I understood unmistakably that it wasn't within my power to remove the senseless gravity from the whole affair, and that I could dispose of it in only one way: to confuse the traces, to lure them away from Klara, to lead them away from her as the partridge leads the hound away from its nest, offering its own body for the sake of its young.

"It's a bad business, I don't remember her name," I said.

"How is it that you don't remember the name of the woman you live with?" questioned the woman with the permanent wave.

"At one time, I used to write all this down, but then it occurred to me that it was stupid and I dropped it. It's hard for a man to rely on his memory."

"Perhaps, Comrade Klima, you have an exemplary relationship with women," said the blonde.

"Perhaps I could remember, but I should have to think about it. Do you know when it was that Mr. Zaturetsky visited me?"

"That was . . . wait a moment," the man with the receding chin looked at his papers, "the fourteenth, on Wednesday afternoon."

"On Wednesday . . . the fourteenth . . . wait . . ."

I held my head in my hand and did some thinking. "Oh I remember. That was Helena." I saw that they were all hanging expectantly on my words.

"Helena what?"

"What? I'm sorry, I don't know. I didn't want to ask her that. As a matter of fact, speaking frankly, I'm not even sure that her name was Helena. I only called her that because her husband seemed to me to be like red-haired Menelaus. But anyway she very much liked being called that. On Tuesday evening I met her in a wineshop and managed to talk to her for a while, when her Menelaus went to the bar to drink a cognac. The next day she came to my place and was there the whole afternoon. Only I had to leave her in the evening for a couple of hours, I had a meeting at the university. When I returned she was disgusted because some little man had molested her and she thought that I had put him up to it; she took offense and didn't want to know me any more. And so, you see, I didn't even manage to learn her correct name."

"Comrade Klima, whether you are telling the truth or not," went on the blonde, "it seems to me to be absolutely incomprehensible that you can educate our youth. Does our life really inspire in you nothing but the desire to carouse and abuse women? Be assured, we shall give our opinion about this in the proper places."

"The porter didn't speak about any Helena," broke in the elderly lady with the permanent wave, "but he did inform us that some unregistered girl from the dress factory has been living with you for a month. Don't forget, comrade, that you are in lodgings. How can you imagine that someone can live with you like this? Do you think that your house is a brothel?"

There flashed before my eyes the ten crowns which I'd given to the porter a couple of days ago, and I understood that the encirclement was complete. And the woman from the local committee continued: "If you don't want to tell us her name, the police will find it out."

11

The ground was slipping away beneath my feet. At the university I began to sense the malicious atmosphere which the professor had told me about. For the time being, I wasn't summoned to any interviews, but here and there I caught an allusion, and now and then Mary let something out, for the teachers drank coffee in her office and didn't watch their tongues. In a couple of days the selection committee, which was collecting evidence on all sides, was to meet. I imagined that its members had read the report of the local committee, a report about which I knew only that it was secret and that I couldn't refer to it.

There are moments in life when a man retreats defensively, when he must give ground, when he must surrender less important positions in order to protect the more important ones. But should it come to the very last, the most important one, at this point a man must halt and stand firm if he doesn't want to begin life all over again with idle hands and a feeling of being shipwrecked.

It seemed to me that this single, most important position was my love. Yes, in those troubled days I suddenly began to realize that I loved my fragile and unfortunate seamstress, who had been both beaten and pampered by life, and that I clung to her.

That day I met Klara at the museum. No, not at home. Do you think that home was still home? Is home a room with glass walls? A room observed through binoculars? A room where you must keep your beloved more carefully hidden than contraband?

Home was not home. There we felt like housebreakers who might be caught at any minute. Footsteps in the corridor made us nervous; we kept expecting someone to start pounding on the door. Klara was commuting from Chelakovits and we didn't feel like meeting in our alienated home for even a short while. So I had asked an artist friend to lend me his studio at night. That day I had got the key for the first time.

And so we found ourselves beneath a high roof in Vinohrady, in an enormous room with one small couch and a huge, slanting window, from which we could see all the lights of Prague. Amid the many paintings propped against the walls, the untidiness, and the carefree artist's squalor, a blessed feeling of freedom returned to me. I sprawled on the couch, pushed in the corkscrew and opened a bottle of wine. I chattered gaily and freely, and was looking forward to a beautiful evening and night.

However, the pressure, which I no longer felt, had fallen with its full weight on Klara.

I have already mentioned how Klara without any scruples and with the greatest naturalness had lived at one time in my attic. But now, when we found ourselves for a short time in someone else's studio, she felt put out. More than put out: "It's humiliating," she said.

"What's humiliating?" I asked her.

"That we have to borrow an apartment."

"Why is it humiliating that we have to borrow an apartment?"

"Because there's something humiliating about it," she replied.

"But we couldn't do anything else."

"I guess," she replied, "but in a borrowed apartment I feel like a whore."

"Good God, why should you feel like a whore in a *borrowed* apartment. Whores mostly operate in their own apartments, not in borrowed ones—"

It was futile to attack with reason the stout wall of irrational feelings that, as is known, is the stuff of which the female mind is made. From the beginning our conversation was ill-omened.

I told Klara what the professor had said, I told her what had happened at the local committee, and I was trying to convince her that in the end we would win if we loved each other and were together.

Klara was silent for a while and then said that I myself was guilty.

"Will you at least help me to get away from those seamstresses?"

I told her that this would have to be, at least temporarily, a time of forbearance.

"You see," said Klara, "you promised and in the end you do nothing. I won't be able to get out, even if somebody else wanted to help me, because I shall have my reputation ruined on your account."

I gave Klara my word that the incident with Mr. Zaturetsky couldn't harm her.

"I also don't understand," said Klara, "why you won't write the review. If you'd write it, then there'd be peace at once."

"It's too late, Klara," I said. "If I write this review they'll say that I'm condemning the work out of revenge and they'll be still more furious."

"And why must you condemn it? Write a favorable review!"

"I can't, Klara. This work is thoroughly absurd."

"So what? Why are you being truthful all of a sudden? Wasn't it a lie when you told the little man that they don't think much of you at *Visual Arts Journal*? And wasn't it a lie when you told the little man that he had tried to seduce me? And wasn't it a lie when you invented Helena? When you've told so many lies, what does it matter if you tell one more and praise him in the review? That's the only way you can smooth things out."

"You see, Klara," I said, "you think that a lie is a lie and it would seem that you're right. But you aren't. I can invent anything, make a fool of someone, carry out hoaxes and practical jokes—and I don't feel like a liar and I don't have a bad conscience. These lies, if you want to call them that, represent myself as I really am. With such lies I'm not simulating anything, with such lies I am in fact speaking the truth. But there are things which I can't lie about, things I've penetrated, whose meaning I've grasped, which I love and take seriously. It's impossible, don't ask me to do it, I can't."

We didn't understand each other.

But I really loved Klara and decided to do everything so that she would have nothing to reproach me for. The following day I wrote a letter to Mrs. Zaturetsky, saying that I would expect her the day after tomorrow at two o'clock in my office.

12

True to her terrifying methodicalness, Mrs. Zaturetsky knocked precisely at the appointed time. I opened the door and asked her in.

Then I finally saw her. She was a tall woman, very tall with a thin peasant's face and pale blue eyes. "Take off your things," I said, and with awkward movements she took off a long, dark coat, narrow at the waist and oddly styled, a coat which God knows why evoked the image of an ancient greatcoat.

I didn't want to attack at once; I wanted my adversary to show me her cards first. After Mrs. Zaturetsky sat down, I got her to speak by making a remark or two.

"Mr. Klima," she said in a serious voice, but without any aggressiveness, "you know why I was looking for you. My husband has always respected you very much as a specialist and as a man of character. Everything depended on your review and you didn't want to do it for him. It took my husband three years to write this study. His life was harder than yours. He was a teacher, he commuted daily twenty miles outside Prague. Last year I forced him to stop that and devote himself to research."

"Mr. Zaturetsky isn't employed?" I asked.

"No . . ."

"What does he live on?"

"For the time being I have to work hard myself. This research, Mr. Klima, is my husband's passion. If you knew how he studied everything. If you knew how many pages he rewrote. He always says that a real scholar must write three hundred pages so as to keep thirty. And on top of it, this woman. Believe me, Mr. Klima, I know him, I'm sure he didn't do it, so why did this woman accuse him? I don't believe it. Let her say it before me and before him. I know women, perhaps she likes you very much and you don't care for her. Perhaps she wanted to make you jealous. But you can believe me, Mr. Klima, my husband would never have dared!"

I was listening to Mrs. Zaturetsky, and all at once something strange happened to me: I ceased being aware that this was the woman for whose sake I should have to leave the university, and that this was the woman who caused the tension between myself and Klara, and for whose sake I'd wasted so many days in anger and unpleasantness. The connection between her and the incident, in which we'd both played a sad role, suddenly seemed vague, arbitrary, accidental, and not our fault. All at once I understood that it had only been my illusion that we ourselves saddle events and control their course. The truth is that they aren't *our* stories at all, that they are foisted upon us from somewhere *outside*; that in no way do they represent us; that we are not to blame for the queer path that they follow. They carry us away, since they are controlled by some *other* forces; no, I don't mean by supernatural forces, but by human forces, by the forces of those people who, when they unite, unfortunately still remain mutually *alien*.

When I looked at Mrs. Zaturetsky's eyes it seemed to me that these eyes couldn't see the consequences of my actions, that these eyes weren't seeing at all, that they were merely swimming in her face; that they were only stuck on.

"Perhaps you're right, Mrs. Zaturetsky," I said in a conciliatory tone: "Perhaps my girl didn't speak the truth, but you know how it is when a man's jealous . . . I believed her and was carried away. This can happen to anyone."

"Yes, certainly," said Mrs. Zaturetsky and it was evident that a weight had been lifted from her heart. "When you yourself see it, it's good. We were afraid that you believed her. This woman could have ruined my husband's whole life. I'm not speaking of the moral light it casts upon him. But my husband swears by your opinion. The editors assured him that it depended on you. My husband is convinced that if his article were published, he would finally be recognized as a scientific worker. I ask you, now that everything has been cleared up, will you write this review for him? And can you do it quickly?"

Now came the moment to avenge myself on everything and appease my rage, only at this moment I didn't feel any rage, and when I spoke it was only because there was no escaping it: "Mrs. Zaturetsky, there is some difficulty regarding the review. I shall confess to you how it all happened. I don't like to say unpleasant things to people's faces. This is my weakness. I avoided Mr. Zaturetsky, and I thought that he would figure out why I was avoiding him. His paper is weak. It has no scientific value. Do you believe me?"

"I find it hard to believe. I can't believe you," said Mrs. Zaturetsky.

"Above all, this work is not original. Please understand, a scholar must always arrive at something new; a scholar can't copy what we already know, what others have written."

"My husband definitely didn't copy."

"Mrs. Zaturetsky, you've surely read this study . . ." I wanted to continue, but Mrs. Zaturetsky interrupted me: "No, I haven't." I was surprised. "You will read it then for yourself."

"I can't see," said Mrs. Zaturetsky. "I see only light and shadow, my eyes are bad. I haven't read a single line for five years, but I don't need to read to know if my husband's honest or not. This can be recognized in other ways. I know my husband, as a mother her children, I know everything about him. And I know that what he does is always honest."

I had to undergo worse. I read aloud to Mrs. Zaturetsky

paragraphs from Mateychek, Pechirka, and Michek, whose thoughts and formulations Mr. Zaturetsky had taken over. It wasn't a question of willful plagiarism, but rather an unconscious submission to those authorities who inspired in Mr. Zaturetsky a feeling of sincere and inordinate respect. But anyone who had seen these passages compared must have understood that no serious scholarly magazine could publish Mr. Zaturetsky's work.

I don't know how much Mrs. Zaturetsky concentrated on my exposition, how much of it she followed and understood; she sat humbly in the armchair, humbly and obediently like a soldier, who knows that he may not leave his post. It took about half an hour for us to finish. Mrs. Zaturetsky got up from the armchair, fixed her transparent eyes upon me, and in a dull voice begged my pardon; but I knew that she hadn't lost faith in her husband and she didn't reproach anyone except herself for not knowing how to resist my arguments, which seemed obscure and unintelligible to her. She put on her military raincoat and I understood that this woman was a soldier in body and spirit, a sad and loyal soldier, a soldier tired from long marches, a soldier who doesn't understand the sense of an order and yet carries it out without objections, a soldier who goes away defeated but without dishonor.

After she'd gone, something remained in my office of her weariness, her loyalty, and her sadness. I suddenly forgot myself and my sorrows. The sorrow which seized me at that moment was purer, because it didn't issue from within me, but flowed from without, from afar.

13

"So now you don't have to be afraid of anything," I said to Klara, when later in the Dalmatian wineshop I repeated to her my conversation with Mrs. Zaturetsky.

"I didn't have anything to fear anyhow," replied Klara with a self-assurance that astonished me.

"How's that, you didn't? If it wasn't for you I wouldn't have met Mrs. Zaturetsky at all!"

"It's good that you did meet her, because what you did to them was cruel. Dr. Kalousek said that it's hard for an intelligent man to understand this."

"When did you meet Kalousek?"

"I've met him," said Klara.

"And did you tell him everything?"

"What? Is it a secret perhaps? Now I know exactly what you are."

"H'm."

"May I tell you what you are?"

"Please."

"A stereotyped cynic."

"You got that from Kalousek."

"Why from Kalousek? Do you think that I can't figure it out for myself? You actually think that I'm not capable of forming an opinion about you. You like to lead people by the nose. You promised Mr. Zaturetsky a review."

"I didn't promise him a review."

"That's one thing. And you promised me a job. You used me as an excuse to Mr. Zaturetsky, and you used Mr.

Zaturetsky as an excuse to me. But you may be sure that I'll get that job."

"Through Kalousek?" I tried to be scornful.

"Not from you. You've gambled so much away and you don't even know yourself how much."

"And do you know?"

"Yes. Your contract won't be renewed and you'll be glad if they'll let you in some gallery as a clerk. But you must realize that all this was only your own mistake. If I can give you some advice: another time be honest and don't lie, because a man who lies can't be respected by any woman."

She got up, gave me (clearly for the last time) her hand, turned, and left.

Only after a while did it occur to me (in spite of the chilly silence which surrounded me) that my story was not of the tragic sort, but rather of the comic variety.

At any rate that afforded me some comfort.

The Golden Apple of Eternal Desire

. . . they do not know that they seek only
the chase and not the quarry.

Blaise Pascal

Martin

Martin is able to do something I'm incapable of—to stop any woman on any street. I must say that during the time I've known Martin I've greatly profited by this skill of his, for I like women not a whit less than he, but I wasn't granted his reckless audacity. On the other hand, through an error of Martin the so-called *arresting* of a woman itself sometimes became the goal of his virtuosity and he would very often stop at that. For this reason he used to say, not without a certain bitterness, that he was like a forward, who unselfishly passes certain balls to his teammate, who then shoots cheap goals and reaps cheap glory.

Last Monday afternoon after work I was waiting for him in a cafe on Vaclav Square, looking through a thick German book on ancient Etruscan culture. It had taken several months for the university library to negotiate its loan from Germany, and now that it had finally come just that day, I carried it off as if it were a relic, and I was actually quite pleased that Martin had kept me waiting for him, and that I could leaf through the book I'd long wanted at a cafe table.

Whenever I think about ancient cultures nostalgia seizes me. Perhaps this is nothing but envy of the sweet slowness of the history of that time: the era of ancient Egyptian culture lasted for several thousand years; the era of Greek antiquity for almost a thousand. In this respect, a single human life imitates the history of mankind; at first it is plunged into immobile slowness and only then gradually does it accelerate more and more. Martin and I unfortunately already found ourselves in that phase, when the days, the months, and the years pass in a mad rush. Just two months ago Martin had turned forty.

But: "Everything depends," Martin would say, "on one's ability to resist the laws." By this he doesn't mean so much the laws of the land as rather more general laws—such as perhaps the laws of biology or time. Martin resists his forty years: his élan, his restlessness, and his incorrigible childishness are his main supports in the resistance.

The Adventure Begins

It was he who disturbed my thoughtful mood. He appeared suddenly in the glass door of the cafe and headed for me, making expressive gestures and grimaces in the direction of a table at which a woman was sitting over a cup of coffee. Without taking his eyes off her, he sat down beside me and said, "What do you say about that?"

I felt humiliated; I'd actually been so engrossed in my thick volume that only now did I notice the girl. I had to admit that she was pretty. And at that moment the girl straightened up and called the man with the black bowtie, saying that she wished to pay.

"Pay too!" ordered Martin.

We thought that we would have to run after the girl, but luckily she was detained at the cloakroom. She had left a shopping bag there and the cloakroom attendant had to hunt for a while before placing it on the counter in front of the girl. As the girl gave the cloakroom attendant a couple of ten-haller pieces, Martin snatched the German book out of my hands.

"It will be better to put it in here," he said with dare-devil nonchalance, and slipped the book carefully into the girl's bag. The girl looked surprised, but didn't know what she was supposed to say.

"It's uncomfortable to carry in one's hand," continued Martin, and when the girl went to pick up the bag herself, he told me off for not knowing how to behave.

The young woman was a nurse in a country hospital. She was in Prague, she said, only for a look around and was hurrying on to the Florents bus terminal. The short distance to the streetcar stop was enough for us to say everything essential and to agree that on Saturday we would come to B. to visit this lovely young woman, who, as Martin meaningfully pointed out, would certainly have some pretty colleague.

The streetcar arrived, I handed the young woman her bag, and she began to take the book out of it, but Martin prevented her with a grand gesture, saying we would come for it on Saturday, and that she should read through it carefully in the meantime. The young woman smiled in a bewildered fashion, the streetcar carried her away, and we waved.

What sense was there in this. The book, which I'd been looking forward to for so long, suddenly found itself in a faraway place. When you came to think of it, it was quite annoying. But nonetheless a certain lunacy happily uplifted me on the wings it promptly provided. Martin immediately began thinking about how to make an excuse for Saturday afternoon and night to his young wife (for this is how things stand: at home he has a young wife; and what is worse, he loves her; and what is still worse, he is afraid of her; and what is still far worse, he is anxious about her).

A Successful Registration

For our excursion I borrowed a neat little Fiat for a small sum and on Saturday at two o'clock I drove up in front of Martin's apartment; Martin was waiting for me and we set off. It was July and oppressively hot.

We wanted to get to B. as soon as possible, but when we saw, in a village through which we were driving, two young men only in swimming trunks and with eloquently wet hair, I stopped the car. The lake was actually not far away, a few paces, a mere stone's throw. I'm no longer able to sleep as I once was, the night before I'd tossed about on account of God knows what worries until three o'clock. I needed to be refreshed. Martin was also for swimming.

We changed into our swimming trunks and leaped into the water. I dove into the water and swam quickly to the other side. Martin, however, barely took a dip, washed himself off, and came out again. When I'd had a good swim and returned to shore, I caught sight of him in a state of intent absorption. On the shore a crowd of kids was yelling; somewhere further off the local young people were playing ball, but Martin was staring at the sturdy little figure of a young girl, who was perhaps fifty feet away with her back toward us. Totally motionless, she was observing the water.

"Look," said Martin.

"I am looking."

"And what do you say?"

"What should I say?"

"You don't know what you should say about that?"

"We'll have to wait until she turns round," I suggested.

"Not at all. We don't have to wait until she turns round. What's showing from this side is quite enough for me."

"As least let's get her registered," said Martin, and turned to a little boy a short distance away who was putting on his swimming trunks: "Say, kid, d'you know the name of that girl over there?" and he pointed to the girl, who, apparently in some curious state of apathy, went on standing in the same position.

"That one there?"

"Yeah, that one there."

"That one is not from here," said the little boy.

Martin turned to a little girl of about twelve, who was sunbathing close by:

"Say, kid, d'you know who that girl over there is, the one standing on the edge?"

The little girl obediently sat up. "That one there?"

"Yeah, that one."

"That's Manka . . ."

"Manka? Manka what?"

"Manka Panku . . . from Traplitse. . . ."

And the girl still stood with her back to us looking at the water. Now she bent down for her swimming cap and when she straightened up again, putting it on her head as she did so, Martin was already at my side saying, "That's a certain Manka Panku from Traplitse. Now we can drive on."

He was completely calmed down and satisfied, and obviously no longer thinking of anything but the rest of the journey.

A Little Theory

That's what Martin calls *registration*. From his vast experience, he has come to the conclusion that it is not so difficult to seduce a girl—if in this area we have high quantitative pretensions—as it is always to know enough girls whom we have not yet seduced.

Therefore, he asserts that it is necessary always, no matter where, and at every opportunity, to compile a wide registration, i.e., to record in a notebook or in our memories (Martin usually relies upon his memory), the names of women who have attracted us and whom we could contact sometime.

Contact is a higher level of activity and means that we will get in touch with a particular woman, make her acquaintance, and gain access to her.

He who likes to look back boastfully will stress the names of the women he's made love to, but he who looks forward, toward the future, must above all see to it that he has plenty of *registered* and *contacted* women.

Above contact there exists only one last level of activity, and I am happy to point out, in deference to Martin, that those who do not go after anything but this last level are wretched, primitive men, who remind me of village footballers, pressing forward thoughtlessly toward the rival goal and forgetting that a rash desire to shoot will not necessarily lead to this goal (or many further goals), but that a competent and fair game on the field will.

"Do you think that you'll go look her up in Traplitse sometime?" I asked Martin, when we were driving again.

"One can never know . . ." said Martin.

Then I said, "In any case the day is beginning propitiously for us."

Game and Necessity

We arrived at the hospital in B. in excellent spirits. It was about three-thirty. We called our nurse on the phone in the lobby. Before long she came down in her cap and white uniform; I noticed that she was blushing and I took this to be a good sign.

Martin began to talk right away and the girl informed us that she finished work at seven and that we should wait for her at that time in front of the hospital.

"Have you already arranged it with your girl friend?" asked Martin and the girl nodded:

"Yes, we'll both come."

"Fine," said Martin, "but we can't confront my colleague here with a fait accompli."

"O.K.," said the girl, "we can drop in on her; Bozhena is in the internal medicine ward."

As we walked slowly across the hospital courtyard I shyly said: "I wonder if you still have that thick book?"

The nurse nodded, saying that she did and in fact it was right here at the hospital. A weight fell from my heart and I insisted that we had to get it first.

Of course it seemed improper to Martin that I should openly give preference to a book over a woman about to be presented to me, but I just couldn't help it.

I confess that I had suffered greatly during those few days, having the book on Etruscan culture out of my sight. And it was only through great self-restraint that I had stoically put up with this, not wishing under any circumstances to spoil the Game, which has such value for me. Over the years I've learned to appreciate the Game and to subordinate to it all my personal interests and desires.

While I was having a touching reunion with my book, Martin continued his conversation with the pretty nurse, and got as far as getting her to promise that she would borrow a cabin by the nearby Hotersky Lake from a colleague for the evening. We were all perfectly happy. Finally we went across the hospital courtyard to a small green building, where the internal medicine ward was.

A nurse and a doctor were just walking toward us. The doctor was a funny-looking bean pole with protruding ears, which fascinated me all the more because at this moment our nurse elbowed me. I let out a short laugh. When they had passed us Martin turned to me: "So you're in luck, fella. You don't deserve such a gorgeous young woman."

I was ashamed to say that I had only looked at the bean pole, so I simulated approbation. After all, there wasn't any hypocrisy on my part. That is to say, I trust in Martin's taste more than in my own, because I believe that his taste is supported by a much greater *interest* than mine. I like objectivity and order in everything, even in love affairs—which only through error are held to be the exclusive realm of caprice. Consequently I have more respect for the opinion of a connoisseur than for that of a dilettante.

Someone might consider it hypocritical for me to call myself a dilettante—I a divorced man who is right now relating one of his (obviously in no way exceptional) affairs. But still I am a dilettante. It could be said that I am *playing* at something which Martin *lives*. Sometimes I have the feeling that the whole of my polygamous life is a consequence of nothing but my imitation of other men; although I am not denying that I take a liking to this imitation. But I cannot rid myself of the feeling that in this liking there remains, all the same, something entirely free, playful, and revocable. It is the same thing that perhaps characterizes visits to art galleries or foreign countries and is in no way reducible to the unconditional imperative which I have suspected at the back of Martin's erotic life. It is precisely the presence of this unconditional imperative that has raised Martin in my eyes. His judgment about a woman seems to me to be that of Nature herself, Necessity herself speaking through his lips.

Home Sweet Home

When we found ourselves outside the hospital Martin pointed out that everything was going tremendously well for us, and then added: "Of course we'll have to hurry this evening. I want to be home by nine."

I was amazed: "By nine? That means we'll have to leave here at eight. But then we came here for no reason! I counted on having the whole night!"

"Why should you want to waste time!"

"But what sense is there in driving here for one hour? What can you do between seven and eight?"

"Everything. As you noticed I got hold of the cabin, so that everything will go swimmingly. It will depend only on you, you'll have to show that you're sufficiently determined."

"But why, I ask, must you be home at nine?"

"I promised Jirzhinka. She's used to playing a game of rummy before going to bed on Saturdays."

"Oh God . . ." I sighed.

"Yesterday again Jirzhinka had a bad time at the

office, so I should give her this little bit of joy on Saturday, shouldn't I? You know, she's the best woman I've ever had. After all," he added, "you should be pleased anyway that you'll still have the whole night before you in Prague."

I understood that it was useless to object. Martin's misgivings about his wife's peace of mind could never be appeased, and his faith in the endless erotic possibilities of every hour or minute could never be shaken by anything.

"Come," said Martin, "there are still three hours till seven! We won't be idle!"

A Delusion

We started on our way along the broad path of the local park, which served the inhabitants as a promenade. We inspected several pairs of girls who walked by us or were sitting on the benches, but we didn't like the look of them too well.

Martin, it must be admitted, accosted two of them, entered into conversation with them, and finally arranged a meeting with them, but I knew that he didn't mean it seriously. This was a so-called *practice contact*, which Martin performed from time to time in order to stay in practice.

Dissatisfied, we went out of the park into the streets, which yawned with small-town vacuity and boredom.

"Let's get something to drink, I'm thirsty," I said to Martin.

We found an establishment above which was the sign CAFE. We entered, but inside there was only self-service. It was a tiled room that gave off an air of coldness and hostility. We went over to the counter and bought ourselves watered-down lemonades from a sullen woman, and then carried them over to a table, which being moist with gravy, invited us to depart hastily.

"Don't worry about it," said Martin. "In our world ugliness has its positive function. No one feels like staying anywhere, people hurry on and thus arises the desirable pace of life. But we won't let ourselves be provoked by this. We can now talk about all sorts of things in the safety of this ugly place." He drank some lemonade and asked: "Have you contacted that medical student yet?"

"Naturally," I replied.

"And what's she like then? Describe to me exactly how she looks!"

I described the medical student to him. This was not very difficult for me to do, even though no medical student existed. Yes. Perhaps this puts me in a bad light, but it's like this: *I invented her.*

I give my word that I didn't do it maliciously, neither to show off in front of Martin nor because I wanted to lead him by the nose. I invented the medical student simply because I couldn't resist Martin's insistence.

Martin's claims about my activities were boundless. Martin was convinced that I met new women every day. He saw me as other than I am, and if I had truthfully told him that not only had I not possessed any new women for a week, but hadn't even come close, he would have taken me for a hypocrite.

For this reason, about a week earlier, I had been forced to dream up my registration of some medical student. Martin was satisfied and he urged me to contact her. And today he was checking up on my progress.

"And about what level is she on? Is she on the level . . ." He closed his eyes and in the darkness searched for a standard of measure: then he remembered a mutual friend: ". . . is she on Marketa's level?"

"She's far better," I said.

"Don't say . . . ," marveled Martin.

"She's on your Jirzhinka's level."

For Martin his own wife was the highest standard of measure. Martin was greatly pleased by my news and fell into a dreamlike state.

A Successful Contact

Then some girl in corduroy pants and a short jacket walked into the room. She went to the counter, waited for a soda, and took it away to drink. She approached a table adjoining ours, put the glass to her lips, and drank without sitting down.

Martin turned to her: "Miss," he said, "we're strangers here and we'd like to ask you a question."

The girl smiled. She was rather pretty.

"We are terribly hot and we don't know what we should do."

"Go and take a swim."

"That's just it. We don't know where to go swimming around here."

"There isn't any swimming here."

"How is that possible?"

"There's one swimming pool, but it's been empty for a month now."

"And what about the river?"

"It's being dredged."

"So where do you go swimming?"

"Only at Hotersky Lake, but it's at least five miles away."

"That's a small matter, we have a car, it would be very nice if you'd accompany us."

"As our guide," I said.

"Rather our guiding light," Martin corrected me.

"Then why not our starlight," said I.

"Our North Star," said Martin.

"And in that case may I say that our star is brighter than Venus," I replied.

"You're simply our constellation and you should go with us," said Martin.

The girl was confused by our foolish banter and finally said that she would go, but that she had to take care of something first and then she'd pick up her bathing suit; she said that we should be waiting for her in exactly an hour at this same spot.

We were glad. We watched her as she walked away, cutely swinging her backside and tossing her black curls.

"You see," said Martin, "life is short. We must take advantage of every minute."

In Praise of Friendship

We went once again into the park. Once again we examined several pairs of girls on the benches; it happened that many a young woman was good-looking, but it never happened that her companion was also good-looking.

"In this there is some special law," I said to Martin. "An ugly woman hopes to gain something from the luster of her pretty friend; a pretty woman, for her part, hopes that she will stand out more lustrously against the background of the ugly woman; and for us it follows from this that our friendship is subjected to continuous trials. And it is precisely this that I value, that we will never leave the choice to the random development of events, nor even to some mutual struggle; choice for us is always a matter of courtesy. We'd offer each other the prettier girl like two old-fashioned gentlemen who can never enter a room because neither wants to be the one who goes first."

"Yes," said Martin with emotion. "You're a great buddy. Come, let's go sit down for a while, my legs are aching."

And thus we sat comfortably with our faces turned up toward the face of the sun, and we let the world around us rush on unnoticed.

The Girl in White

All of a sudden Martin got up (moved evidently by some mysterious sense) and stared along a secluded path of the park. A girl in a white dress was coming our way. Already from afar, before it was possible to ascertain with complete confidence the proportions of her body or the features of her face, we saw that she possessed unmistakable, special, and very perceptible charm, that there was a certain purity or tenderness in her appearance.

When the girl was fairly close to us, we realized that she was quite young, something between a child and a young woman, and this at once threw us into a state of complete agitation. Martin shot up off the bench: "Miss, I am the director Jasny, the film director; you must help us."

He gave her his hand and the young girl with an utterly astonished expression shook it.

Martin nodded in my direction and said: "This is my cameraman."

"Kalish," I offered my hand.

The girl nodded.

"We are in an awkward situation here. I am looking for outdoor locations for my film. Our assistant, who knows this area well, was supposed to meet us here, but he hasn't arrived, so that right now we are wondering how to get about in this town and in the surrounding countryside. My friend Kalish here," joked Martin, "is always studying his fat German book, but unfortunately it is not to be found in there."

The allusion to the book, which I had been deprived of for the whole week, somehow irritated me all of a sudden: "It's a pity that you don't take a greater interest in this book," I attacked my director. "If you prepared thoroughly and didn't leave the studying to your cameramen maybe your films wouldn't be so superficial and there wouldn't be so much nonsense in them . . . forgive me." I turned then to the girl with an apology. "Anyhow, we won't bother you with our quarrels about our work; our film is to be a historical film and will touch upon Etruscan culture in Bohemia. . . ."

"Yes," the girl nodded.

"It's a rather interesting book—look." I handed the girl the book and she took it in her hands with a certain religious awe, and when she saw that I wanted her to, turned the pages lightly.

"The Phachek castle must surely not be far from here," I continued. "It was the center of the Bohemian Etruscans . . . but how can we get there?"

"It's only a little way," said the girl and beamed all over, because her secure knowledge of the road to Phachek gave her a little bit of firm ground in the somewhat obscure conversation that we were carrying on with her.

"Yes? Do you know the area around there?" asked Martin, feigning great relief.

"Sure I know it!" said the girl. "It's an hour away!"

"On foot?" asked Martin.

"Yes, on foot," said the girl.

"But luckily we have a car here," I said.

"Wouldn't you like to be our guide?" said Martin, but I didn't continue the customary ritual of witticisms, because I have a more precise sense of psychological judgment than Martin, and I felt that frivolous joking would be more inclined to harm us in this case and that our best weapon was absolute propriety.

"We do not want, miss, to disturb you in any way," I said, "but if you would be so kind as to devote a short time to us and show us some of the places we're looking for, you would help us a great deal—and we would both be very grateful."

"But yes," the girl nodded again, "I am happy . . . but I . . ." Only now did we notice that she had a shopping bag in her hand and in it two heads of lettuce. "I must take Mom the lettuce, but it's only a little way away and I would come right back . . ."

"Of course you must take the lettuce to Mom on time and intact," I said. "We will be happy to wait here."

"Yes. It won't take more than ten minutes," said the girl and once again she nodded, and then she walked off quickly and anxiously.

"God!" said Martin and sat down.

"Isn't it great, eh?"

"I should say so. For this I'd be willing to sacrifice our two female barber surgeons."

Deceived by Excessive Faith

But ten minutes passed, a quarter of an hour, and the girl didn't come.

"Don't be afraid," Martin consoled me. "If anything is certain, then it's this, that she'll come. Our performance was completely plausible and the girl was in raptures."

I too was of this opinion, and so we went on waiting, with each moment becoming more and more eager for this childish young girl. In the meanwhile, also, the time appointed for our meeting with the girl in corduroy pants went by, but we were so set on our little girl in white that it didn't even occur to us to leave.

And time was passing.

"Listen, Martin, I think that she won't come now," I said at last.

"How do you explain it? After all, that girl believed in us as in God Himself."

"Yes," I said, "and in that lies our misfortune. That is to say she believed us only too well!"

"What? Perhaps you'd have wanted her not to believe us?"

"It would perhaps have been better like that. Too much faith is the worst ally." A thought took my fancy; I got really involved in it: "When you believe in something literally, through your faith you'll turn it into something absurd. One who is a genuine adherent, if you like, of some political outlook, never takes its *sophistries* seriously, but only its practical aims, which are concealed beneath these sophistries. Political rhetoric and sophistries do not exist, after all, in order that they be believed; rather, they have to serve as a *common and agreed upon alibi*. Foolish people, who take them in earnest, sooner or later discover inconsistencies in them, begin to protest, and finish finally and infamously as heretics and apostates. No, too much faith never brings anything good—and not only to political or religious systems but even to our own system, the one we used to convince the girl."

"Somehow I'm not quite following you any more."

"It's quite simple: for the girl we were actually two serious and respectable gentlemen, and she, like a well-behaved child who offers her seat to an older person on a streetcar, wanted to please us."

"So why didn't she please us?"

"Because she believed us so completely. She gave Mom the lettuce and at once told her enthusiastically all about us: about the historical film, about the Etruscans in Bohemia, and Mom . . ."

"Yes, the rest is perfectly clear to me . . ." Martin interrupted me and got up from the bench.

The Betrayal

The sun was already slowly going down over the roofs of the town. It was cooling off a bit and we felt sad. We went to the cafe just in case the girl in the corduroy pants was by some mistake still waiting for us. Of course she wasn't there. It was six-thirty. We walked down to the car, and feeling all of a sudden like two people who had been banished from a foreign city and its pleasures, we said to ourselves that nothing remained for us but to retire to the extraterritorial domain of our own car.

"Come on!" remonstrated Martin in the car. "Anyhow, don't look so gloomy! We don't have any reason for that! The most important thing is still before us!"

I wanted to object that we had no more than an hour for this most important thing, because of Jirzhinka and her rummy—but I chose to keep silent.

"Anyway," continued Martin, "it was a fruitful day; the registration of that girl from Traplitse, contact with the girl in the corduroy pants; after all, we have it all set up whenever we feel like it. We don't have to do anything but drive here again!"

I didn't object at all. Yes. The registration and the contact had been excellently brought off. This was quite in order. But at this moment it occurred to me that for the last year, apart from countless registrations and contacts, Martin had not come by anything more worthwhile.

I looked at him. As always his eyes shone with a lustful glow. I felt at that moment that I liked Martin and that I also liked the banner under which he had been marching all his life: the banner of the eternal pursuit of women.

Time was passing and Martin said, "It's seven o'clock."

We drove to within about thirty feet of the hospital gates, so that in the rear-view mirror I could safely observe who was coming out.

I was still thinking about that banner. And also about the fact that in this pursuit of women from year to year it had become less a matter of women and much more a matter of the pursuit itself. Assuming that the pursuit is known to be *vain* in advance, it is possible to pursue any number of women and thus to make the pursuit *an absolute pursuit*.

Yes, Martin had attained the state of being in absolute pursuit.

We waited five minutes. The girls didn't come.

It didn't put me out in the least. It was a matter of complete indifference to me whether they came or not. Even if they came, could we in a mere hour drive with them to the isolated cabin, become intimate with them, make love to them, and at eight o'clock say goodbye pleasantly and take off? No, at that moment when Martin limited our available time to ending on the stroke of eight, he had shifted the whole affair to the sphere of a self-deluding game. Yes, that is the word for it! All these registrations and contacts are nothing but a *self-deluding game* with which Martin wants to retain for himself the illusion that nothing has changed, that the beloved comedy of youth continues to be played, that the labyrinth of women is endless, and that it is still his preserve.

Ten minutes went by. No one appeared at the gates.

Martin became indignant and almost yelled: "I'll give them five more minutes! I won't wait any longer!"

Martin hasn't been young for quite a while now. I speculated further—he truly loves his wife, as a matter of fact he has the most regular sort of marriage. This is a fact. And yet—above this (and simultaneously with it), Martin's youth continues on the level of touchingly innocent self-deception: a restless, gay, and erring youth transformed into a mere game, a game that was no longer in any way up to crossing the line into real life and realizing itself as a fact. And because Martin is the knight obsessed by Necessity, he has transformed his love affairs into the harmlessness of a game, *without knowing it*. So he continues to put his whole inflamed soul into them.

O.K., I said to myself. Martin is the captive of his

self-deception, but what am I? What am I? Why do I assist him in this ridiculous game? Why do I, who know that all of this is a delusion, pretend along with him? Am I not then still more ridiculous than Martin? Why at this time should I behave as if an amorous adventure lay before me, when I know that at most a single aimless hour with unknown and indifferent girls awaits me.

At that moment in the mirror I caught sight of two young women at the hospital gates. Even from that distance they gave off a glow of powder and rouge. They were strikingly chic and their delay was obviously connected with their well made-up appearance. They looked around and headed toward our car.

"Martin, there's nothing to be done." I renounced the girls. "It's over a quarter of an hour. Let's go." And I put my foot on the gas.

Repentance

We drove out of B. We passed the last little houses and drove into the countryside through fields and woods, toward whose treetops a large sun was sinking.

We were silent.

I thought about Judas Iscariot, about whom a brilliant author relates that he betrayed Jesus just because he *believed* in him infinitely: he couldn't wait for the miracle through which Jesus was to have shown all the Jews his divine power. So he handed Him over to His tormentors in order to provoke Him at last to action. He betrayed Him, because he longed to hasten His victory.

Oh God, I said to myself, I've betrayed Martin from

far less noble motives. I betrayed him in fact just because I stopped believing in him (and in the divine power of his womanizing). I am a vile compound of Judas Iscariot and of the man whom they called Doubting Thomas. I felt that as a result of my wrongdoing my sympathy for Martin was growing and that his banner of the eternal chase (which was to be heard still fluttering above us) was reducing me to tears. I began to reproach myself for my overhasty action.

Does perhaps some magnet not attract me to lead expeditions back to the time of freedom and wandering, of choice and searching, to the time of lack of commitment and initial choice? Shall I be in a position more easily to part with these gestures which signify youth for me? And will there remain for me perhaps something other than a feeling that I should at least *imitate* them and endeavor to find a small, safe place for this foolish activity within my otherwise sensible life?

What does it matter that it's all a futile game? What does it matter that I *know* it. Will I stop playing the game just because it is futile?

I knew that this would not be the case; I knew that soon we'd drive out of Prague again, we'd stop girls and think up new escapades.

In all this I shall rightly remain a split character, doubting and vacillating, while Martin, like a character from mythology, will forever be an internally integrated being, fighting the great metaphysical battle against time and against those damnably narrow confines, within which our life cowers.

The Golden Apple of Eternal Desire

He was sitting beside me and little by little his indignation subsided.

"Listen," he said, "is that medical student really so high-class?"

"I'm telling you she's on Jirzhinka's level."

Martin put further questions to me. I had to describe the medical student to him once again.

Then he said: "Perhaps you could hand her over to me afterward, eh?"

I wanted to appear plausible. "That may be quite difficult. It would bother her that you're my buddy. She has firm principles . . ."

"She has firm principles . . . ," said Martin sadly, and it was plain that he was upset by this.

I didn't want to upset him.

"Unless I could pretend I don't know you," I said. "Perhaps you could pass yourself off as someone else."

"Fine! Perhaps as Jasny, like today!"

"She doesn't give a damn about film directors. She prefers athletes."

"Why not?" said Martin, "it's all within the realm of possibility," and we spent some time involved in this discussion. From moment to moment the plan became clearer and after a while it dangled before us in the advancing twilight like a beautiful, ripe, shining apple.

Permit me to name this apple with a certain ceremoniousness The Golden Apple of Eternal Desire.

Symposium

1

The Staff Room

The doctors' staff room (in any ward of any hospital in any town you like) brought together five characters and intertwined their actions and speech into a trivial, yet, for all that, most enjoyable episode.

Dr. Havel and Nurse Alzhbeta are here (today both of them are on the night shift) and there are two additional doctors (some less than important pretext led them here, so that they could sit with the two who are on duty over a couple of bottles of wine that had been brought in): the bald chief physician of this ward and a comely, thirty-year-old woman doctor from another ward, whom the whole hospital knew were going with each other.

(The chief physician is, of course, married, and just a moment before he had uttered his favorite maxim, which should give evidence not only of his wit but also of his intentions: "My dear colleagues, as you know, I am very unhappily married: my wife is so perfect that I haven't the slightest hope of a divorce.")

In addition to the four named there is still a fifth, but he is not actually here, because, as the youngest, he has just been sent for another bottle. And there is a window here, important because it's open and because through it from the darkness outside there enters into the room a warm, fragrant, and moonlit summer's night. And finally, there is an agreeable mood here, manifesting itself in the appreciative chatter of all, especially, however, of the chief physician, who listens to his own adages with enamored ears.

A little later in the evening (and only here in fact does our story begin), certain tensions could be noted: Alzhbeta drank more than was advisable for a nurse on duty, and on top of that, began to behave toward Havel with defiant flirtatiousness, which went against the grain with him and provoked him to admonishing invective.

Havel's Admonition

"My dear Alzhbeta, I don't get you. Every day you rummage about in festering wounds, you jab old men in their wrinkled backsides, you give enemas, you take out bedpans. Your lot has provided you with the enviable opportunity to understand human corporeality in all its metaphysical vanity. But your vitality is incorrigible. It is impossible to shake your tenacious desire to be flesh and nothing but flesh. Your breasts know how to rub against a man standing fifteen feet away from you. My head is already spinning from those eternal gyrations, which your untiring butt describes when you walk. Go to the devil, get away from me! Those boobs of yours are ubiquitous—like God! You should have given the injections ten minutes ago!"

Dr. Havel Is Like Death. He Takes Everything

When Nurse Alzhbeta (ostentatiously offended) had left the staff room, condemned to jab two very old backsides, the chief physician said: "I ask you, Havel, why do you insist on turning down poor Alzhbeta?"

Dr. Havel took a sip of wine and replied: "Sir, don't

get mad at me on this account. It's not because she isn't pretty and is getting on in years. Believe me, I've had women still uglier and far older."

"Yes, it's a well-known fact about you: you're like death, you take everything. But if you take everything, why don't you take Alzhbeta?"

"Maybe," said Havel, "it's because she shows her desire so conspicuously that it resembles an order. You say that I am like death in relation to women. But not even death likes to be given an order."

The Chief Physician's Greatest Success

"I think I understand you," answered the chief physician. "When I was some years younger, I knew a girl who went with everyone and because she was pretty I was determined to have her. And imagine, she turned me down. She went with my colleagues, with the chauffeurs, with the boilerman, with the cook, even with the undertaker, only not with me. Can you imagine that?"

"Sure," said the woman doctor.

"Let me tell you, Miss Novak." The chief physician got angry; in front of people he called his mistress Miss Novak rather than Anna. He went on, "It was then a couple of years after graduation and I was a big shot. I believed that every woman was attainable, and I had succeeded in proving this in the case of women relatively hard to get. And look, I came to grief with this readily attainable girl."

"If I know you, you certainly must have your theory about it," said Dr. Havel.

"I do," replied the chief physician. "Eroticism is not

only a desire for the body, but to an equal extent a desire for honor. The partner, whom you've won, who cares about you and loves you, is your mirror, the measure of what you are and what you stand for. In eroticism we seek the image of our own significance and importance. But for my tart, this was difficult. She went with everyone, so there were so many of these mirrors that they gave a quite confusing and ambiguous image. And too, when you go with everyone you stop believing that such a commonplace thing as making love can have a real meaning for you. And so you seek the true meaning precisely in the opposite. The only man who could provide that girl with a clear gauge of her human worth was one who cared about her, but whom she herself had rejected. And because she understandably longed to verify to herself that she was the most beautiful and best of women, she went about choosing this one man, whom she would honor with her refusal, very strictly and captiously. When in the end she chose me, I understood that this was a remarkable honor and up to the present time I consider this my greatest erotic success."

"It's quite marvelous the way you are able to turn water into wine," said the woman doctor.

"Did it offend you that I don't consider you my greatest success?" said the chief physician. "You must understand me. Though you are a virtuous woman, all the same, for you I am not (nor do you know how this grieves me) your first and last, while for that tart I was. Believe me, she has never forgotten me, and to this day nostalgically remembers how she rejected me. After all, I related this story only to bring out the analogy to Havel's rejection of Alzhbeta."

In Praise of Freedom

"Good God, sir." Havel let out a groan. "I hope that you don't want to say that in Alzhbeta I am seeking an image of my human worth!"

"Certainly not," said the woman doctor caustically. "After all, you've already explained to us that Alzhbeta's provocativeness strikes you as an order, and you wish to retain the illusion that it is you who are choosing the woman."

"You know, although we talk about it in those terms, Doctor, it isn't like that." Havel did a bit of thinking. "I was only trying to make a joke, when I said to you that Alzhbeta's provocativeness bothered me. To tell the truth, I've had women far more provocative than she, and their provocativeness suited me quite well, because it pleasantly speeded up the course of events."

"So why the hell don't you take Alzhbeta?" cried the chief physician.

"Sir, your question isn't as stupid as it seemed to me at first, because I see that as a matter of fact it's hard to answer. If I'm going to be frank, then I don't know why I don't take Alzhbeta. I've slept with women more hideous, more provocative, and older. From this it follows that I should necessarily sleep with her too. All the statistics would have worked it out that way. All the cybernetic machines would have assessed it that way. And you see, perhaps for those very reasons, I don't take her. Perhaps I want to resist necessity. To trip up causality. To throw off the predictability of the world's course through the whimsicality of caprice."

"But why did you pick Alzhbeta for this?" cried the chief physician.

"Just because it's groundless. If there had been a reason, it would have been possible to find it in advance, and it would have been possible to determine my action in advance. Precisely in this groundlessness is a tiny scrap of freedom granted us, for which we must untiringly reach out, so that in this world of iron laws there should remain a little human disorder. My dear colleagues, long live freedom," said Havel, and sadly raised his tumbler in a toast.

Whither the Responsibility of Man Extends

At this moment, a new bottle appeared in the room; it drew the attention of all the doctors present. The charming, lanky young man, who was standing in the doorway with it, was the ward intern, Flaishman. He put the bottle (very slowly) on the table, searched (a long time) for the corkscrew, then (slowly) pushed the corkscrew into the cork, and (quite slowly) screwed it into the cork, which he then (thoughtfully) drew out. From the parentheses that have been introduced, Flaishman's slowness is evident; however, it testified far more to his slothful self-love than to clumsiness. With self-love, the young intern would gaze peacefully into his own heart, overlooking the insignificant details of the external surroundings.

Dr. Havel said: "All the stuff we've been chattering about here is nonsense. It isn't I who am rejecting Alzhbeta, but she me. Unfortunately. Anyhow, she's crazy about Flaishman."

"About me?" Flaishman raised his head from the bottle, then with slow steps returned the corkscrew to its place, came back to the table, and poured wine into the tumblers.

"You're a fine one," the chief physician supported Havel. "Everybody knows this except you. Since you appeared in our ward, it's been hard to put up with her. It's been like that for two months now."

Flaishman looked (for a long time) at the chief physician and said: "I really didn't know that." And then he added, "And anyway it doesn't interest me at all."

"And what about those gentlemanly speeches of yours? That quacking about respect for women?" Havel attacked Flaishman. "Doesn't it interest you that you cause Alzhbeta pain?"

"I feel pity for women and I could never knowingly hurt them," said Flaishman. "But what I bring about involuntarily doesn't interest me, because I'm not in a position to influence it, and so I'm not responsible for it."

Then Alzhbeta came into the room. She evidently considered that it would be better to forget the insult and behave as if nothing had happened, so she behaved extremely unnaturally. The chief physician pushed a chair up to the table for her and filled a tumbler: "Drink, Alzhbeta, and forget all the wrongs that have been done you."

"Sure." Alzhbeta threw a big smile at him and emptied the glass.

And the chief physician turned once again to Flaishman: "If a man were responsible only for what he is aware of, blockheads would be absolved in advance from any guilt whatever. Only, my dear Flaishman, man is obliged to know. A man is responsible for his ignorance. Ignorance is a fault. And that is why nothing absolves you from your guilt, and I declare that you are a boor in regard to women, even if you dispute it."

In Praise of Platonic Love

"I'm wondering if you've got that sublet for Miss Klara yet, you know, the one you promised her?" Havel laid into Flaishman, reminding him of his vain attempts to win the heart of a certain medical student (known to all those present).

"No, I haven't, but I'm taking care of it."

"It just happens that Flaishman behaves like a gentleman toward women. Our colleague Flaishman doesn't lead women by the nose." The woman doctor stood up for the intern.

"I can't bear cruelty toward women, because I have pity for them," repeated the intern.

"All the same, Klara hasn't given herself to you," said Alzhbeta to Flaishman, and started to laugh in a very improper way, so that the chief physician was once again forced to take the floor:

"She gave herself, she didn't give herself, it isn't nearly so important as you think, Alzhbeta. It is well known that Abelard was castrated, but that he and Heloise nonetheless remained faithfully in love. Their love was immortal. George Sand lived for seven years with Frederic Chopin, intact, like a virgin, and there isn't a chance in a million that you could compete with them when it comes to love! I don't want to introduce into this sublime context the case of the girl who by rejecting me gave me the highest reward of love. But note this well, my dear Alzhbeta, love is connected far more loosely with what you so incessantly think about than it might seem. Surely you don't doubt that Klara loves Flaishman! She's nice to him, but nevertheless she rejects him. This sounds illogical to you, but love is precisely that which is illogical."

"What's illogical in that?" Alzhbeta once again laughed in an improper way. "Klara cares about the apartment. That's why she's nice to Flaishman. But she doesn't feel like sleeping with him, maybe because she is sleeping with someone else. But that guy can't get her an apartment."

At that moment, Flaishman raised his head and said: "You're getting on my nerves. You're like an adolescent. What if shame restrains a woman? This wouldn't occur to you, would it? What if she has some disease, which she is hiding from me? A scar after an operation, which disfigures her? Women are capable of being terribly ashamed. Only you, Alzhbeta, know almost nothing about this."

"Or else," the chief physician came to Flaishman's aid, "when Klara is face to face with Flaishman, she is so petrified by the anguish of love that she cannot make love with him. You, Alzhbeta, are not able to imagine that you could love someone so terribly that just because of it you couldn't sleep with him?"

Alzhbeta confessed that she couldn't.

The Signal

At this point we can stop following the conversation for a while (they went on uninterruptedly discussing trivia) and mention that all this time Flaishman has been trying to catch the woman doctor's eye, for he has found her damned attractive since the time (it was about a month before) he first saw her. The sublimity of her thirty years dazzled him. Till now, he'd known her only in passing and today for the first time he had the opportunity of spending a longer time in the same room with her. It seemed to him that every now and then she returned his look, and this excited him.

After one such exchange of glances, the woman doctor got up for no reason at all, walked over to the window, and said, "It's gorgeous outside. There's a full moon . . . ," and then again reached out to Flaishman with a fleeting look.

Flaishman wasn't blind in such situations and he at once grasped that it was a signal—a signal for him. He felt his chest swelling. His chest was a sensitive instrument, worthy of Stradivarius's workshop. From time to time he would feel the aforementioned swelling, and each time was certain that this swelling had the inevitability of soothsaying through which is announced the advent of something great and unprecedented, something exceeding all his dreams.

This time he was partly stupefied by the swelling and partly (in that corner of his mind which the stupor hadn't reached) amazed. How was it that his desire had such power that at its summons reality submissively hurried to come into being? Continuing to marvel at its power, he was on the lookout for when the conversation would become more heated and the arguers would forget about his presence. As soon as this happened, he slipped out of the room.

The Handsome Young Man with His Arms Folded

The ward where this impromptu symposium was taking place was on the ground floor of an attractive pavilion, situated (close to other pavilions) in the large hospital garden. Now Flaishman entered this garden. He leaned against the tall trunk of a plane tree, lit a cigarette, and gazed at the sky. It was summer, fragrances were floating through the air, and a round moon was suspended in the black sky.

He tried to imagine the course of future events: the woman doctor who had indicated to him a little while before that he should step outside would bide her time until her baldpate was more involved in the conversation than in watching her, and then probably she would inconspicuously announce that a small, intimate need compelled her to absent herself from the company for a moment.

And what else would happen? He deliberately didn't want to imagine anything else. His swelling chest was apprising him of a love affair, and that was enough for him. He believed in his own good fortune, he believed in his star of love, and he believed in the woman doctor. Spoiled by his self-assurance (a self-assurance that was always a bit amazed at itself), he lapsed into agreeable passivity. That is to say, he always saw himself as an attractive, successful, well-loved man, and it gratified him to await a love affair with his arms folded, so to speak. He believed that precisely this posture was bound to provoke both women and fate.

Perhaps at this opportunity it is worth mentioning that Flaishman very often, if not uninterruptedly (and with self-love), *saw* himself; so he was continuously accompanied by a double and this made his solitude quite amusing. This time he not only stood leaning against the plane tree smoking, but simultaneously observed himself with self-love. He saw how he was standing (handsome and boyish) leaning against the plane tree, nonchalantly smoking. He diverted himself for some time with this sight, until finally he heard light footsteps coming in his direction from the pavilion. He purposely didn't turn around. He drew once more on his cigarette, blew out the smoke, and looked at the sky. When the steps had got quite close to him, he said in a tender, winning voice: "I knew that you would come . . ."

Urination

"That wasn't so hard to figure," replied the chief physician, "I always prefer to take a leak in nature rather than in civilized facilities, which are foul. Here my little golden fountain will before long wondrously unite with the soil, the grass, the earth. For, Flaishman, I arose from the dust and now at least in part I shall return to the dust. A leak in nature is a religious ceremony, by means of which we promise the earth that in the end we'll return to it entirely."

As Flaishman was silent, the chief physician questioned him: "And what about you? Did you come to look at the moon?" And as Flaishman stubbornly continued to be silent the chief physician said: "You're a real lunatic, Flaishman. And I like you just because of it." Flaishman perceived the chief physician's words as mockery, and wanting to keep his image he said with his mouth half-open: "Let's leave the moon out of it. I came to take a piss too."

"My dear Flaishman," said the chief physician very gently, "from you I consider this an exceptional show of kindness toward your aging boss."

Then they both stood under the plane tree performing the act, which the chief physician with untiring rapture and in ever new images described as a divine service.

2

The Handsome and Sarcastic Young Man

Then they went back together down the long corridor and the chief physician put his arm round the intern's shoulder in a brotherly fashion. The intern didn't doubt that the jealous baldpate had detected the woman doctor's signal and was now mocking him with his friendly effusions. Of course he couldn't remove his boss's arm from his shoulder, but all the more did anger accumulate in his heart. And the only thing that consoled him was that not only *was* he full of anger, but also he immediately *saw* himself in this angry state, and was pleased with the young man who returned to the staff room and to everyone's surprise was suddenly an utterly different person: scathingly sarcastic, aggressively witty, almost demonic.

When they both actually entered the staff room, Alzhbeta was standing in the middle of the room, twisting about horribly from the waist and emitting some singing sounds in a low voice. Dr. Havel looked at the floor, and the woman doctor, so as to relieve the shock of the two new arrivals, explained: "Alzhbeta is dancing."

"She's a bit drunk," added Havel.

Alzhbeta didn't stop swaying her hips while gyrating the upper part of her body around the lowered head of the seated Havel.

"Wherever did you learn such a beautiful dance?" asked the chief physician.

Flaishman, bursting with sarcasm, let out a conspicuous laugh: "Hahaha! A beautiful dance! Hahaha!"

"I saw it at the striptease in Vienna," replied Alzhbeta.

"Now, now," the chief physician scolded her gently. "Since when do our nurses go to striptease shows?"

"I suppose it isn't forbidden, sir." Alzhbeta gyrated the upper part of her body around the chief physician.

Bile shot up through Flaishman's body and longed to escape through his lips. And so Flaishman said, "You should take a bromide, instead of stripping. Or we'll be scared that you might rape us!"

"You don't have to be scared. I don't go cradle-snatching," snapped back Alzhbeta, and gyrated the upper part of her body around Havel.

"And did you like the striptease?" The chief physician went on questioning her in a fatherly way.

"Yes, I did," replied Alzhbeta. "There was a Swedish girl there with gigantic breasts, but see, mine are prettier" (with those words she caressed her breasts). "And also there was a girl who pretended to be bathing in soap bubbles in some sort of paper bath, and a colored girl, who masturbated right in front of the audience—that was the best of all . . ."

"Haha!" said Flaishman at the height of his fiendish sarcasm, "masturbation, that's just the thing for you!"

Grief in the Shape of a Backside

Alzhbeta went on dancing, but her audience was probably far worse than the one at the Vienna strip joint: Havel lowered his head, the woman doctor watched scornfully, Flaishman negatively, and the chief physician with fatherly forbearance. And Alzhbeta's backside, covered with the white material of a nurse's apron, circled around the room like a beautifully round sun, but an extinct and dead sun (wrapped up in a white shroud), a sun doomed to pitiful redundance by the indifferent and distracted eyes of the doctors present.

At one moment when it seemed that Alzhbeta would really begin to throw off parts of her clothing, the chief physician protested in an uneasy voice: "Come, Alzhbeta dear! I hope you don't want to demonstrate the Vienna show here for us!"

"What are you afraid of, sir! At least you'd see how a naked female should really look!" screeched Alzhbeta, and then she turned again to Havel, threatening him with her breasts: "Whatever is it, Havel my pet? You're acting as if you were at a funeral. Raise your head! What, did someone die on you? Did someone die on you? Look at me! I am alive anyhow! I'm not dying! For the time being I am still alive! I'm alive!" and with these words her backside was no longer a backside, but grief itself, splendidly formed grief, dancing around the room.

"You should quit, Alzhbeta," said Havel in the direction of the floor.

"Quit?" said Alzhbeta. "After all, I'm dancing for your sake. And now I'll perform a striptease for you! A great striptease!" and she undid her apron, and with a dancing movement cast it onto the desk.

The chief physician once again protested timidly: "Alzhbeta, my dear, it would be beautiful if you performed your striptease for us, but somewhere else. You must realize that here we are at our place of work."

The Great Striptease

"Sir, I know what I'm allowed to do!" replied Alzhbeta. She was now in her pale blue state uniform with the white collar, and she didn't stop wiggling about.

Then she put her hands on her hips and slid them up both sides of her body and all the way up above her head. Then she ran her right hand along her raised left arm and then her left hand along her right arm, then with both arms made a violent movement in Flaishman's direction which scared him so that he started. "You milksop, you dropped it," she yelled at him.

Then she put her hands on her hips again and this time slid them down both legs. When she had bent down entirely, she raised first her right and then her left leg. Then, staring at the chief physician, she made a violent movement with her right arm. At the same time the chief physician extended his hand with the fingers spread out, and immediately clasped them into a fist. Then he put this hand on his knee and with the fingers of the other hand blew Alzhbeta a kiss.

After some more wiggling and dancing Alzhbeta rose onto her tiptoes, bent her arms at the elbows, and put them behind her back, trying with her fingers to reach as high as she could up her spine. Then with dancing movements, she brought her arms forward, stroked her left shoulder with her right palm and her right shoulder with her left palm and again made a gliding movement with her arm, this time in Havel's direction. He also distractedly moved his arm a little.

Now Alzhbeta straightened up and began to stride

majestically about the room; she went around to all four spectators in turn, thrusting upon each of them the symbolic nakedness of the upper part of her body. Eventually she stopped in front of Havel, once again began wiggling her hips, and bending down slightly, slid both her arms down her sides and again (as before) raised first one, then the other leg. After that she triumphantly stood up straight, raising her right hand, the thumb and index finger of which she pressed together. With this hand she again waved with a gliding movement in Havel's direction.

Then she stood on her tiptoes again, posing in the full glory of her fictional nakedness. She was no longer looking at anyone, not even at Havel, but with the half-closed eyes of her half-turned head she was staring down at her own twisting body.

Suddenly her showy posture relaxed and Alzhbeta sat down on Dr. Havel's knee. "I'm bushed," she said yawning. She stretched out her hand for Havel's glass and took a drink. "Doctor," she said to Havel, "you don't have some kind of pep pill, do you? After all, I don't want to sleep!"

"Anything for you, dear Alzhbeta," said Havel. He lifted Alzhbeta off his knees, set her on a chair, and went over to the dispensary. There he found some strong sleeping pills and gave two to Alzhbeta.

"Will this pick me up?" she asked.

"As sure as my name's Havel," said Havel.

Alzhbeta's Words at Parting

When Alzhbeta had chased down both the pills, she wanted to sit on Havel's knee again, but Havel moved his legs aside so that she fell on the floor.

Havel immediately felt sorry about this, because in fact he hadn't intended to let Alzhbeta fall in this ignominious way, and if he moved his legs aside, it was an unconscious movement, caused by his simple aversion to touching Alzhbeta's backside with his legs.

So he tried now to lift her up again, but Alzhbeta in pitiful defiance was clinging to the floor with her whole weight.

At this moment, Flaishman stood up in front of her and said: "You're drunk, you should go to bed."

Alzhbeta looked up from the floor with boundless scorn and (relishing the masochistic pathos of her being on the floor) said to him: "You beast. You idiot." And once again: "You idiot."

Havel once more attempted to lift her up, but she broke away from him furiously and began to sob. No one knew what to say, so her sobbing echoed through the silent room like a solo violin. Only a bit later did it occur to the woman doctor to start whistling quietly. Alzhbeta got up brusquely, went to the door, and as she was catching hold of the door handle, half-turned toward the room and said: "You beasts. You beasts. If you only knew. You don't know anything. You don't know anything."

The Chief Physician's
Indictment of Flaishman

After her departure there was silence, which the chief physician was the first to break. "You see, Flaishman my boy. You say you feel sorry for women. But if you are sorry for them, why aren't you sorry for Alzhbeta?"

"Why should I care about her?" Flaishman protested.

"Don't pretend that you know nothing. We told you about it a little while ago. She's crazy about you."

"Can I help it?" asked Flaishman.

"You can't," said the chief physician, "but you can help being rude to her and tormenting her. The whole evening it mattered a great deal to her what you would do, if you would look at her and smile, if you would say something nice to her. And remember what you did say to her."

"I didn't say anything so terrible to her," protested Flaishman, but his voice sounded fairly uncertain.

"Nothing so terrible, eh?" laughed the chief physician. "You made fun of her dance, even though she was dancing only for your sake, you recommended a bromide for her, you claimed there was nothing for her but masturbation. Nothing terrible? When she was doing her striptease you let her apron fall on the floor."

"What apron?" protested Flaishman.

"Her apron," said the chief physician. "And don't play the fool. In the end you sent her to bed, although a moment before she had taken a pep pill."

"But, after all, she was running after Havel, not me," Flaishman continued to protest.

"Don't dissemble," said the chief physician sternly.

"What could she do if you weren't paying attention to her? She was trying to provoke you. And she was only longing for a few crumbs of jealousy from you. You are a gentleman."

"Don't torment him any more," said the woman doctor. "He is cruel, but, still, he is young."

"He is the chastising archangel," said Havel.

Mythological Roles

"Yes, indeed," said the woman doctor, "look at him; a wicked, handsome archangel."

"We are a real mythological group," the chief physician sleepily observed, "because you are Diana. Frigid, sportive, and spiteful."

"And you are a satyr. Grown old, lecherous, and garrulous," the woman doctor spoke again. "And Havel is Don Juan. He's not old, but he's getting old."

"Not at all. Havel is death," the chief physician objected, putting forward his old thesis.

The End of the Don Juans

"If I should pass judgment on whether I'm Don Juan or death, I must incline, albeit unhappily, toward the chief physician's opinion," said Havel, taking a long drink. "Don Juan. He, after all, was a conqueror. Rather in capital letters. A Great Conqueror. But I ask you, how can you be a conqueror in a domain where no one refuses you, where everything is possible and everything is permitted? Don Juan's era has come to an end. Today, Don Juan's descendant no longer *conquers*, but only *collects*. The figure of the Great Collector has taken the place of the Great Conqueror, only the Collector is no longer really Don Juan at all. Don Juan was a tragic figure. He was burdened by his guilt. He sinned gaily and laughed at God. He was a blasphemer and ended up in hell.

"Don Juan bore on his shoulders a dramatic burden about which the Great Collector doesn't even have a suspicion, because in his world every burden has lost its weight. Boulders have become feathers. In the Conqueror's world, a single glance was as important as ten years of the most ardent love-making in the Collector's realm.

"Don Juan was a master, while the Collector is a slave. Don Juan arrogantly transgressed conventions and laws. The Great Collector only obediently, by the sweat of his brow, complies with conventions and the law, because collecting has become good manners, good form, and almost an obligation. After all, if I'm burdened by any guilt, then it's only because I don't take Alzhbeta.

"The Great Collector knows nothing of tragedy or drama. Eroticism, which used to be the greatest instigator of catastrophes, has become, thanks to him, like breakfasts and dinners, like stamp-collecting and ping-pong, if not like a ride on the streetcar or shopping. He has introduced it into the ordinary round of events. He has transformed it into a stage, on which genuine drama should by now have stepped. Alas, my friends," ranted Havel, "my loves (if I may call them that) are a stage upon which nothing is taking place.

"My dear doctor and you, dear sir. You've placed Don Juan and death in opposition to each other. By sheer chance and inadvertence, you've grasped the essence of the matter. Look. Don Juan struggled against the impossible. And that is a very human thing to do. But in the realm of the Great

Collector, nothing's impossible, because it is the realm of death. The Great Collector is death, who has come to fetch tragedy, drama, and love. Death, who has come to fetch Don Juan. In hell fire, where the commander sent him, Don Juan is alive. But in the world of the Great Collector, where passions and feelings flutter through space like feathers—in this world, he is forever dead.

"Not at all, my dear doctor," said Havel sadly, "Don Juan and I, not at all! What would I have given to have seen the commander and to have felt in my soul the terrible burden of his curse and to have felt the greatness of the tragedy growing within me. Not at all, Doctor, I am at most a figure of comedy, and I do not owe even that to my own efforts, but to Don Juan, because only against the historical background of his tragic gaiety can you to some extent perceive the comic sadness of my womanizing existence, which without this gauge would be nothing but gray banality in a tedious setting."

Further Signals

Havel, fatigued by his long speech (in the course of it the sleepy chief physician had almost nodded off twice), fell silent. Only after an appropriate instant full of emotion did the woman doctor break the silence: "I hadn't suspected, Doctor, that you could speak so fluently. You portrayed yourself as a figure of comedy, gray, dull, a zero in fact. Unfortunately, the way you spoke was somewhat too sublime. You're so damned cunning: calling yourself a beggar, but choosing words so majestic that you would after all sound more like a king. You're an old fraud, Havel. Vain even as you vilify yourself. You're simply an old fraud."

Flaishman laughed loudly, for he fancied to his satisfaction that in the woman doctor's words he could detect scorn for Havel. So, encouraged by her mockery and his own laughter, he went over to the window and said meaningfully: "What a night!"

"Yes," said the woman doctor, "a gorgeous night. And Havel is going to play death! Have you noticed, Havel, what a beautiful night it is?"

"Of course he hasn't," said Flaishman, "for Havel one woman is like another, one night like another, winter like summer. Dr. Havel refuses to distinguish the secondary characteristics of things."

"You've seen right through me," said Havel.

Flaishman concluded that this time his rendezvous with the woman doctor would be successful. The chief physician had drunk a great deal and the sleepiness, which had come over him in the last few minutes, had considerably blunted his wariness. That being so, Flaishman inconspicuously remarked: "Oh, this bladder of mine!" and throwing a glance in the woman doctor's direction, he went out the door.

Gas

Walking along the corridor, he recalled how throughout the evening the woman doctor had been ironically making fun of both the men, the chief physician and Havel, whom she just now had very aptly called a fraud. He was astonished that it was happening once again; he marveled anew each time it happened, because it happened so regularly. Women liked him, they preferred him to experienced men; in the case of the woman doctor. This was a great, new, and unexpected triumph, since she was obviously choosy, intelligent, and a bit (but pleasantly) uppity.

It was with these pleasant thoughts that Flaishman was walking down the long corridor to the exit. When he was almost at the swinging doors leading to the garden, he suddenly smelled the offensive odor of gas. He stopped and sniffed. The smell was concentrated around the door leading to the nurses' little room. All at once Flaishman realized that he was terribly frightened.

First he wanted to run back quickly and bring Havel and the chief physician, but then he decided to take hold of the door handle (perhaps because he assumed that it would be locked, if not barricaded). But surprisingly enough the door was open. In the room a strong ceiling light was on, illuminating a large, naked, female body lying on the couch. Flaishman looked round the room and hurried over to the small range. He turned off the open gas jet. Then he ran to the window and flung it wide open.

A Remark in Parentheses

(One can say that Flaishman acted promptly and with great presence of mind. There was one thing, however, that he wasn't able to record with a sufficiently cool head. It is true that for an instant he stood gaping at Alzhbeta's naked body, but shock overcame him to such a degree that beneath its veil he did not realize what we from an advantageous distance can fully appreciate:

Alzhbeta's body was magnificent. She was lying on her back with her head turned slightly to the side and one shoulder slightly bent inward toward the other, so that both her beautiful breasts pressed against each other and showed their full shape. One of her legs was stretched out and the other was slightly bent at the knee, so that it was possible to see the remarkable fullness of her thighs and the exceptionally dense black of her bush.)

The Appeal for Help

When he had opened the door and window wide, Flaishman ran out into the corridor and began to shout. Everything which followed then took place in a brisk and matter of fact way: artificial respiration, a call to the internal medicine ward, a bed for moving the sick woman, conveying her to the doctor on duty in the internal medicine ward, more artificial respiration, resuscitation, a blood transfusion, and finally deep exhalation, at which point Alzhbeta's life had clearly been saved beyond any doubt.

3
Who Said What

When all four doctors emerged from the internal medicine building into the courtyard, they looked exhausted.

The chief physician said: "Poor Alzhbeta spoiled our symposium."

The woman doctor said: "Unsatisfied women always bring bad luck."

Havel said: "It's curious. She had to turn on the gas so that we'd find out that she has such a beautiful body."

At these words Flaishman gave Havel a (long) look and said: "I'm no longer in the mood for booze or witticisms. Good night." And he walked toward the hospital exit.

Flaishman's Theory

The words of his colleagues disgusted Flaishman. In them he saw the callousness of aging men and women, the cruelty of their mature years, which rose before his youth like a hostile barrier. For this reason he was glad to be alone, and he purposely went on foot, because he wanted to fully experience and enjoy his agitation. With pleasurable terror he kept repeating that Alzhbeta had been within an ace of death, and that he would have been guilty of this death.

Of course he well knew that a suicide does not have a single cause but, for the most part, a whole bunch, yet on the other hand he just couldn't deny that the one (and probably the decisive) cause was he himself partly through the simple fact of his existence, partly as a result of his behavior that night.

Now he touchingly blamed himself. He called himself an egotist, who out of vanity had been engrossed in his own amorous successes. He derided himself for allowing himself to be dazzled by the woman doctor's interest. He blamed himself for turning Alzhbeta into a mere thing, a vessel into which he'd poured his rage when the jealous chief physician had thwarted his nocturnal rendezvous. By what right, by what right had he behaved like this toward an innocent human being?

The young intern, however, didn't have a primitive mind. Each of his spiritual states encompassed a dialectic of assertion and negation, so that now his inner counsel for the defense was immediately objecting to his inner prosecutor: certainly the sarcastic remarks that he had made about Alzhbeta had been uncalled for, but they would hardly have had such tragic results if it hadn't been for the fact that Alzhbeta loved him. However, was Flaishman to blame because someone had fallen in love with him? As a result of this did he perhaps automatically become responsible for it?

At this question he paused for a moment. It seemed to him to be the key to the whole mystery of human existence. He finally stopped altogether and with complete seriousness answered himself: Yes, he had been wrong today when he had tried to persuade the chief physician that he was not responsible for what he caused involuntarily. However, was it possible to reduce himself only to that part of him which was conscious and intentional? After all, that which he had caused involuntarily also belonged to the sphere of his personality, and who else but he could be responsible for that? Yes, it was his fault that Alzhbeta loved him; it was his fault that he didn't know; it was his fault that he paid no attention; it was his fault. It would have taken only a little and he could have killed a human being.

The Chief Physician's Theory

While Flaishman was absorbed in his self-searching deliberations, the chief physician, Havel, and the woman doctor returned to the staff room. They really no longer felt like drinking. For a while they remained silent and then Havel sighed: "I wonder what put that crazy idea into Alzhbeta's head."

"No sentimentality, please, Doctor," said the chief physician. "When a person does something so asinine, I refuse to be moved. Besides, if you hadn't been so obstinate and had done long ago with her what you don't hesitate to do with everyone else, it wouldn't have come to this."

"Thank you for making me the reason for the attempted suicide," said Havel.

"Let's be precise," replied the chief physician. "It was not a question of suicide but of a demonstration of suicide set up in such a way that a disaster would not occur. My dear doctor, when someone wants to get poisoned with gas, to start with he closes the door. And not only that, he seals up the crevices well so that the gas won't be located until as late as possible. Only in Alzhbeta's case it was not a question of death, but of you.

"God knows how many weeks she's been looking forward to being on night duty with you, and since the beginning of the evening she's been brazenly making advances to you. But you were hardhearted. And the more hardhearted you were, the more she drank and the more blatant she became. She talked nonsense, danced, wanted to do a striptease . . .

"You see, in the end there is perhaps, after all, something touching in this. When she could attract neither your eyes nor your ears she staked everything on your sense of smell and turned on the gas. Before turning it on, she undressed. She knows that she has a beautiful body, and she wanted to force you to discover this. Remember how when she was standing in the doorway she said: *If you only knew. You don't know anything. You don't know anything.* So now you do know, Alzhbeta has a hideous face but a beautiful body. You yourself admitted it. You see, she didn't reason so altogether stupidly. Maybe you will now finally be prevailed upon."

"Maybe." Havel shrugged his shoulders.

"Certainly," said the chief physician.

Havel's Theory

"What you say, sir, has some plausibility, but there's an error in your reasoning: You overestimate my role in this drama. I wasn't the person in question. After all, it wasn't only I who refused to sleep with Alzhbeta. Nobody wanted to sleep with Alzhbeta.

"When you asked me earlier why I didn't want to take Alzhbeta, I told you some rubbish about the beauty of caprice and how I wanted to retain my freedom. But those were only stupid jokes with which I obscured the truth. For the truth is just the reverse and not at all flattering: I refused Alzhbeta just because I don't in the least know how to be free. Not to sleep with Alzhbeta, that's the fashion. No one sleeps with her, and even if someone did sleep with her, he would never admit it because everyone would laugh at him. Fashion is a terrible martinet and I've slavishly submitted to it. At the same time, Alzhbeta is a mature woman and this has dulled her wits. And maybe it's *my* refusal that's dulled her wits the most, because, after all, it's well known that I take everything. But the fashion was dearer to me than Alzhbeta's wits.

"And you are right, sir, she knows that she has a beautiful body, and so she considered her situation sheer absurdity and injustice and was protesting against it. Remember how the whole evening she kept unceasingly referring to her body. When she spoke about the Swedish girl at the strip-tease in Vienna she stroked her own breasts and declared that they were prettier than the Swedish girl's. Remember how her breasts and her backside filled the room this evening like a mob of demonstrators. Actually, sir, it was a demonstration!

"And remember that striptease of hers, just remember how deeply she was experiencing it! It was the saddest striptease I've ever seen! She was passionately trying to strip and at the same time she still remained in the hated confinement of her nurse's clothing. She was trying to strip and couldn't. And although she knew that she wouldn't strip, she was trying to, because she wanted to communicate to us her sad and unrealizable desire to strip. Sir, she wasn't stripping, she was singing about stripping, about the impossibility of stripping, about the impossibility of making love, about the impossibility of living! And we didn't even want to hear it. We looked at the floor and we were unsympathetic."

"You romantic womanizer! Do you really believe that she wanted to die?" the chief physician shouted at Havel.

"Remember," said Havel, "how while she was dancing, she kept saying to me: *I am still alive! For the time being I am still alive!* Do you remember? From the moment she began to dance, she knew what she was going to do."

"And why did she want to die naked, eh? What kind of an explanation do you have for that?"

"She wanted to step into the arms of death as one steps into the arms of a lover. That's why she undressed, did her hair, and put on makeup . . ."

"And that's why she left the door unlocked, what about that? Please, don't try to persuade yourself that she really wanted to die!"

"Maybe she didn't know exactly what she wanted. After all, do you know what you want? Which of us knows that? She wanted and she didn't want. She quite sincerely wanted to die and at the same time (equally sincerely) she wanted to prolong the state she found herself in, engaged in the act leading to death and feeling great on account of this act. You do know this, she didn't want us to see her after she had turned quite brown and became bad-smelling and disfigured. She wanted us to see her in all her glory, to see her drifting away in her beautiful, underestimated body to have intercourse with death. She wanted us, at least at so vital a moment as this, to envy death this body and long for it."

The Woman Doctor's Theory

"My dear gentlemen," protested the woman doctor, who had been silent till now listening attentively to both the doctors, "so far as I, as a woman, can judge, you've both spoken logically. Your theories are plausible in themselves and astonishing, because they reveal such a deep knowledge of life. But they contain one little mistake. There isn't an iota of truth in them. That is, Alzhbeta didn't want to commit suicide. Not genuine suicide, nor staged. Neither."

For a moment the woman doctor relished the effect of her words, then went on, "My dear gentlemen, I detect a bad conscience in you. When we were coming back from the internal medicine building, you avoided Alzhbeta's little room. You no longer even wanted to see it. But I took a good look around while they were giving Alzhbeta artificial respiration. A small pot was on the range. Alzhbeta was making herself some coffee and she fell asleep. The water boiled over and put out the flames."

Both the male doctors hurried with the woman doctor

to Alzhbeta's little room, and, indeed, on the burner stood a small pot and in it there even remained a little water.

"But I ask you, why was she naked?" said the chief physician with surprise.

"Look." The woman doctor pointed to three corners of the room: on the floor beneath the window lay a pale blue uniform, up on the white medicine chest hung a bra, and in the opposite corner on the floor was a pair of white panties. "Alzhbeta threw her clothes in different directions, bearing witness to the fact that she wanted at least to make the strip-tease come true for herself. It was you, cautious sir, who had prevented this.

"When she was naked, she apparently felt tired. This didn't suit her, because she'd in no way given up hope for tonight. She knew that we were all going to leave and that Havel would remain here alone. That's surely why she asked for pep pills. She decided to make some coffee for herself and put the pot on the burner. Then once again she caught sight of her body and this excited her. My dear gentlemen, Alzhbeta had one advantage over all of you. She saw herself without her own head. So to herself she was completely beautiful. She got excited by this and eagerly lay down on the couch. But sleep overcame her apparently before sensual delight."

"Of course," Havel now remembered, "after all, I gave her sleeping pills!"

"That's just like you," said the woman doctor. "So is anything still not clear to you?"

"There is," said Havel. "Remember those things she said: *I'm still not dying! I'm alive. For the time being I'm still alive!* And those last words of hers: she said them so pathetically, as if they were words of farewell: *If you only knew. You don't know anything. You don't know anything.*"

"But Havel," said the woman doctor, "as if you didn't

know that ninety-nine percent of all statements are idle talk. Don't you yourself talk mostly just for the sake of talking?"

The doctors went on talking for a little while longer and then all three went out in front of the pavilion. The chief physician and the woman doctor shook hands with Havel and walked away.

Fragrances Floated Through the Night Air

Flaishman finally arrived at the suburban street, where he lived with his parents in the family house, which was surrounded by a garden. He opened the little gate, but didn't go indoors. He sat down on a bench, above which twined the roses so carefully tended by his mom.

Through the summer night floated the fragrance of flowers, and the words "guilty," "egotism," "beloved," "death" rose in Flaishman's chest and filled him with uplifting delight, so that he had the impression wings were growing out of his back.

In the first flush of melancholy happiness he realized that he was loved as never before. Certainly several women had expressed their affection for him, but now he would be soberly truthful with himself: had it always been love? Hadn't he sometimes been subject to illusions? Hadn't he sometimes talked himself into things? Wasn't Klara perhaps actually more calculating than enamored? Didn't the apartment, which he had been searching for, matter more to her than he himself? In the light of Alzhbeta's act, everything paled.

Through the air floated only important words, and Flaishman said to himself that love has but one measure, and that is death. At the end of true love is death, and only that love which ends in death is love.

Through the air, fragrances floated and Flaishman asked himself: would anyone ever love him as much as this ugly woman? But what is beauty or ugliness compared with love? What is the ugliness of a face compared with an emotion in whose greatness the absolute itself is mirrored?

(The absolute? Yes. This was a young man only recently cast out into the adult world, which is full of uncertainties. However much he ran after girls, above all he was seeking a comforting embrace, never-ending and vast, which would redeem him from the infernal relativity of the freshly discovered world.)

4

The Woman Doctor's Return

Dr. Havel had been lying on the couch for a while, covered with a light woolen blanket, when he heard a tapping on the window. In the moonlight he caught sight of the woman doctor's face. He opened the window and asked: "What's the matter?"

"Let me in!" said the woman doctor and hurried toward the entrance to the building.

Havel did up the buttons on his shirt, heaved a sigh, and left the room.

When he unlocked the pavilion door, the woman doctor without so much as an explanation rushed into the staff room, and only when she had seated herself in an armchair opposite Havel did she begin to explain that she hadn't been able to go home. Only now, she said, did she realize how upset she was. She couldn't have slept at all and asked Havel to talk to her for a bit, so she could calm down.

Havel didn't believe a word of what the woman doctor was telling him, and was so ungentlemanly (or careless) that this was apparent from the expression on his face.

That is why the woman doctor said: "Of course you don't believe me, because you're convinced that I came just to sleep with you."

The doctor made a gesture of denial, but the woman doctor continued: "You're conceited, Don Juan. Naturally, all the women who set eyes on you think of nothing but that. And you, bored and careworn, carry out your sad mission."

Once again Havel made a gesture of denial, but the woman doctor, when she had lit a cigarette and nonchalantly exhaled some smoke, continued: "You poor Don Juan, don't be afraid, I haven't come to trouble you. You're not at all like death. That is just our dear chief physician's little joke. You don't take everything, because not every woman would allow you to take her. I guarantee that I, for example, am quite immune to you."

"Did you come to tell me that?"

"Perhaps. I came to comfort you, by telling you that you are not like death. That I wouldn't let myself be taken."

Havel's Morality

"It's nice of you," said Havel. "It's nice that you wouldn't let yourself be taken and that you came to tell me. I'm really not like death. Not only won't I take Alzhbeta, but I wouldn't even take you."

"Oh," the woman doctor was surprised.

"By this I don't mean that I'm not attracted by you. On the contrary."

"That's better," said the woman doctor.

"Yes, you do attract me very much."

"So why wouldn't you take me? Because I don't care about you?"

"No, I don't think it has anything to do with that," said Havel.

"Then with what?"

"You're going with the chief physician."

"So?"

"The chief physician is jealous. It would hurt him."

"Have you moral inhibitions?" laughed the woman doctor.

"You know," said Havel, "in my life I've had enough affairs with women to teach me to respect friendship between men. This relationship unblemished by the idiocy of eroticism is the only value I've found in life."

"Do you consider the chief physician a friend?"

"He's done a lot for me."

"More, no doubt, for me," objected the woman doctor.

"Maybe," said Havel, "but, after all, it isn't a question of gratitude. I just like him. He's a great guy. And he really cares about you. If I did happen to make a play for you, I would have to consider myself a real villain."

Slander of the Chief Physician

"I didn't suspect," said the woman doctor, "that I would hear such heartfelt odes to friendship from you. You present me, Doctor, with a new, unexpected image of yourself. Not only do you, contrary to all expectations, have a capacity for emotion, but you bestow it (and this is touching) on an old, bald, gray-haired gentleman, who is noteworthy only because of how funny he is. Did you notice him this evening? How he continuously shows off? He's always trying to prove several things, which no one can believe:

"First, he wants to prove that he's witty. Did you notice? He incessantly talked nonsense; he entertained the company; he made cracks—'Dr. Havel is like death'; he concocted paradoxes about the fact that he is unhappily married (as if I wasn't hearing it for the fiftieth time!); he took pains to lead Flaishman by the nose (as if it required any brilliance to do that!).

"Second, he tries to show that he's a friendly man. In reality, of course, he doesn't like anybody with hair on his head, but because of this he tries all the harder. He flattered you, he flattered me, he was kind to Alzhbeta in a fatherly way, and even kidded Flaishman so cautiously that he wouldn't notice it.

"And third, and this is the main thing, he tries to prove that he's a big shot. He tries desperately to hide his present appearance beneath his former appearance. Unfortunately, it no longer exists and not one of us remembers it. Surely you noticed how neatly he introduced the incident about the tart who refused him, only because this gave him the opportunity to evoke his youthful, irresistible face and with it make us forget his pitiful bald head."

A Defense of the Chief Physician

"Everything that you say is pretty much true, Doctor," replied Havel. "But all that provides even more reasons for me to like the chief physician, because all this is closer to me than you suspect. Why should I mock a bald spot which I won't escape? Why should I mock those earnest efforts of the chief physician not to be who he is?

"An old man will either make the best of the fact that he is what he is, a lamentable wreck of his former self, or he won't. But what should he do if he doesn't make the best of it? There remains nothing but to pretend not to be what he is. There remains nothing but to create, by means of a difficult pretense, everything that he no longer is, that has been lost: to invent, create, and demonstrate his gaiety, vitality, and friendliness; to evoke his youthful self and to try to merge with it and have it replace what he has become. In the chief physician's game of pretense I see myself, my own future—if, of course, I have enough strength to defy resignation, which is certainly a worse evil than this sad pretense.

"Maybe you've diagnosed the chief physician correctly. But I like him even better for it and I could never hurt him, so it follows that I could never do anything with you."

The Woman Doctor's Reply

"My dear doctor," replied the woman doctor, "there are fewer differences between us than you suppose. After all, I like him too. After all, I'm also sorry for him—just like you. And I have more to be grateful for from him than you. Without him I wouldn't have such a good position. (Anyhow, you know this, everybody knows this only too well!) You think that I lead him by the nose? That I cheat on him? That I have other lovers? With what relish they'd inform him about that! I don't want to hurt him or myself, and that's why I'm more tied down than you can imagine. But I'm happy that we two have understood each other now. Because you are the one man with whom I can afford to be unfaithful to the chief physician. You really do like him and you would never hurt him. You will be scrupulously discreet. I can depend on you. I can make love with you . . ." and she sat down on Havel's knee and began to unbutton his clothes.

What Did Dr. Havel Do?

Ah, that's some question . . .

5

In a Vortex of Noble Sentiments

After the night came morning and Flaishman went into the back garden to cut some flowers. Then he took the streetcar to the hospital.

Alzhbeta was in a private room in the internal medicine ward. Flaishman took a seat near her bed, put the flowers on the night table, and caught hold of her hand to take her pulse.

"Well now, are you feeling better?" he asked.

"Sure," said Alzhbeta.

And Flaishman said warmly: "You shouldn't play the fool, my girl."

"Well sure," said Alzhbeta, "but I fell asleep. I put on the coffee water and I fell asleep like an idiot."

Flaishman sat gaping at Alzhbeta, because he hadn't expected such nobility. Alzhbeta didn't want to burden him with remorse, she didn't want to burden him with her love so she was renouncing it.

He stroked her face and carried away by emotion addressed her tenderly: "I know everything. You musn't tell lies. But I do thank you for that lie."

He understood that he wouldn't find such refinement, devotion, and consideration in any other woman, and a terrible desire to give in to this fit of rashness and ask her to become his wife swept over him. At the last moment, however, he regained his self-control (there's always enough time for the marriage proposal), and he said only this:

"Alzhbeta, Alzhbeta, my girl. I brought these roses for you."

Alzhbeta gaped at Flaishman and said: "For me?"

"Yes, for you. Because I'm happy to be here with you. Because I'm happy that you exist at all. My dear Alzhbeta. Perhaps I do like you. Perhaps I like you very much. But perhaps just for this reason it would be better if we remain as we are. Possibly a man and a woman are closer to each other when they don't live together and when they know about each other only that they exist, and when they are grateful to each other for the fact that they exist and that they know about each other. And that alone is enough for their happiness. I thank you, dear Alzhbeta, I thank you for existing."

Alzhbeta didn't understand anything, but a foolish,

blissful smile full of vague happiness and indistinct hope spread across her face.

Then Flaishman got up, squeezed Alzhbeta's shoulder (as a sign of discreet, self-restrained love), turned, and left.

The Uncertainty of All Things

"Our beautiful female colleague, who looks absolutely radiant with youth today, has perhaps actually offered the most correct interpretation of the events," said the chief physician to the woman doctor and to Havel, when all three of them met in the ward. "Alzhbeta was making some coffee and fell asleep. At least that's what she claims."

"You see," said the woman doctor.

"I don't see anything," objected the chief physician. "As a matter of fact no one knows anything about how it really was. The pot could have been on the range already. If Alzhbeta wanted to turn the gas on herself, why would she take off the pot?"

"But she herself explains it that way!" argued the woman doctor.

"After she had performed for us properly and scared us properly, why couldn't she, in the end, put the blame on the pot? Don't forget that would-be suicides are sent to an asylum to be treated in this country. No one would like to go there."

"Suicides have taken your fancy, sir," said the woman doctor.

And the chief physician began to laugh: "I would like for once to burden Havel's conscience thoroughly."

Havel's Repentance

Havel's bad conscience heard in the chief physician's words a reproach in cipher, by means of which the heavens were mysteriously admonishing him, and he said: "The chief physician is right. This need not have been a suicide attempt, but it could have been. Besides, if I am to speak frankly, I wouldn't hold it against Alzhbeta. Tell me, where in life is there a value that would make us consider suicide uncalled for on principle! Love? Or friendship? I guarantee that friendship is not a bit less fickle than love and it is impossible to build anything on it. Self-love? I wish it were possible," now said Havel almost ardently, and it sounded like repentance. "But, sir, I swear to you that I don't like myself at all."

"My dear gentlemen," said the woman doctor smiling, "if it will make the world more beautiful for you and will save your souls, please, let's agree that Alzhbeta really did want to commit suicide. Agreed?"

A Happy Ending

"Nonsense," the chief physician waved his hand, "quit it. Havel, don't pollute the beautiful morning air with your speeches! I'm fifteen years older than you. I have an unhappy marriage, because I'll never be able to get divorced from my perfect wife. And I have an unhappy love, because the woman I love is unfortunately this doctor here. Yet all the same I like being alive, you sly dog!"

"That's right, that's right," said the woman doctor to the chief physician with unusual tenderness, seizing him by the hand. "I too like to be alive!"

At this moment, Flaishman came up to the trio of doctors and said, "I've been to see Alzhbeta. She is an astonishingly honorable woman. She denied everything. She's taken it all on herself."

"You see," laughed the chief physician, "and Havel here will lure us all to suicide!"

"Of course," said the woman doctor. And she went over to the window. "It will be a beautiful day again. Outside it's so blue. What do you say about that, my dear Flaishman?"

Only a moment before Flaishman had been almost reproaching himself for having acted cunningly when he had settled everything with a bunch of roses and some nice words, but now he was glad that he hadn't rushed into anything. He heard the woman doctor's signal and he understood it perfectly. The thread of the romance was being resumed where it had been broken off yesterday, when the gas had thwarted his meeting with the woman doctor. He couldn't help smiling at the woman doctor even in front of the jealous chief physician.

So the story continues there, where it finished yesterday, and it seems to Flaishman that he is entering it a far older and far stronger man. He has known a love as great as death. His chest swelled and it was the most beautiful and biggest swelling he'd experienced till now. For that which was inflating him so pleasurably was death; he had been made a present of death, splendid and invigorating death.

Dr. Havel
After Ten Years

1

When Dr. Havel was leaving to take a cure at a spa, his beautiful wife had tears in her eyes. She had them there partly out of sympathy (some time ago he had been stricken with gall bladder attacks and until that time she had never seen him sick), but she also had them there because the coming three weeks of separation aroused jealous anguish in her.

What? Could this actress, admired, beautiful, so many years younger than he, be jealous of an aging gentleman, who in recent months had not left the house without slipping into his pocket a small bottle of tablets to relieve the pain which would attack insidiously?

That was the case, but no one understood her. Not even Dr. Havel, for she seemed to him invulnerably majestic, judging by her appearance. It had charmed him all the more when they became closer several years before and he had discovered her simplicity, her skill as a housekeeper, and her insecurity. It was curious; even after they were married, the actress altogether disregarded the superiority of her youth. She was bewitched by love and by her husband's formidable reputation as a womanizer, so that he seemed to her to always be elusive and unfathomable, and even though he tried to convince her every day with infinite patience (and absolute sincerity) that he did not have and never would have anyone but her, she was still bitterly and madly jealous. Only her refinement kept this nasty feeling hidden, but it continued to torment her even more.

Havel knew all this. At times it moved him, at times it angered him, sometimes it wearied him, but because he was fond of his wife, he did everything to relieve her anguish.

This time again he made an attempt to help her. He greatly exaggerated his pains and the dangerous state of his health, for he knew that fear on account of his being ill was uplifting and cheering to her, whereas fear on account of his being healthy (a fear of infidelities and mysterious escapades) was destructive to her. He often directed his conversation to Dr. Frantishka, who was going to treat him at the spa. The actress knew her and the thought of her physical appearance, completely benign and completely alien to any lecherous ideas, soothed her.

When Dr. Hável was seated in the bus, looking at the tearful eyes of the beauty standing on the sidewalk, to tell the truth he felt relieved. For her love was not only sweet, it was also oppressive. But at the spa he didn't feel so well. After partaking of the mineral waters, which he had to do three times a day and which went right through his body, he had pains and felt tired. When he met good-looking women in the colonnade, with dismay he found that he felt old and that he didn't desire them. The only woman whom he had been granted among the boundless number was the good Frantishka, who jabbed injections into him, took his blood pressure, prodded his stomach, and supplied him with information about what was going on at the spa and about her two children, especially her son, whom, she said, looked like her.

He was in such a state of mind when he received a letter from his wife. Ah alas, this time her refinement kept a poor watch over her passionate jealousy. The letter was full of grievances and complaints. She said she didn't want to reproach him with anything, but that she hadn't slept the whole night. She said she well knew that her love was a burden to him, and she was able to imagine how happy he was now that he was without her and could rest a bit. Yes, she understood that he couldn't stand her, and she also knew that she was too weak to change his fate, which was always to be besieged by hordes of women; yes she knew it, she didn't protest against it, but she cried and couldn't sleep.

When Dr. Havel had read through this list of complaints, he recalled the three years during which he had tried patiently, but in vain, to portray himself to his wife as a reformed libertine and a loving husband; he felt immense weariness and hopelessness. In anger, he crumpled up the letter and threw it into the waste basket.

2

Surprisingly enough, the following day he felt a little better; his gall bladder no longer hurt at all, and he felt a slight but unmistakable desire for several of the women whom he had seen walking through the colonnade in the morning. This small gain was, however, wiped out by his recognition of something far worse: these women passed him by without the least show of interest; to them he blended with the other pale sippers of mineral water into a single crowd of sick people.

"You see, it's getting better," said Dr. Frantishka, when in the morning she was prodding him. "But stick strictly to the diet. The women patients, whom you met at the colonnade, are fortunately rather old and sick, so they shouldn't upset you, and for you it's better that way, because you need rest."

Havel was tucking his shirt into his pants; he was standing in front of a small mirror hanging in a corner above the washbasin and ill-humoredly examining his face. Then he said very sadly: "You're wrong. I clearly noticed that among the majority of old women there was a minority of quite pretty women strolling through the colonnade. Only they didn't spare me so much as a glance."

"I'll believe anything you like, but not that," the woman doctor smiled at him, and Dr. Havel, having torn his eyes away from the sad spectacle in the mirror, peered into her unquestioning, loyal eyes. He felt much gratitude toward her, even though he knew she was expressing only a faith in tradition, a faith in her role of many years, during which she had become accustomed to viewing him with mild disapproval (but nevertheless in a kindly way).

Then someone knocked at the door. When Frantishka opened it a little, the head of a young man, nodding in greeting, could be seen. "Ah, it's you! I had completely forgotten!" She asked the young man to come into the consulting room and explained to Havel, "The editor of the spa magazine has been searching for you for the past two days."

The young man began to apologize at length for disturbing the doctor at such an awkward time, and tried to assume (unfortunately it turned out somewhat forced and unpleasant) a facetious air. He said that Havel should not be angry with the lady doctor for betraying him, for the editor would have caught up with him anyway, maybe even in the carbonic water bath, and also that the doctor should not be angry at his impudence, for this attribute was one of the necessities of the journalistic profession and, without it, he wouldn't have been able to earn his living. Then he became talkative about the illustrated magazine, which the spa put out once a month, and explained that in every issue there was an interview with some prominent patient who was then taking the cure. He mentioned a few names, among which one was that of a member of the government, one of a woman singer, and one of a hockey player.

"You see," said Frantishka, "the beautiful women at the colonnade have not shown an interest in you; on the other hand, you attract the attention of journalists."

"That's an awful step down," said Havel. He was, however, quite pleased with this attention and smiled at the editor, refusing his proposal with touchingly transparent insincerity. "I, my dear sir, am neither a member of the government, nor a hockey player, even less a woman singer. And although I don't want to underestimate my scientific research, it is after all for experts rather than for the general public."

"But I don't want to interview you; that didn't even occur to me," replied the young man with prompt sincerity. "I want to talk with your wife. I heard that she is supposed to come visit you at the spa."

"Then you are better informed than I," said Havel rather coldly. He then approached the mirror again and looked at his face—it didn't please him. He buttoned the top button of his shirt, and kept silent, while the young editor became embarrassed and lost his avowed journalistic impudence as he said goodbye. He apologized to the woman doctor, he apologized to Dr. Havel, and was glad to be leaving.

3

The editor was scatter-brained rather than stupid. He didn't think much of the spa magazine, but, being its sole editor, every month he had to do the things necessary to fill the twenty-four pages with the requisite photographs and words. In the summer it was tolerably easy, because the spa teemed with prominent guests, various orchestras alternated at the promenade concerts, and there was no need for petty sensations. On the other hand, in the damp and cold months the colonnades were filled with provincial women and boredom, so he couldn't let any opportunity escape him. When yesterday he had heard somewhere that the husband of a well-known actress was taking a cure here (the husband of the very one who was appearing in the new detective film which was currently and successfully distracting the bored spa guests), he sniffed him out and began immediately to hunt for him.

But now he was ashamed. He was always unsure of himself and for this reason slavishly and entirely dependent upon the people with whom he came in contact. It was in their sight and judgment that he timidly found out what he was like and how much he was worth. Now he concluded that he had been recognized as wretched, stupid, and tiresome, and took it all the more to heart, because the man who had so judged him he'd rather liked at first glance. And so, troubled, he telephoned the woman doctor the same day to ask her who in fact the actress's husband was, and learned that he was not only well known as a physician, but was very famous in other ways too; had the editor really never heard of him?

The editor confessed that he hadn't, and the woman doctor indulgently said: "Well, of course, you are after all still a child. And luckily you are not up in the field in which Havel excelled."

When more questions to more people revealed that by "this field" was meant erotic knowledge, in which Dr. Havel was said to have no competition in his native land, the editor was mortified to have been called an ignoramus, and even to have confirmed this by never having heard of Havel. And because he had always longingly dreamed of someday being an expert like this man, it bothered him that he had acted like a disagreeable fool precisely in front of him, in front of his master. He remembered his chatter, his silly jokes, his lack of tact, and he humbly agreed that the punishment, which the master had meted out by way of his negative silence and absentminded glance at the mirror, was justified.

The spa town in which this story takes place is not large and people meet each other several times a day, whether they want to or not. And so it wasn't difficult for the young editor to soon come across the man he was thinking about. It was late afternoon and a crowd of gall bladder sufferers was slowly moving among the pillars of the colonnade. Dr. Havel was sipping the smelly water from a porcelain bowl and grimacing slightly. The young editor went up to him and began confusedly to apologize. He had never suspected, he said, that the husband of the well-known actress, Havlova, was he, *the* Dr. Havel, and not a different Havel; he said that in Bohemia there were many Havels and unfortunately the actress's husband had not been associated in the editor's mind with that famous doctor, about whom the editor had, of course, long ago heard, and not only as an outstanding physician, but—perhaps he might venture to say this—also on account of the most varied tales and anecdotes.

There's no reason to deny that the young man's words pleased Dr. Havel in his ill-humored state of mind, especially the remarks about the tales, for Havel well knew that they were subject to the laws of aging and extinction, like man himself.

"You don't have to make any apologies to me," he said to the young man, and because he saw the editor's embarrassment, he took him gently by the arm and got him to take a stroll through the colonnade. "Anyhow, it's not worth talking about," he consoled him. At the same time, though, he himself dwelled on the apology and several times said: "So you've heard about me?" and each time without fail smiled contentedly. "Yes," the editor eagerly assented. "But I didn't imagine you at all like this!"

"Well, how did you imagine me?" asked Dr. Havel with genuine interest, and when the editor stammered something, not knowing what to say, Havel said gloomily, "I know. Unlike real people the characters in stories, legends, and anecdotes are made of a substance not subject to the corruption of old age. No, by this I don't mean to say that legends and anecdotes are immortal, certainly they too age and with them their characters, only they grow old in such a way that their appearance does not change and deteriorate, but pales slowly, becomes transparent, and eventually merges with the transparentness of space. So in the end Cohen disappears from an anecdote and Havel-the-Collector, and also Moses and Pallas Athena or Francis of Assisi. But consider that Francis will slowly grow pale and with him the little birds which are sitting on his shoulder, and the fawn which rubs against his leg, and the grove of olive trees which provides him with shade; that his whole landscape will become transparent with him and together they will slowly turn into comforting azure, while we, my dear friend, will fade out against the background of a derisive, colored landscape and before the eyes of derisive, living youth."

Havel's speech puzzled and excited the young man, and they kept on walking together for a long time through the deepening dusk. When they parted, Havel declared that he was tired of his diet and that tomorrow he would like to go for a proper dinner; he asked the editor if he would like to accompany him. By all means the young man wanted to.

4

"Don't tell my doctor," said Havel, when he had taken a seat across the table from the editor and had picked up the menu, "but I have my own conception of a diet: I strictly avoid all those foods I don't enjoy." Then he asked the young man what aperitif he would have.

The editor was not used to drinking aperitifs before dinner, and because nothing else occurred to him, he said: "Vodka."

Dr. Havel looked displeased: "Vodka stinks of the Russian alphabet."

"That's true," said the editor, and from that moment was lost. He was like a candidate for the high school oral examination before his committee. He didn't try to say what he thought and do what he wanted, but attempted to satisfy the examiners. He tried to divine their thoughts, their whims, their taste; he wanted to be worthy of them. Not for anything in the world would he have admitted that his meals were usually poor and rudimentary, and that he didn't have a clue about which wine went with which meat. And Dr. Havel unwittingly tormented him when he persisted in conferring with him about the choice of hors d'oeuvre, main course, wine, and cheese. His generosity of spirit compelled him to treat every person as an equal.

When the editor realized that the committee had taken off many points in the part on epicureanism, he wanted more than ever to make up the loss, and now in the interval between the hors d'oeuvre and the main course, he conspicuously looked around at the women present in the restaurant and by various remarks tried hard to demonstrate his interest and knowledge. But once again he was the loser. When he stated, in regard to a red-haired lady sitting two tables away, that she would certainly be an excellent mistress, Havel without malice questioned him as to why he believed so. The editor replied vaguely, and when the doctor asked about his experiences with redheads, he became entangled in incredible lies and soon fell silent.

By contrast, Dr. Havel felt happy and relaxed with the editor's admiring eyes fixed on him. He ordered a bottle of red wine with the meat, and the young man, incited by the alcohol, made a further attempt to become worthy of the master's favor. He commented at length about a girl he'd recently discovered, whom he'd been trying to make for the past several weeks, with, he said, great hope of success. His statement was not too substantial, and the unnatural smile which covered his face and was supposed, with its artificial ambiguity, to state what he'd left unsaid, was capable only of conveying that he was attempting to overcome his insecurity. Havel was well aware of all this and, moved by pity, asked the editor about the most diverse physical attributes of the girl he'd mentioned, so as to detain him on this agreeable topic for as long as possible and to give him a chance to converse freely. However, even this time the young man was an incredible failure. It turned out that he wasn't able to describe with sufficient precision the general architecture of the girl's body, or particular features of it, and even less the girl's mind. And so Dr. Havel himself finally talked expansively and, becoming elated by the coziness of the evening and by the wine, overwhelmed the editor with a witty monologue of his own reminiscences, anecdotes, and ideas.

The editor sipped his wine, listened, and at the same time experienced ambiguous emotions. On the one hand he was unhappy—he felt his own insignificance and stupidity, he felt like a questionable apprentice in front of an unquestionable master and he was ashamed to open his mouth; but at the same time he was also happy: it flattered him that the master was sitting opposite him, having a nice, long, friendly chat with him and confiding to him the most varied, intimate, and valuable observations.

When Havel's speech had already lasted too long, the young man yearned, after all, to open his own mouth, to put in his two bits, to join in, to prove his ability to be a partner. He spoke, therefore, once more about his girl and sociably invited Havel to take a look at her the next day, and let him know how she appeared to him according to the standards set by his experience; put differently (yes, in his whimsical frame of mind he used these words), to *check her out*.

What was he thinking of? Was it only an involuntary notion born of wine and the intense desire to say something?

However spontaneous the idea may have been, still, through it the editor was pursuing at least a three-fold benefit:

—by means of the conspiracy involving a common and secret judgment (the checking out), a close bond would be established between himself and the master, they would become real buddies, a thing the editor craved;

—if the master voiced his approval (and the young man expected this, for he himself was greatly taken with the girl in question), this would be approval of the young man, of his judgment and taste, so that in the master's eyes he would change from an apprentice into a journeyman, and in his own eyes he would also be more important than before;

—and lastly, the girl would then mean more to the young man than before, and the pleasure that he experienced in her presence would change from fictional to real (for the young man occasionally realized that the world in which he lived was for him a labyrinth of values, the worth of which he only quite dimly surmised and, consequently, illusory values could become real values only when they were *endorsed*).

5

When Dr. Havel awoke the next day he felt a slight pain in his gall bladder on account of yesterday's dinner; and when he looked at his watch he found that in half an hour he had to be at a cure and would therefore have to hurry, which of all things in life he liked to do least. And when, combing his hair, he caught sight of his face in the mirror, it didn't please him. The day was beginning badly.

He didn't even have time for breakfast (he considered this a bad sign as well) and he hurried to the building which housed the baths. There was a long corridor with many doors opening off of it. He knocked on one and a pretty blonde in a white uniform peeped out. She ill-humoredly chided him for being late and asked him in. A moment after Dr. Havel went behind a screen in a cubicle to undress, he heard, "So hurry up then!" The masseuse's voice became more and more impolite. It offended Havel and provoked him to retaliate (and alas, over the years Dr. Havel had become accustomed to only one way of retaliating against women!). Therefore, he took off his underpants, pulled in his stomach, stuck out his chest and was about to step forward out of the cubicle. But this effort disgusted him; it was beneath his dignity and would have seemed ridiculous to him in others. He comfortably relaxed his stomach again and with nonchalance, which was the only thing he considered respectable for himself, walked toward the large bath and submerged himself in the lukewarm water.

The masseuse, completely disregarding both his chest and his stomach, meanwhile turned several faucets on a large switchboard. Dr. Havel was lying already stretched out on the bottom of the bath. She seized his right foot under the water and put the nozzle of a hose, from which there issued a stinging stream, against his sole. Dr. Havel, who was ticklish, jerked his foot, so that the masseuse had to rebuke him.

It would certainly not have been too difficult to get the blonde to abandon her cold and impolite tone by means of some joke, gossip, or facetious question, only Havel was too angry and insulted for this. He said to himself that the blonde deserved to be punished and didn't deserve his making her situation easier. As she ran the hose over his groin and he covered his genitals with his hands so that the stinging stream shouldn't hurt them, he asked her what she was doing that evening. Without looking at him, she asked him why he wanted to know. He explained to her that he was staying alone in a single bedroom and that he wanted her to come to him there that evening. "Maybe you've confused me with someone else," said the blonde, and told him to turn over onto his stomach.

And so Dr. Havel lay with his stomach on the bottom of the bath, holding his chin up high so that he could breathe. He felt how the stinging stream was massaging his calves, and was satisfied with the correct way he had addressed the masseuse. Dr. Havel had for a long time been in the habit of punishing recalcitrant, insolent, or spoiled women by leading them over to his couch coldly, without any tenderness, almost without a word, and also by then dismissing them in an equally chilly manner. Only after a moment did it occur to him that though he had no doubt addressed the masseuse with appropriate coldness and without any sort of tenderness, still he had not led her to the couch and was not likely to do so. He understood that he had been rejected and that this was a new insult. For this reason he was glad when at last he was drying himself with a towel in the cubicle.

He quickly left the building and hurried to the Time Cinema to see the display case; three publicity stills were displayed there, and in one of them his wife was kneeling in terror over a corpse. Dr. Havel looked at that sweet face, distorted by fright, and felt boundless love and boundless nostalgia. For a long time he couldn't drag himself away from the display case. Then he decided that he'd drop in on Frantishka.

6

"Get me long-distance, please, I have to talk to my wife," he said to her, when she had seen her patient out and asked him into the consulting room.

"Has something happened?"

"Yes," said Havel, "I feel lonely!"

Frantishka looked at him mistrustfully, dialed the long-distance operator, and gave the number which Havel indicated to her. Then she hung up the receiver and said: "So you're lonely?"

"And why shouldn't I be?" Havel became angry. "You're like my wife. You see in me someone whom I haven't been for a long time. I'm humble, I'm forlorn, I'm sad. The years weigh heavily on me. And I'm telling you that this is not a pleasant thing."

"You should have children," the woman doctor replied. "You wouldn't think so much about yourself. The years also weigh heavily on me and I don't think about it. When I see my son, how he is changing from a baby into a boy, I look forward to seeing how he will look as a man, and I don't complain about the passing of time. Imagine what he said to me yesterday: 'Why,' he said, 'are there doctors in the world when everyone will die anyway?' What do you say to that? What would you have said to him?"

Luckily, Dr. Havel didn't have to answer because the telephone rang. He picked up the receiver, and when he heard his wife's voice, he immediately blurted out how sad he was, how he had no one to talk to or look at here, how he couldn't bear it alone here.

Through the receiver a low voice was heard, distrustful at first, startled, almost faltering, which under the impact of her husband's words unbent a little.

"Please, come here to see me; come to see me as soon as you can!" said Havel into the receiver, and heard his wife reply that she'd like to but that nearly every day she had to do a show.

"Nearly every day is not every day," said Havel and he heard that his wife had the following day free, but that she didn't know if it would be worthwhile for one day.

"How can you talk like that? Don't you realize what wealth one day constitutes in this short life of ours?"

"And you really aren't angry with me?" asked the low voice into the receiver.

"Why should I be angry?" said Havel becoming angry.

"Because of that letter. You are in pain and I bore you stiff with such a silly, jealous letter."

Dr. Havel murmured sweet nothings into the mouthpiece and his wife (in a voice already grown quite tender) declared that she would come the next day.

"Anyway, I envy you," said Frantishka, when Havel had hung up the receiver. "You have everything. Girls at your beck and call and a happy marriage too."

Havel looked at his friend, who talked to him of envy, but because of the very goodness of her heart, probably wasn't capable of that emotion. And he felt sorry for her, for he knew that the pleasure to be had from children cannot compensate for other pleasures, and, besides, a pleasure burdened with the obligation to substitute for other pleasures will soon become too wearisome a pleasure.

He then left for lunch. After lunch he slept, and when he woke up he remembered that the young editor was awaiting him in a café, to present his girl to him. So he dressed and went out.

As he walked down the stairs of the patients' building, in the hall near the cloakroom he caught sight of a tall woman who resembled a beautiful riding horse. Ah, this should not have happened; that is to say, Havel always found precisely this type of woman damnably attractive. The cloakroom attendant was handing the tall woman a coat and Dr. Havel ran over to help her into it. The woman who resembled a horse casually thanked him and Havel said: "Can I do anything else for you?" He was smiling at her, but she replied, without a smile, that he couldn't, and dashed out of the building.

Dr. Havel felt as if he'd been slapped in the face and, in a renewed state of gloom, started for the café.

7

The editor had already been sitting in a booth beside his girl friend for quite a while (he'd picked a place from which the entrance was visible) and wasn't up to concentrating on conversation, which at other times used to bubble up between them gaily and unflaggingly. He was shy at the thought of Havel's arrival. For the first time today he had attempted to look at his girl friend with a more critical eye. And while she was saying something (fortunately she went on saying something so that the young man's inner anxiety remained unnoticed), he discovered several minor flaws in her beauty. This greatly disturbed him, even if in no time he was assuring himself that these minor flaws in fact made her beauty more interesting and that it was precisely these things that gave him a warm feeling of closeness to her whole being.

That is to say he liked the girl.

But if he liked her, why had he proceeded with this venture which would be so humiliating to her; checking her out with the dissipated doctor? And if we grant him extenuating circumstances, allowing that this was only a game for him, how was it that he had become so shy and put out by a mere game?

This was not a game. The young man really did not know what his girl was like, he wasn't able to pass judgment on the degree of her beauty and attractiveness.

But was he really so naive and so totally inexperienced that he could not distinguish a pretty woman from one who was not pretty?

Not at all. The young man wasn't so totally inexperienced; he had already known a few women and had affairs with them, but while they were going on he had been concentrating far more on himself than on them. Let us take a look at what had appeared noteworthy to him: the young man recalled precisely when and how he had been dressed with which woman; he knew on what occasion he had worn pants that were too wide and had suffered from his consciousness of their impropriety; he knew that at some other time he had worn a white sweater in which he had felt like a stylish sportsman, but he had no idea how his girl friends had been dressed.

Yes, this is noteworthy: during his brief friendships he had undertaken long and detailed studies of himself in the mirror, while he had only an overall, general impression of his female counterparts; it was far more important to him how he himself was seen through the eyes of his female partner than how she appeared to him. By this I don't mean to say that it didn't matter to him whether the girl with whom he was going was or was not pretty. It did matter. For he himself was not merely seen by the eyes of his partner, but both of them together were seen and judged by the eyes of others (by the eyes of the world), and it was very important to him that the world should be pleased with his girl, for he knew that through her was judged his choice, his taste, his status, thus he himself. But precisely because what concerned him was the judgment of others, he had not relied too much on his own eyes, but until now had considered it sufficient to listen to the voice of general opinion and to accept it.

But what was the voice of general opinion against the voice of a master and an expert? The editor was looking anxiously toward the entrance, and when at last he caught sight of Havel's figure in the glass door, he pretended to be astonished and said to the girl that by sheer chance a certain remarkable man, whom he wanted to interview for his magazine within the next few days, was just coming in. He went to meet Havel and led him over to their table. The girl, interrupted for a moment by the introduction, soon picked up the thread of her incessant conversation and continued to chatter away.

Dr. Havel, rejected ten minutes before by the woman who resembled a riding horse, looked slowly at the prattling girl and sank deeper and deeper into a surly mood. The girl wasn't a beauty but she was quite cute and there was no doubt that Dr. Havel (who was alleged to be like death, because he took everything) would have taken her any time and been very glad to do it. She possessed several marks indicative of a curious, esthetic ambiguity: at the base of her nose she had a shower of freckles, which could be taken as a flaw in the whiteness of her complexion, but also conversely as a natural gem. She was very frail, which could be taken as the inadequate filling out of ideal feminine proportions, but also conversely as the provocative delicacy of the child continuing to exist within the woman. She was immensely talkative, which could be taken as inconvenient blather, but also conversely as a useful trait, which would allow her partner to give himself up to his own thoughts in the shelter of her words whenever he liked and without fear of being caught.

The editor secretly and anxiously examined the doctor's face, and when it seemed to him that it was dangerously (and for his hopes unfavorably) lost in thought, he called over a waiter and ordered three cognacs. The girl protested that she would not drink, and then again slowly let herself be persuaded that she could drink and should, and Dr. Havel sullenly realized that this esthetically ambiguous creature, revealing in her stream of words all the simplicity of her inward nature, would with the greatest probability be, if he were to make a play for her, his third failure of the day. For he, Dr. Havel, once powerful as death, was no longer the man he once had been.

Then the waiter brought the cognacs, they all three raised them to clink glasses, and Dr. Havel looked into the girl's blue eyes as into the hostile eyes of someone who was not going to belong to him. And when he understood the total significance of these eyes as hostile, he reciprocated with hostility, and saw before himself suddenly a creature esthetically quite unambiguous: a sickly girl, her face splattered with smudges of freckles, insufferably garrulous.

Even if this change, together with the young man's gaze fixed on him with an anxious and questioning look, gratified Havel, these pleasures were small in comparison with the deep gloom which left a gaping hole inside him. It occurred to Havel that he ought not to prolong this meeting, which could not bring him any satisfaction. So he quickly took over the conversation, uttered several charming witticisms before the young man and the girl, then expressed his pleasure at having been able to spend an agreeable moment with them, stated that he was in a hurry to get somewhere, and took his leave.

When the doctor got to the glass door, the young man tapped his forehead and told the girl that he had completely forgotten to come to an agreement with the doctor about the interview for the magazine. He rushed out of the booth and only caught up with Havel in the street. "Well, what do you say about her?" he asked.

Havel stared for a long while into the eyes of the young man, whose imploring look cheered him up.

On the other hand, Havel's silence made the editor shudder, so that already in advance he began to retreat: "I know that she isn't a beauty . . ."

Havel said: "No, she isn't a beauty."

The editor lowered his head: "She talks a little too much. But in other respects she's nice!"

"Yes, that girl is really nice," said Havel, "but a dog, a canary, or a duckling waddling about in a farmyard can also be nice. In life, my friend, it is not a question of winning the greatest number of women, because that is too external a success. Rather, it is a question of cultivating one's own demanding taste, because in it is mirrored the extent of one's personal worth. Remember, my friend, that a real fisherman throws small fish back into the water."

The young man began to make excuses and claimed that he himself had considerable doubts about the girl, which after all was borne out by the fact that he had asked Havel for his judgment.

"Sure, it's nothing," said Havel, "don't worry about it."

However, the young man went on apologizing and making excuses and pointed out that in the fall there is a dearth of beautiful women in the spa town and a man has to put up with what there is.

"I don't agree with you in this matter," Havel dismissed his remarks. "I've seen several remarkably attractive women here. But I'll tell you something. There exists a certain external shapeliness in a woman, which small-town taste mistakenly considers beauty. And then there exists the genuine erotic beauty of a woman. Of course, it is no small matter to recognize this at a mere glance. It is an art." Then he shook the young man's hand and left.

8

The editor fell into a terrible state. He understood that he was an incorrigible fool, lost in the unbounded (yes, it seemed to him unbounded and interminable) wilderness of his own youth. He realized that he had fallen in Dr. Havel's esteem, and had discovered beyond a shadow of a doubt that his girl was uninteresting, insignificant, and not pretty. When he sat down again beside her in the booth, it seemed to him that all the clientele at the café as well as both the busy waiters knew this and felt maliciously sorry for him. He called for the check, and explained to the girl that he had pressing work and must be off. The girl became downcast and the young man's heart was wrung with grief. Even though he knew that he was throwing her back into the water like a real fisherman, all the same, deep down, he still (secretly and ashamedly) liked her.

The next morning did not bring any light into his gloomy mood, and when he saw Dr. Havel walking toward him with a fashionably dressed woman, he felt within himself an envy akin almost to hatred. This lady was too blatantly beautiful and Dr. Havel's mood, as he nodded gaily to the editor, was too blatantly buoyant, so that the young man felt even more wretched.

"This is the editor of the local magazine; he made my acquaintance only so that he could meet you," Havel introduced him to the beautiful woman.

When the young man learned that before him was the woman whom he knew from the movie screen, his insecurity increased even more. Havel forced him to walk with them, and the editor, because he didn't know what to say, began to explain his former journalistic project and supplemented it with a new idea; he said that he would do an interview with both the doctor and Mrs. Havel.

"But my dear friend," Havel admonished him, "the conversations that we engaged in were pleasant and through your efforts also interesting, but tell me, why should we make them public in a periodical destined for gall bladder sufferers and the owners of duodenal ulcers?"

"I can imagine those conversations of yours," said Mrs. Havel smiling.

"We talked about women," said Dr. Havel. "In this gentleman here I found an excellent partner and debater for this subject, a fair friend for damp, dreary days."

Mrs. Havel turned to the young man. "He didn't bore you?"

The editor was delighted that the doctor had called him his fair friend, and, once again, grateful devotion began to be mixed in with his envy. He declared that perhaps rather it was he who had bored the doctor; that is, he was too well aware of his inexperience and colorlessness, yes—he even added—of his worthlessness.

"Ah, my dear," laughed the actress, "you must have done a horrible lot of showing off!"

"That's not true." The editor stood up for the doctor. "You, my dear lady, do not know what a small town is like, what this backwater where I live is like."

"But it's beautiful here!" protested the actress.

"Yes, for you, when you've come here just for a while. But I live here and will go on living here. Always the same circle of people, whom I already know only too well. Always the same people, who all think alike, and the things they think are nothing but superficialities and foolishness. Whether I like it or not I have to get along with them and I don't always even realize that I'm being assimilated by them. It's dreadful—I could become one of them! It's terrible to see the world through their shortsighted eyes!"

The editor spoke with increasing excitement and it seemed to the actress that in his words she heard the eternal protest of youth. This captivated her, this took her fancy, and she said, "You mustn't conform! You musn't!"

"I musn't," the young man agreed. "The doctor here opened my eyes yesterday. At any price I must get outside the vicious circle of this milieu. The vicious circle of this pettiness, of this mediocrity. Oh, to get outside it!" The young man repeated the phrase, "Oh, to get outside it!"

"We talked about the fact," explained Havel to his wife, "that the banal taste of a small town creates a false ideal of beauty, which is essentially unerotic, even anti-erotic. Whereas genuine, explosive erotic magic remains unnoticed by those with this taste. Women walk past us who would be capable of leading a man to the most dizzying heights of sensual adventure, and no one here sees them."

"That's how it is," confirmed the young man.

"No one sees them," the doctor went on, "because they do not correspond to the norms of the local tailors; that is to say, erotic magic is exhibited by deformation rather than regularity, loudness rather than restraint, and originality rather than ready-made prettiness."

"Yes," agreed the young man.

"You know Frantishka," said Havel to his wife.

"Yes," said the actress.

"And surely you know how many of my friends would have given all their worldly goods for one night with her. I'd bet my life that in this town no one even notices her. Come tell me, my dear editor, after all, you know the doctor; have you ever noticed what an extraordinary woman she is?"

"No, actually I haven't!" said the young man. "It never occurred to me for a moment to look at her as a woman!"

"Of course," said Havel. "She seemed a little skinny to you. In her you missed the freckles and the talkativeness."

"Yes," said the young man unhappily, "yesterday you found out what an idiot I am."

"But have you ever noticed how she walks?" continued Havel. "Have you ever noticed how expressive her legs are when she walks? My dear editor, if you heard what her legs were saying, you would blush, even though I know that in other respects you are an experienced libertine."

9

"You're making fools of innocent people," said the actress to her husband, when they had taken leave of the editor.

"You know very well that in me that is a sign of good humor. And I swear to you that this is the first time I've been in a good mood since I arrived here."

This time Dr. Havel was not lying. That morning when he'd seen the bus coming into the terminal, and caught sight of his wife behind the glass, and then seen her laughing on the step, he had been happy. And because the preceding days had stored up in him reserves of untouched gaiety, throughout the whole day he displayed a delight that was almost crazy. They strolled together through the colonnade, nibbled on sweet, round wafers, looked in on Frantishka and heard fresh information about her son's latest statements, completed the walk with the editor described in the foregoing chapter, and made fun of the patients, who were walking through the streets for their health's sake. Upon this occasion, Dr. Havel noticed that several of the people who were walking about were staring at the actress; when he turned around he discovered that they were standing and looking back at them.

"You've been discovered," said Havel. "The people here have nothing to do and they've become passionate moviegoers."

"Does it bother you?" asked the actress, who considered the publicity of her profession some sort of offense, for like all true lovers she longed for a love that was peaceful and hidden.

"On the contrary," said Havel and laughed. Then for a long time he amused himself with the childish game of trying to guess who, out of those people walking about, would recognize the actress and who would not, and he made bets with her as to how many people would recognize her on the next street. And old men, peasant women, children did turn around, but so also did several of the good-looking women who were to be found at the spa at that time.

Havel, who in recent days had been experiencing humiliating invisibility, was pleasantly gratified by the attention of the passersby, and longed for the sparks of interest to alight, as much as possible, upon him also. To this end, he put his arm around the actress's waist, bent down toward her, and whispered into her ear the most varied mixture of sweet-talk and lasciviousness, so that she too pressed herself against him in return and raised her merry eyes to his face. And Havel, beneath the many glances, felt how once more he was regaining his lost visibility, how his dim features were becoming perceptible and conspicuous, and again he felt proud joy emanating from his body, from his gait, from his being.

When they were hanging around on the main street in front of the window displays, entwined in loverlike fashion, Havel caught sight of the blonde masseuse, who had treated him so impolitely yesterday; she was standing in an empty hunting goods store, gabbing with the salesgirl. "Come," he said to his startled wife, "you are the best creature in the whole world; I want to give you a present," and he took her by the hand and led her into the store.

Both the chattering women fell silent. The masseuse

took a long look at the actress, then a brief one at Havel, another look at the actress, and again one at Havel. Havel noted this with satisfaction but, without directing a single glance toward her, quickly scrutinized the goods on display; he saw antlers, haversacks, shotguns, binoculars, walking sticks, muzzles for dogs.

"What would you like to see?" the salesgirl asked him.

"Just a minute," said Havel. Finally he caught sight of some black whistles under the glass of the counter and pointed to one of them. The salesgirl handed it to him, Havel put the whistle to his lips, whistled, then inspected it from all sides and once again whistled weakly. "Excellent," he praised it to the salesgirl and placed before her the required five crowns. He gave the whistle to his wife.

The actress saw in this gift her husband's childishness and roguishness, which she adored, and also his feeling for absurdity. She thanked him with a beautiful, amorous look. But that wasn't enough for Havel; he whispered to her: "Is that all your thanks for such a lovely present?" And so the actress kissed him. Neither woman took her eyes off them, even after they had left the store.

They went back to hanging around in the streets and in the park, they nibbled on wafers, whistled on the whistle, sat on a bench, and made bets as to how many passersby would look around at them. When in the evening they went into a restaurant, they nearly bumped into the woman who resembled a horse. She looked at them in surprise, stared at the actress for a long time, glanced briefly at Havel, then once again at the actress and, when she looked at Havel once more, involuntarily nodded to him. Havel nodded too, and bending toward his wife's ear, in a low voice asked if she loved him. The actress looked at him amorously and stroked his face.

Then they sat down at a table, ate modestly (for the

actress took scrupulous care of her husband's diet), drank red wine (for Havel was allowed to drink only that), and a wave of emotion swept over Mrs. Havel. She leaned toward her husband, took him by the hand, and told him that this was one of the nicest days that she had ever spent. She opened her heart to him, saying how unhappy she had been when he had left for the spa; once again she apologized for the crazy, jealous letter and thanked him for calling her and asking her to come to him. She told him that it would have been worthwhile for her to come see him, even if it had been for only a minute. She talked at length about how life with him was a life of continuous agitation and uncertainty, how Havel would eternally elude her, but that just for this reason every day was a new experience for her, a new falling in love, a new gift.

Then they went off together to Havel's single bed room, and the actress's joy soon reached its zenith.

10

Two days later, Havel went again to his so-called underwater massage and again arrived somewhat late, because, to tell the truth, he was never on time anywhere. And there again was the blonde masseuse, only this time she didn't scowl at him, on the contrary, she smiled and addressed him as *doctor*, so Havel knew that she'd gone to look up his medical records, or else she'd inquired about him. Dr. Havel noted this interest with satisfaction and began to undress behind the screen in the cubicle. When the masseuse called to him that the bath was full, he self-assuredly stepped forward with his paunch thrust out and, with relish, sprawled in the water.

The masseuse turned on a faucet and asked him whether his wife was still at the spa. Havel said that she wasn't, and the masseuse asked if his wife would be playing again in some nice film. Havel said that she would, and the masseuse lifted up his right leg. When the stream of water tickled his sole the masseuse smiled and said that the doctor, as was evident, had a very sensitive body. Then they went on talking and Havel mentioned that it was boring at the spa. The masseuse smiled very meaningfully and said that the doctor certainly knew how to arrange his life so as not to be bored. And when she was bending down low over him, running the nozzle of the hose over his chest, Havel praised her breasts, whose upper halves he could easily see from where he was lying, and the masseuse replied that the doctor had certainly already seen more beautiful ones.

From all this it seemed quite obvious to Havel that his wife's presence had thoroughly transformed him in the eyes of this pleasant, muscular girl, that he had all of a sudden acquired charm and appeal, and, what is more, that his body was for her undoubtedly an opportunity which could secretly put her on intimate terms with the well-known actress, make her equal to the celebrated woman whom everybody turned round to look at. Havel understood that suddenly everything was permitted for him, everything was quietly promised in advance.

Only, as usually happens, when a man is contented, he is glad to turn down an opportunity which presents itself, so as to be reassured about his blissful satiety. It was quite enough for Havel that the blonde girl had lost her impolite inaccessibility, that she had a sweet voice and meek eyes, that she offered herself to him indirectly in this way—and he didn't long for her at all.

Then he had to turn over on his stomach, thrust his

chin up out of the water, and let the stinging stream of
water be run over him from his heels to the nape of his neck.
This position seemed to him the ritual position of humility
and thanksgiving. He thought about his wife, about how beautiful she was, about how he loved her and she loved him, and
also about how she was his lucky star, which brought him the
favor of chance occurrences and of muscular misses.

And when the massage was over and he stood up to
step out of the bath, the masseuse, wet with perspiration,
seemed to him so wholesomely and succulently pretty and
her eyes so submissively affectionate, that he longed to make
an obeisance in the direction where, far away, he supposed
his wife to be. It appeared to him that the masseuse's body
was standing in the actress's large hand and that this hand
was offering it to him like a message of love, like a gift. And
it suddenly struck him as rudeness to his own wife to refuse
this gift, to refuse this tender consideration. Therefore he
smiled at the perspiring girl and said to her that he had freed
himself this evening for her and would be waiting for her at
seven o'clock at the hot springs. The girl consented and Dr.
Havel wrapped himself up in a large towel.

When he had dressed and combed his hair, he discovered that he was in an extraordinarily good mood. He felt
like gossiping and for this reason stopped by Frantishka's.
His visit suited her, for she too was in excellent spirits. She
talked confusedly about all sorts of things, but always returned
to the subject which they'd touched upon at their last meeting. She spoke about her age and, in unclearly formulated
sentences, implied that a person should not give in to his age,
that a person's age is not always a disadvantage, and that it
is a terribly beautiful feeling when a person finds out that he
or she can safely be a match for younger people. "And children
aren't everything either," she said all at once for no reason.

"No, I love my children," she clarified herself, "you know how I love them, but there are other things in the world also . . ."

Frantishka's reflections did not depart even for an instant from their vague abstractness and they would have unmistakably appeared to be mere idle talk to an uninitiated person. Only Havel wasn't an uninitiated person and he discerned the purport hidden behind this idle talk. He gathered that his own happiness was only a link in a whole chain of happiness, and because he had a generous heart, he felt doubly good.

11

Yes, Dr. Havel had guessed correctly: the editor had dropped in on the woman doctor the very same day that his master had praised her. After just a few sentences, he discovered within himself a surprising boldness, and he told her that he found her attractive and that he wanted to go out with her. The woman doctor stammered in alarm that she was older than he and that she had children. At this, the editor gained self-confidence and his words simply poured out: he claimed that she possessed a hidden beauty, which was worth more than banal shapeliness; he praised her walk and told her that when she walked her legs were most expressive.

And two days after this declaration, at the same time that Dr. Havel was contentedly arriving at the hot springs, where already, from a distance, he could see the muscular blonde, the editor was impatiently pacing up and down in his narrow attic. He was almost certain of success, but this made him all the more fearful of some error or mishap which could deprive him of it. Every little while he would open the door and look down the stairs. At last he caught sight of her.

The care with which Frantishka was dressed and made up changed her somewhat from the everyday woman who wore white pants and a white gown. To the excited young man it seemed that her erotic magic, heretofore only suspected, was now standing before him almost brazenly exposed, so that respectful diffidence assailed him. To overcome it, he embraced the woman doctor in the doorway and began to kiss her frantically. She was alarmed by this sudden assault and begged him to let her sit down. He did let her, but he immediately sat at her feet and, on his knees, kissed her stockings. She put her hand in his hair and attempted to gently push him away.

Let us note what she said to him. First she repeated several times: "You must behave yourself, you must behave yourself, promise me that you will behave yourself." When the young man said: "Yes, yes, I will behave myself," and at the same time moved his mouth further up the rough material, she said: "No, no, not that, not that"; and when he moved it still higher, she suddenly began to use his first name and declared, "You are a young devil, oh you are a young devil!"

Everything was decided by this declaration. The young man no longer ran up against any resistance. He was carried away; he was carried away by himself, he was carried away by the swiftness of his success, he was carried away by Dr. Havel, whose genius had entered into him and now dwelled with him, he was carried away by the nakedness of the woman who was lying beneath him in amorous union. He longed to be a master, he longed to be a virtuoso, he longed to demonstrate his sensuality and savagery. He raised himself slightly above the woman doctor, with a passionate eye he examined her body lying there, and murmured: "You're beautiful, you're magnificent, you're magnificent . . ."

The doctor covered up her belly with both arms and said, "You mustn't make fun of me . . ."

"What are you raving about? I'm not making fun of you, you're magnificent!"

"Don't look at me," she clasped him to her, so that he shouldn't see her: "I've already had two children, you know."

"Two children?" the young man didn't understand.

"You can see it on me, you mustn't look."

This slowed the young man down a bit in his initial flight and it was only with difficulty that he once again attained the proper ecstasy. In order to manage this better, he tried hard to reinforce the diminishing excitement of the reality with words, and he whispered into the doctor's ear how beautiful it was that she was here with him naked, absolutely naked.

"You're sweet, you're terribly sweet," said the woman doctor.

The young man went on repeating the words about her nakedness and asked her whether it was also exciting for her that she was here with him naked.

"You're a child," said the woman doctor, "yes, it is exciting." But after a short while she added that so many doctors had already seen her naked that it didn't even faze her. "More doctors than lovers," she laughed, and launched into an account of her difficulties in childbirth. "But it was worth it," she ended by saying: "I have two beautiful children. Beautiful, beautiful!"

The ecstasy, come by with difficulty, was slipping away from the editor again. He even had the impression that they were sitting in a cafe and that he was chatting with the woman doctor over a cup of tea. This exasperated him. He began to make violent love to her again, and endeavored to engage her in more sensual thoughts: "When I came to see you last time, did you know that we would make love?"

"Did you?"

"I *wanted* to," said the editor, "I *wanted* to terribly!" and into the word "wanted" he put immense passion.

"You're like my son," the woman doctor laughed in his ear. "That kid wants everything too. I always ask him, and wouldn't you like the moon perhaps?"

And so they made love and Frantishka talked to her heart's content.

Then when they were sitting next to each other on the couch, naked and tired, the woman doctor stroked the editor's hair and said, "You have a cute little mop like him."

"Who?"

"My son."

"You're always thinking about your son," said the editor with timid disapproval.

"You know," she said proudly, "he is his mother's pet, he is his mother's pet."

Then she got up and dressed. And all of a sudden the feeling came over her in this young man's little room that she was young, that she was a really young girl, and she felt foolishly good. As she left she embraced the editor and her eyes were moist from gratitude.

12

After a beautiful night, a beautiful day began for Havel. At breakfast he exchanged a few meaningful words with the woman who resembled a riding horse, and at ten o'clock, when he returned from the cure, a loving letter from his wife awaited him in his room. Then he went to take a walk through the colonnade among the crowd of patients. He held the porcelain bowl to his lips and beamed with good humor. The women, who at one time had passed by him without any show of interest, now fastened their eyes upon him, so that he nodded slightly to them in greeting. When he caught sight of the editor, he beckoned gaily to him: "I visited Frantishka this morning and according to certain signs, which cannot escape a good psychologist, it seems to me that you've met with success!"

The young man wanted nothing more than to confide in his master, but the events of the past evening had somewhat confused him. He wasn't sure if it had really been as great as it should have been, and that being so, he didn't know whether a precise and truthful account would raise or lower him in Havel's estimation. He was hesitant about what he should confide and what he shouldn't.

But when he now saw Havel's face beaming with gaiety and insolence, he could do nothing but answer in a similar tone, gay and impudent and, with enthusiastic words, praise the woman whom Havel had recommended. He related how he had found her attractive when he had looked at her for the first time with eyes devoid of small-town prejudice, how she had quickly agreed to come to his place, and with what remarkable speed he had gained possession of her.

When Dr. Havel put various questions and subquestions to him, so as to exhaust all the nuances of the carefully analyzed affair, the young man willy-nilly came closer and closer to the truth, and finally pointed out that although he was remarkably satisfied with everything, still, the conversation he had had with the woman doctor had put him out somewhat.

Dr. Havel found this very interesting, and, having persuaded the editor to repeat the dialogue to him in detail, he would interrupt the account with enthusiastic exclamations: "That's excellent! Well, that's simply fantastic!" "Oh, that eternal mother's heart!" and "My friend, I really envy you!"

At that moment, the woman who resembled a riding horse stopped in front of the two men. Dr. Havel bowed and the woman offered him her hand: "Don't be angry," she apologized, "I'm a tiny bit late."

"Never mind," said Havel. "I've been enjoying myself enormously with my friend here. You must forgive me if I finish my conversation with him."

And, not letting go of the tall woman's hand, he turned to the editor, "My dear friend, what you've told me surpassed all my expectations. You must understand that the pleasures of the body left undiscussed are tiresomely similar. In this silence one woman becomes like another and all of them are forgotten in all the others. And surely we throw ourselves into amorous pleasures above all in order to remember them! So that their luminous points should connect our youth with our old age by means of their shining band! So that they should preserve our memory in an eternal flame! And take it from me, my friend, only a word uttered at this most banal of moments is capable of illuminating it in such a way that it remains unforgettable. They say of me that I'm a collector of women. In reality, I'm far more a collector of words. Believe me, you will never forget yesterday evening, and be happy for that!"

Then he nodded to the young man, and holding the tall woman who resembled a horse by the hand, he moved away slowly with her along the spa promenade.

Edward
and God

1

We can advantageously begin Edward's story in his elder brother's little house in the country. His brother was lying on the couch and saying to Edward, "Ask the old hag. Never mind, just go and talk to her. Of course she's a pig, but I believe that even in such creatures a conscience exists. Just because she once did me dirt, now perhaps she'll be glad if you'll allow her to make amends for her past wrongdoings."

Edward's brother was still the same, a good-natured guy and a lazy one. Just this way perhaps had he been lolling on the couch in his university attic when, many years ago (Edward was still a little boy then), he had lazed and snored away the day of Stalin's death. The next day he had unsuspectingly gone to the department and caught sight of his fellow student, Miss Chehachkova, standing in ostentatious rigidity in the middle of the hall like a statue of grief. Three times he circled her and then began to roar with laughter. The offended girl denounced her fellow student's laughter as political provocation and Edward's brother had had to leave school and go to work in a village, where since that time he had acquired a little house, a dog, a wife, two children, and even a cottage.

In this village house, then, was he now lying on the couch and speaking to Edward. "We used to call her the chastising scourge of the working class. But as a matter of fact this needn't concern you. Today she's an aging female and she was always after young boys, so she'll meet you halfway."

Edward was at that time very young. He had just graduated from teachers' college (the course his brother had not completed), and was looking for a position. The next day, following his brother's advice, he knocked on the director's door. Then he saw a tall, bony woman with the greasy black hair of a gypsy, black eyes, and black down under her nose. Her ugliness relieved him of the shyness to which feminine beauty still always reduced him, so that he managed to talk to her in a relaxed manner, amiably, even courteously. The directress was evidently delighted by his approach and several times said with perceptible elation, "We need young people here." She promised to find a place for him.

2

And so Edward became a teacher in a small Czech town. This made him neither happy nor sad. He always tried hard to distinguish between the important and the unimportant, and he put his teaching career into the category of *unimportant*. Not that teaching itself was unimportant; after all, it constituted his livelihood (in this respect, in fact, he was deeply attached to it, because he knew that he would not be able to earn a living any other way). But he considered it unimportant in terms of his true nature. He hadn't selected it. Social demand, his party record, the certificate from high school, entrance examinations had selected it for him. The interlocking conjunction of all these forces eventually dumped him (as a crane drops a sack onto a truck) from secondary school into teachers' college. He didn't want to go there (it was superstitiously stigmatized by his brother's failure), but eventually he acquiesced. He understood, however, that his occupation would be among the fortuitous aspects of his life. It would be attached to him like a false beard—which is something laughable.

If, however, his professional duties were something not important (laughable, in fact), perhaps on the contrary, what he did voluntarily was. In his new place of work Edward soon found a young girl who struck him as beautiful, and he began to pursue her with a seriousness that was almost genuine. Her name was Alice and she was, as he discovered to his sorrow on their first dates, very reserved and virtuous.

Many times during their evening walks he had tried to put his arm around her so that he could touch the region of her right breast from behind, and each time she'd seized his hand and pushed it away. One day when he was repeating this experiment once again and she (once again) was pushing his hand away, she stopped and asked: "Do you believe in God?"

With his sensitive ears Edward caught secret overtones in this question and immediately forgot about the breast.

"Do you?" Alice repeated her question and Edward didn't dare answer. Do not let us condemn him for fearing to be frank; in his new place of work he felt lonely and was too attracted to Alice to risk losing her favor over a single solitary answer.

"And you?" he asked in order to gain time.

"Yes, I do." And once again she urged him to answer her.

Until this time it had never occurred to him to believe in God. He understood, however, that he must not admit this. On the contrary, he saw that he should take advantage of the opportunity and knock together from faith in God a nice Trojan horse, within whose belly, according to the ancient example, he would enter the girl's heart unobserved. Only it wasn't so easy for Edward to say to Alice simply *yes, I believe in God.* He wasn't at all cynical and was ashamed to lie; the vulgar and uncompromising nature of a lie went against the grain with him. If he absolutely had to tell a lie, even so he wanted it to remain as close as possible to the truth. For that reason he replied in an exceptionally thoughtful voice:

"I don't really know, Alice, what I should say to you about this. Certainly I believe in God. But . . ." He paused and Alice glanced up at him in surprise. "But I want to be completely frank with you. May I?"

"You must be frank," she said. "Otherwise surely there wouldn't be any sense in our being together."

"Really?"

"Really," said Alice.

"Sometimes I'm bothered by doubts," said Edward in a low voice. "Sometimes I doubt whether He really exists."

"But how can you doubt that!" Alice almost shrieked.

Edward was silent, and after a moment's reflection a familiar thought struck him: "When I see so much evil around me, I often wonder how it is possible that God would permit it all."

This sounded so sad that Alice seized his hand. "Yes, the world is indeed full of evil, I know this only too well. But for just that reason you must believe in God. Without Him all this suffering would be in vain. Nothing would have any meaning. And if that were so, I couldn't live at all."

"Perhaps you're right," said Edward thoughtfully, and on Sunday he went to church with her. He dipped his fingers in the font and crossed himself. Then there was the Mass and people sang, and with the others he sang a hymn whose tune was familiar, but to which he didn't know the words. Instead of the prescribed words he chose only various vowels and always started to sing a fraction of a second behind the others, because he only dimly recollected even the tune. Yet the moment he became certain of the tune, he let his voice ring out fully, so that for the first time in his life he realized that he had a beautiful bass. Then they all began to recite the Lord's Prayer and some old ladies knelt. He could not hold back a compelling desire to kneel too on the stone floor. He crossed himself with impressive arm movements and experienced the incredible feeling of being able to do something that he'd never done in his life, neither in the classroom nor on the street, nowhere. He felt magnificently free.

When it was all over, Alice looked at him with a radiant expression in her eyes. "Can you still say that you have doubts about Him?"

"No."

And Alice said, "I would like to teach you to love Him just as I do."

They were standing on the broad steps of the church and Edward's soul was full of laughter. Unfortunately, just at that moment the directress was walking by and she saw them.

3

This was bad. We must recall (for the sake of those to whom perhaps the historical background of the story is missing) that although it is true people weren't forbidden to go to church, all the same, churchgoing was not without a certain danger.

This is not so difficult to understand. Those who had been leading the fight for the revolution were very proud, and their pride went by the name of: *standing on the correct side of the front lines*. When ten or twelve years have already passed since the revolution (as had happened approximately at the time of our story), the front lines begin to melt away, and with them the correct side. No wonder former adherents of the revolution feel cheated and are quick to seek *substitute* fronts. Thanks to religion they can (as atheists opposing believers) stand again in all their glory on the correct side and retain that so habitual and precious sense of their own superiority.

But to tell the truth, the substitute front was also useful to others, and it will perhaps not be too premature to disclose that Alice was one of them. Just as the directress wanted to be on the *correct* side, Alice wanted to be on the *opposite* side. During the revolution they had nationalized her dad's business and Alice hated those who had done this to him. But how should she show her hatred? Perhaps by taking a knife and avenging her father? But this sort of thing is not the custom in Bohemia. Alice had a better alternative for expressing her opposition: she began to believe in God.

Thus the Lord came to the aid of both sides (who had already almost lost the living reason for their positions), and, thanks to Him, Edward found himself between Scylla and Charybdis.

When on Monday morning the directress came up to Edward in the staff room, he felt very insecure. There was no way he could invoke the friendly atmosphere of their first talk because since that time (whether through artlessness or carelessness) he had never again engaged in polite conversation with her. The directress therefore had good reason to address him with a conspicuously cold smile:

"We saw each other yesterday, didn't we?"

"Yes, we did," said Edward.

The directress went on, "I can't understand how a young man can go to church." Edward shrugged his shoulders in bewilderment and the directress shook her head. "A young man."

"I went to see the baroque interior of the cathedral," said Edward by way of an excuse.

"Ah, so that's it," said the directress ironically, "I didn't know you had such artistic interests."

This conversation wasn't a bit pleasant for Edward. He remembered how his brother had circled his fellow student three times and then roared with laughter. It seemed to him that family history was repeating itself and he felt afraid. On Saturday he made his excuses over the telephone to Alice, saying that he wouldn't be going to church because he had a cold.

"You are a real mollycoddle," Alice rebuked him after Sunday and it seemed to Edward that her words sounded cold. So he began to tell her (enigmatically and vaguely, because he was ashamed to admit his fear and his true reasons) about the wrongs being done him at school, and about the horrible directress who was persecuting him for no reason. He wanted to get her pity and sympathy, but Alice said:

"My woman boss, on the contrary, isn't bad at all," and giggling, she began to relate stories about her work. Edward listened to her merry voice and became more and more gloomy.

4

Ladies and gentlemen, these were weeks of torment. Edward longed hellishly for Alice. Her body fired him up and yet this very body was utterly inaccessible to him. The settings in which their dates took place were also agonizing. Either they hung about together for an hour or two in the streets after dark or they went to the movies. The banality and the negligible erotic possibilities of these two variants (there weren't any others) prompted Edward to think that perhaps he would achieve more outstanding successes if they could meet in a different environment. Once, with an ingenuous face, he proposed that for the weekend they go to the country and visit his brother, who had a cottage in a wooded valley by a river. He excitedly described the innocent beauties of nature. However, Alice (naive and credulous in every other respect) swiftly saw through him and categorically refused. It wasn't Alice alone who was repulsing him. It was Alice's God Himself (eternally vigilant and wary).

This God embodied a single idea (He had no other wishes or concerns): He forbade extramarital sex. He was therefore a rather comical God, but let's not laugh at Alice for that. Of the ten commandments which Moses gave to the people, fully nine didn't trouble her at all; she didn't feel like killing or not honoring her father, or coveting her neighbor's wife. But the one remaining commandment she felt to be not *self-evident*, and therefore a genuine inconvenience and imposition, the famous seventh: *Thou shalt not commit adultery*. If she wanted to put her religious faith into practice somehow, to prove and demonstrate it, she had then to fasten onto this single commandment. She had thereby created for herself from an obscure, diffuse, and abstract God, a God who was quite specific, comprehensible, and concrete: the God of No Fornication.

I ask you where in fact does fornication begin? Every woman fixes this boundary for herself according to totally mysterious criteria. Alice quite happily allowed Edward to kiss her, and after many, many attempts she eventually became reconciled to letting him stroke her breasts. However, at the middle of her body, let's say at her navel, she drew a strict and uncompromising line below which lay the area of sacred prohibitions, the area of Moses's denial and of the anger of the Lord.

Edward began to read the Bible and to study basic theological literature. He had decided to fight Alice with her own weapons.

"Alice dear," he then said to her, "if we love God, nothing is forbidden. If we long for something, it's because of His will. Christ wanted nothing but that we should all be ruled by love."

"Yes," said Alice, "but a different love from the one you're thinking of."

"There's only one love," said Edward.

"That would certainly suit you," she said, "only God set down certain commandments, and we must abide by them."

"Yes, the Old Testament God," said Edward, "but not the Christian God."

"How's that? Surely there's only one God," objected Alice.

"Yes," said Edward, "only the Jews of the Old Testament understood him a little differently from the way we do. Before the coming of Christ, men had to abide above all by a specific system of God's commandments and laws. What a man was like inside was not so important. But Christ considered some of these prohibitions and regulations to be external. For Him, the most important thing was what a man is like inside. When a man is true to his own ardent, believing heart, everything he does will be good and pleasing to God. After all, that's why St. Paul said, 'Everything is pure to the man who is pure at heart.' "

"Only I wonder if you are this pure-hearted man."

"And St. Augustine," continued Edward, "said, 'Love

God and do what it pleases you to do.' Do you understand, Alice? Love God and do what it pleases you to do!"

"Only what pleases you will never please me," she replied, and Edward understood that his theological assault had foundered completely this time, therefore he said:

"You don't like me."

"I do," said Alice in a terribly matter-of-fact way. "And that's why I don't want us to do anything that we shouldn't do!"

As we have already mentioned, these were tormenting weeks. And the torment was that much greater because Edward's desire for Alice was not only the desire of a body for a body; on the contrary, the more she refused him her body, the more lonesome and afflicted he became and the more he coveted her heart as well. However, neither her body nor her heart wanted to do anything about it; they were equally cold, equally wrapped up in themselves, and contentedly self-sufficient.

It was precisely this unruffled moderation of hers which exasperated Edward most in his relations with Alice. Although in other respects he was quite a sober young man, he began to long for some extreme action through which he could drive Alice out of her unruffled state. And because it was too risky to provoke her through blasphemy or cynicism (to which by nature he was attracted), he had to go to the opposite (and therefore far more difficult) extreme, which would coincide with Alice's own position but would be so overdone that it would put her to shame. To put it more simply: Edward began to exaggerate his religiousness. He didn't miss a single visit to church (his desire for Alice was greater than his fear of unpleasantnesses) and once there he behaved with eccentric humility: at every opportunity he knelt, while Alice prayed beside him and crossed herself standing, because she was afraid for her stockings.

One day he criticized her for her lukewarm religiosity. He reminded her of Jesus's words: "Not everyone who says to me 'Lord, Lord' shall enter the kingdom of heaven." He criticized her, saying that her faith was formal, external, shallow. He criticized her for being too pleased with herself. He criticized her for not being aware of anyone except herself.

As he was saying all this (Alice was not prepared for his attack and defended herself feebly), he suddenly caught sight of a cross on the opposite corner of the street, an old, neglected, metal cross with a rusty, iron Christ. He pretentiously slipped his arm out from under Alice's, stopped and (as a protest against her indifferent heart and a sign of his new offensive) crossed himself with stubborn conspicuousness. He did not even really get to see how this affected Alice, because at that moment he spied on the other side of the street the woman janitor who worked at the school. She was looking at him. Edward realized that he was lost.

5

His fears were confirmed when two days later the woman janitor stopped him in the corridor and loudly informed him that he was to present himself the next day at twelve o'clock at the directress's office: "We have something to talk to you about, comrade."

Edward was overcome by anxiety. In the evening he met Alice so that, as usual, they could hang about for an hour or two in the streets, but Edward no longer pursued his religious crusade. He was downcast and longed to confide what had happened to him, but he didn't dare, because he knew that in order to save his unloved (but indispensable) job, he was ready to betray the Lord without hesitation the next morning. For this reason he preferred not to say a word about the inauspicious summons, so he couldn't even get any consolation. The following day he entered the directress's room in a mood of utter dejection.

In the room four judges awaited him: the directress, the woman janitor, one of Edward's colleagues (a tiny man with glasses), and an unknown (gray-haired) gentleman, whom the others called Comrade Inspector. The directress asked Edward to be seated, and told him they had invited him for just a friendly and unofficial talk. For, she said, the manner in which Edward had been conducting himself in his extracurricular life was making them all uneasy. As she said this she looked at the inspector, who nodded his head in agreement, then at the bespectacled teacher, who had been watching her attentively the whole time. Now, intercepting her glance, he launched into a fluent speech about how we wanted to bring up healthy young people without prejudices and how we had complete responsibility for them because we (the teachers) served as models for them. Precisely for this reason, he said, we could not countenance a religious person within our walls. He developed this thought at length and finally declared that Edward's behavior was a disgrace to the whole school.

Even a few minutes earlier Edward had been convinced that he would deny his recently acquired God and admit that his church attendance and his crossing himself in public were only jokes. Now, however, face to face with the real situation, he felt that he couldn't do it. He could not, after all, say to these four people, so serious and so excited, that they were getting excited about some misunderstanding, some bit of foolishness. He understood that to do that would be to involuntarily mock their earnestness, and he also realized that what they were expecting from him were only quibbles and excuses which they were prepared in advance to reject. He understood (in a flash, there wasn't time for lengthy cogitation) that at that moment the most important thing was for him to appear truthful—more precisely, that his statements should resemble the ideas they had constructed about him. If he was to succeed in correcting these ideas to a certain extent, he would also have to play their game to a certain extent. Therefore he said:

"Comrades, may I be frank?"

"Of course," said the directress. "After all, that's why you're here."

"And you won't be angry?"

"Just talk," said the directress.

"Very well, I shall confess to you then. I really do believe in God."

He glanced at his judges and it seemed to him that they all exhaled with satisfaction. Only the woman janitor snapped at him. "In this day and age, comrade? In this day and age?"

Edward went on. "I knew that you would get angry if I told the truth. But I don't know how to lie. Don't ask me to lie to you."

The directress said (gently): "No one wants you to lie. It's good that you are telling the truth. Only, please tell me how you, a young man, can believe in God!"

"Today, when we fly to the moon!" The teacher lost his temper.

"I can't help it," said Edward. "I don't want to believe in Him. Really, I don't."

"How come you say you don't want to believe, if you

do?" The gray-haired gentleman (in an exceedingly kind tone of voice) joined the conversation.

"I don't want to believe, but I do believe." Edward quietly repeated his confession.

The teacher laughed, "But there's a contradiction in that!"

"Comrades, I'm telling it the way it is," said Edward. "I know very well that faith in God leads us away from reality. What would socialism come to if everyone believed that the world was in God's hands? No one would do anything and everyone would just rely on God."

"Exactly," agreed the directress.

"No one has ever yet proved that God exists," stated the teacher with glasses. Edward continued: "The history of mankind is distinguished from prehistory by the fact that people have taken their fate into their own hands and do not need God."

"Faith in God leads to fatalism," said the directress.

"Faith in God belongs to the Middle Ages," said Edward, and then the directress said something again and the teacher said something and Edward said something and the inspector said something, and they were all in complete accord, until finally the teacher with glasses exploded, interrupting Edward:

"So why do you cross yourself in the street, when you know all this?"

Edward looked at him with an immensely sad expression and then said, "Because I believe in God."

"But there's a contradiction in that!" repeated the teacher joyfully.

"Yes," admitted Edward, "there is. There is a contradiction between knowledge and faith. Knowledge is one thing and faith another. I recognize that faith in God will lead us to obscurantism. I recognize that it would be better if He didn't exist. But when here inside I . . ." he pointed with his finger to his heart, "feel that He exists . . . You see, comrades, I'm telling it to you the way it is. It's better that I confess to you, because I don't want to be a hypocrite. I want you to know what I'm really like," and he hung his head.

The teacher's brain was no larger, proportionally, than his body. He didn't know that even the strictest revolutionary considers force only a necessary evil and believes the intrinsic *good* of the revolution lies in re-education. He, who had become a revolutionary overnight, did not enjoy too much respect from the directress and did not suspect that at this moment Edward, who had placed himself at his judges' disposal as a difficult case and yet as an object capable of being remolded, had a thousand times more value than he. And because he didn't suspect it, he attacked Edward with severity and declared that people who did not know how to part with their medieval faith belonged in the Middle Ages and should leave the modern school.

The directress let him finish his speech then administered her rebuke: "I don't like it when heads roll. This comrade was frank; he told us everything just as it was. We must know how to respect this." Then she turned to Edward. "The comrades are right, of course, when they say that religious people cannot educate our youth. What do you yourself suggest?"

"I don't know, comrades," said Edward unhappily.

"This is what I think," said the inspector. "The struggle between the old and the new goes on not only between classes, but also within each individual man. Just such a struggle is going on inside our comrade here. With his reason he knows, but feeling pulls him back. We must help our comrade in this struggle, so that reason may triumph."

The directress nodded. Then she said: "I myself will take charge of him."

6

Edward had thus averted the most pressing danger. His fate as a teacher was now in the hands of the directress exclusively, which was entirely to his satisfaction. He remembered his brother's observation that the directress was always after young men, and with all his vacillating, youthful self-confidence (now deflated, then exaggerated) he resolved to win the contest by gaining as a man the favor of his ruler.

When, according to an agreement, he visited her a few days later in her office, he tried to assume a light tone. He used every opportunity to slip an intimate remark or bit of subtle flattery into the conversation, or to emphasize by way of discreet double-talk his curious position as a man in the hands of a woman. But he was not to be permitted to choose the tone of the conversation. The directress spoke to him affably, but with the utmost restraint. She asked him what he was reading, then she herself named some books and recommended that he should read them. She evidently wanted to embark upon the lengthy job to be done on his thinking. Their short meeting ended with her inviting him to her place.

As a result of the directress's reserve, Edward's self-confidence was deflated again, so he entered her bachelor apartment meekly, with no intention of conquering her with his masculine charm. She seated him in an armchair and, assuming a friendly tone, asked him what he felt like having: some coffee perhaps? He said that he didn't. Some alcohol then? He was embarrassed: "If you have some cognac . . ." and was immediately afraid that he had been presumptuous. But the directress replied affably: "No, I don't have cognac, but I do have a little wine," and she fetched a half-empty bottle, whose contents were just sufficient to fill two tumblers.

Then she told Edward that he must not look upon her as some inquisitor; after all, everyone had a complete right to profess what he recognized as right. Naturally, it is another matter (she added at once) whether he is then fit or not fit to be a teacher; for that reason, she said, they had had (although they hadn't been happy about it) to summon Edward and have a talk with him and they (at least she and the inspector) were very pleased with the frank manner in which he had spoken to them, and the fact that he had not denied anything. Then she said she had talked with the inspector about Edward for a very long time and they had decided that they would summon him for another interview in six months' time and that until then the directress would help his development through her influence. And once again she emphasized that she merely wanted *to help him in a friendly way*, that she was neither an inquisitor nor a policeman. Then she mentioned the teacher who had attacked Edward so sharply, and said, "That man is hiding something himself and so he would be ready to sacrifice others. Also, the woman janitor is letting it be known everywhere that you were insolent, and pig-headedly stuck to your opinions, as she puts it. She's not to be talked out of the view that you should be dismissed from the school. Of course, I don't agree with her, but you cannot startle her so completely again. I wouldn't be happy either if someone who crosses himself publicly in the street were teaching my children."

Thus the directress showed Edward in a single outpouring of sentences how attractive were the prospects of her mercy, and also how menacing the prospects of her severity.

And then to prove that their meeting was genuinely a friendly one, she digressed to other subjects; she talked about books and led him to her bookcase. She raved about Rolland's *Enchanted Soul* and scolded him for not having read it. Then she asked how he was getting on at the school, and after his conventional reply, she herself spoke at length. She said that she was grateful to fate for her position; she liked her work because it was a means for her to educate children and thus be in continuous and real touch with the future, and only the future could, in the end, justify all this suffering, of which she said ("Yes, we must admit it") there was plenty. "If I did not believe that I was living for something more than just my own life, I couldn't perhaps live at all."

These words suddenly sounded very ingenuous and it was not clear whether the directress was trying to confess or to commence the expected ideological polemic about the meaning of life. Edward decided to interpret them in their personal sense and asked her in a low, discreet voice:

"And how about your own life?"

"My life?" she repeated after him.

"Wouldn't it have been satisfying in itself?"

A bitter smile appeared on her face and Edward felt almost sorry for her at that moment. She was pitifully hideous: her black hair cast a shadow over her bony, elongated face and the black down under her nose began to look as conspicuous as a mustache. Suddenly he glimpsed all the sorrow of her life. He perceived her gypsylike features, revealing passion, and he perceived her ugliness, revealing the hopelessness of that passion; he imagined how she had passionately turned into a living statue of grief upon Stalin's death, how she had passionately sat up late at hundreds of thousands of meetings, how she had passionately struggled against poor Jesus. And he understood that all this was only a sad outlet for her desire, which could not flow where she wished it to. Edward was young and his compassion was not used up. He looked at the directress with sympathy. She, however, as if ashamed of having involuntarily fallen silent, now assumed a brisk tone and went on:

"It doesn't depend on that at all, Edward. Anyhow, a man is not in the world only for his own sake. He always lives for something." She looked deeply into his eyes: "However, the question is for what. For something real or for something fictitious? God—that is a beautiful fiction. But the future of the people, Edward, that is reality. And I have lived for reality, I have given up everything for reality."

She spoke with such an air of commitment, that Edward did not stop feeling that sudden rush of human sympathy which had awoken in him a short while before. It struck him as stupid that he should be lying to another human being (one fellow creature to another), and it seemed to him that this intimate moment in their conversation offered him the opportunity to cast away finally the unworthy (and after all difficult) pretense of being a believer.

"But I quite agree with you," he quickly assured her. "I too prefer reality. Don't take this religion of mine so seriously."

He soon learned that a man should never let himself be led astray by a rash fit of emotion. The directress looked at him in surprise and said with perceptible coldness: "Don't pretend. I liked you because you were frank. Now you're pretending to be something that you aren't."

No, Edward was not to be permitted to step out of the religious costume in which he had originally clothed himself. He quickly reconciled himself to this and tried hard to correct the bad impression: "No, I didn't mean to be evasive. Of course I believe in God, I would never deny that. I only wanted to say that I also believe in the future of humanity, in progress and all that. After all, if I didn't believe in that, what would my work as a teacher be for? Why should children be born and why should we live at all? And I've come to think that it is also God's will that society continue to advance toward something better. I have thought that a man can believe in God and in communism, that it is possible for them to be combined."

"No," the directress smiled with maternal authoritativeness, "it isn't possible for those two things to be combined."

"I know," said Edward sadly. "Don't be angry with me."

"I'm not angry. You are still a young man and you obstinately stick to what you believe. No one understands you the way I do. After all I was young once too. I know what it's like to be young. And I like your youthfulness. Yes, I rather like you."

And now it finally happened. Neither earlier nor later, but now, at precisely the right moment. It is evident that Edward was not the instigator but merely the instrument. When the directress said she rather liked him he replied, not too expressively:

"I like you too."

"Really?"

"Really."

"Well I never! I'm an old woman . . ." objected the directress.

"That's not true," Edward had to say.

"But it is," said the directress.

"You're not at all old, that's nonsense," he had to say very resolutely.

"You think so?"

"It happens that I like you very much."

"Don't lie. You know you mustn't lie."

"I'm not lying. You're pretty."

"Pretty?" The directress made a face to show that she didn't really believe it.

"Yes, pretty," said Edward, and because he was struck by the obvious incredibility of his assertion, he at once took pains to support it: "I'm mad about black-haired women like you."

"You like black-haired women?" asked the directress.

"I'm mad about them," said Edward.

"And why haven't you come by all the time that you've been at the school? I had the feeling that you were avoiding me."

"I was ashamed," said Edward. "Everyone would have said that I was sucking up to you. No one would have believed that I was coming to see you only because I liked you."

"But you must not be ashamed," said the directress. "Now it has *been decided* that you must meet with me from time to time."

She looked into his eyes with her large brown irises (let us admit that in themselves they were beautiful), and just before he left she lightly stroked his hand, so that this foolish fellow went off with the sprightly feelings of a winner.

7

Edward was sure that the unpleasant affair had been settled to his advantage, and the next Sunday, feeling carefree and impudent, he went to church with Alice. Not only that, he went full of self-confidence—for (although this arouses in us a compassionate smile) in retrospect, he perceived the events at the directress's apartment as glaring evidence of his masculine appeal.

In addition, this particular Sunday in church he noticed that Alice was somehow different; as soon as they met she slipped her hand under his arm and even in church clung to him. Formerly she had behaved modestly and inconspicuously; now she kept looking around and smilingly greeted at least ten acquaintances.

This was curious and Edward didn't understand it.

Then two days later as they were walking together along the streets after dark, Edward became aware to his amazement that her kisses, once so unpleasantly matter-of-fact, had become damp, warm, and passionate. When they stopped for a moment under a street lamp he found that her eyes were looking amorously at him.

"Let me tell you this, I like you," blurted out Alice and immediately covered his mouth. "No, no, don't say anything; I'm ashamed, I don't want to hear anything."

Again they walked a little way and again they stopped. This time Alice said, "Now I understand everything. I understand why you reproached me for being too comfortable in my faith."

Edward, however, didn't understand anything. So he also didn't say anything. When they'd walked a bit further, Alice said, "And you didn't say anything to me. Why didn't you say anything to me?"

"And what should I have said to you?" asked Edward.

"Yes, that's you all over," she said with quiet enthusiasm. "Others would put on airs; but you are silent. But that's exactly why I like you."

Edward began to suspect what she was talking about, but nevertheless he questioned her. "What are you talking about?"

"About what happened to you."

"And who told you about it?"

"Come on! Everybody knows about it. They summoned you, they threatened you, and you laughed in their faces. You didn't retract anything. Everyone admires you."

"But I didn't tell anyone about it."

"Don't be naive. A thing like that gets around. After all, it's no small matter. How often today do you find someone who has a little courage?"

Edward knew that in a small town every event is quickly turned into a legend, but he hadn't suspected that the worthless episodes he'd been involved in, whose significance he'd never overestimated, possessed the stuff of which legends are made. He hadn't sufficiently realized how very useful he was to his fellow countrymen who, as is well-known, do not really like *heroes* (men who struggle and conquer), but rather *martyrs*, for such men soothingly reassure them about their loyal inactivity, and corroborate their view that life provides only two alternatives: to be submissive or to be destroyed. Nobody doubted that Edward would be destroyed, and admiringly and complacently they all passed this on, until now, through Alice, he himself encountered the beautiful image of his own crucifixion. He accepted it cold-bloodedly and said:

"But my not retracting anything was after all a matter of course. Anyone would have done that much."

"Anyone?" blurted out Alice. "Look around you at what they all do! How cowardly they are! They would renounce their own mothers!"

Edward was silent and Alice was silent. They walked along holding hands. Then Alice said in a whisper: "I would do anything for you."

No one had ever said such words to Edward. They

were an unexpected gift. Of course, Edward knew that they were an undeserved gift, but he said to himself that if fate withheld from him deserved gifts, he had a complete right to accept these undeserved ones. Therefore he said:

"No one can do anything for me any more."

"How's that?" whispered Alice.

"They'll drive me from the school and those who speak of me today as a hero won't lift a finger for me. Only one thing is certain. I shall remain entirely alone."

"You won't," Alice shook her head.

"I will," said Edward.

"You won't!" Alice almost shrieked.

"They've all abandoned me."

"I'll never abandon you," said Alice.

"You will," said Edward sadly.

"No, I won't," said Alice.

"No, Alice," said Edward, "you don't like me. You've never liked me."

"That's not true," whispered Alice and Edward noticed with satisfaction that her eyes were wet.

"You don't, Alice; a person can feel that sort of thing. You were always cold to me. A woman who loves a man doesn't behave like that. I know that very well. And now you feel pity for me, because you know they want to ruin me. But you don't really like me and I don't want you to deceive yourself about it."

They walked still further, silently, holding hands. Alice cried quietly for a while, then all at once she stopped walking and amid sobs said, "No, that's not true. You mustn't believe that. That's not true."

"It is," said Edward, and when Alice did not stop crying, he suggested that on Saturday they go to the country.

In a beautiful valley by the river was his brother's cottage, where they could be alone.

Alice's face was wet with tears as she dumbly nodded her assent.

8

That was on Tuesday, and when on Thursday he was again invited to the directress's bachelor apartment, he made his way there with gay self-assurance, for he had absolutely no doubt that his natural charm would definitively dissolve the church scandal into little more than a cloud of smoke, a mere nothing. But this is the way life goes: a man imagines that he is playing his role in a particular play, and does not suspect that in the meantime they have changed the scenery without his noticing, and he unknowingly finds himself in the middle of a rather different performance.

He was again seated in the armchair opposite the directress. Between them was a little table and on it a bottle of cognac and two glasses. And this bottle of cognac was precisely that new prop by which a bright man with a sober temperament would have immediately recognized that the church scandal was no longer the matter in question.

But innocent Edward was so intoxicated with himself that at first he didn't realize this at all. He quite gaily took part in the opening conversation (the subject matter of which was vague and general). He drank the glass that was offered him, and was quite ingenuously bored. After half an hour or an hour the directress inconspicuously changed to more personal topics; she talked a lot about herself and from her words there emerged before Edward the image that she wanted: that of a sensible, middle-aged woman, not too happy, but reconciled to her lot in a dignified way; a woman who regretted nothing and even expressed satisfaction that she was not married, because only in this way, after all, could she fully enjoy her independence and privacy. This life had provided her with a beautiful apartment, where she felt happy and where perhaps now Edward was also not too uncomfortable.

"No, it's really very nice here," said Edward, and he said it glumly, because just at that moment he had stopped feeling good. The bottle of cognac (which he had inadvertently asked for on his first visit and which was now hurried to the table with such menacing readiness), the four walls of the bachelor apartment (creating a space which was becoming ever more constricting and confining), the directress's monologue (focusing on subjects ever more personal), her glance (dangerously fixed), all this caused *the change of program* to begin finally to get to him. He understood that he had entered into a situation, the development of which was irrevocably predetermined. He realized that his livelihood was jeopardized not by the directress's aversion, but just the contrary, by his physical aversion to this skinny woman with the down under her nose, who was urging him to drink. His anxiety made his throat contract.

He listened to the directress and had a drink, but now his anxiety was so strong that the alcohol had no effect on him at all. On the other hand, after a couple of drinks the directress was already so thoroughly carried away that she abandoned her usual sobriety, and her words acquired an exaltation that was almost threatening. "One thing I envy you," she said, "that you are so young. You cannot know yet what disappointment is, what disillusion is. You still see the world as full of hope and beauty."

She leaned across the table in Edward's direction and in gloomy silence (with a smile that was rigidly forced) fixed her frightfully large eyes on him, while he said to himself that if he didn't manage to get a bit drunk, he'd be in real trouble before the evening was over. To that end he poured some cognac into his glass and downed it quickly.

And the directress went on: "But I want to see it like that! The way you do!" And then she got up from the armchair, thrust out her chest, and said, "That I am not a boring woman! That I'm not!" And she walked around the little table and grabbed Edward by the sleeve. "That I'm not!"

"No," said Edward.

"Come, let's dance," she said, and letting go of Edward's arm she skipped over to the radio and turned the dial until she found some dance music. Then she stood over Edward with a smile.

Edward got up, seized the directress, and began to guide her around the room to the rhythm of the music. Every now and then the directress would tenderly lay her head on his shoulder, then suddenly raise it again, to gaze into his eyes, then, after another little while, she would sing along with the melody in a low voice.

Edward felt so out of sorts that several times he stopped dancing to have a drink. He longed for nothing more than to put an end to the discomfort of this interminable trudging around, but also he feared nothing more. For the discomfort of what would follow the dancing seemed to him even more unbearable. And so he continued to guide the lady who was singing to herself around the room and at the same time steadily (and meticulously) observe in himself the influence of the alcohol, which he longed for. When it finally seemed to him that his brain was sufficiently deadened, with his right arm he firmly pressed the directress against his body and put his left hand on her breast.

Yes, he did the very thing that had been frightening him the whole evening. He would have given anything not to have had to do this, but if he did it all the same, then believe me, it was only because he really *had to*. The situation, which he had got into at the very beginning of the evening, was so compelling that, though it was no doubt possible to slow down its course, it was not possible to stop it, so that when Edward put his hand on the directress's breast, he was merely submitting to totally irreversible necessity.

The results of his action exceeded all expectations. As if by magic command, the directress began to writhe in his arms and in no time had placed her hairy upper lip on his mouth. Then she dragged him onto the couch and, wildly writhing and loudly sighing, bit his lip and the tip of his tongue, which hurt Edward a lot. Then she slipped out of his arms, said, "Wait!" and ran off to the bathroom.

Edward licked his finger and found out that his tongue was bleeding slightly. The bite hurt so much that his painstakingly induced intoxication receded, and once again his throat contracted from anxiety at the thought of what awaited him. From the bathroom could be heard a loud running and splashing of water. He picked up the bottle of cognac, put it to his lips, and drank deeply.

But by this time the directress had already appeared in the doorway in a transparent nylon nightgown (thickly decorated with lace over the breasts), and was walking steadily toward Edward. She embraced him. Then she stepped back and reproachfully asked, "Why are you still dressed?"

Edward took off his jacket and, looking at the directress (who had her big eyes fixed on him), he couldn't think of anything but the fact that there was the greatest likelihood that his body would sabotage his assiduous will. Wishing therefore to arouse his body somehow or other, he said in an uncertain voice, "Undress completely."

With a violent and enthusiastically obedient movement she flung off her nylon nightie and bared her skinny white body, in the middle of which her thick black bush protruded in gloomy desolation. She came slowly toward him and with terror Edward discovered what he already knew anyway: his body was completely fettered by anxiety.

I know, gentlemen, that in the course of the years you have become accustomed to the occasional insubordination of your own bodies, and that this no longer upsets you at all. But understand, Edward was young then! His body's sabotage threw him into an incredible panic each time and he bore it as an inexpiable disgrace, whether the witness to it was a beautiful face or one as hideous and comical as the directress's. The directress was now only a step away from him, and he, frightened and not knowing what to do, all at once said, he didn't even know how (it was rather the fruit of inspiration than of cunning reflection): "No, no, oh Lord, no! No, it is a sin, it would be a sin!" and jumped away.

The directress kept coming toward him muttering in a husky voice: "What sin? There is no sin!"

Edward retreated behind the round table, where they had been sitting a while before: "No, I can't do this, I can't do it."

The directress pushed aside the armchair, standing in her path, and went after Edward, never taking her large brown eyes off him: "There is no sin! There is no sin!"

Edward went around the table, behind him was only the couch and the directress was a mere step away. Now he could no longer escape and perhaps his very desperation advised him at this moment of impasse to command her: "Kneel!"

She stared at him uncomprehendingly, but when he once again repeated in a firm (though desperate) voice, "Kneel!" she enthusiastically fell to her knees in front of him and embraced his legs.

"Take those hands off," he called her to order. "Clasp them!"

Once again she looked at him uncomprehendingly.

"Clasp them! Did you hear?"

She clasped her hands.

"Pray," he commanded.

She had her hands clasped and she glanced up at him devotedly.

"Pray, so that God may forgive us," he hissed.

She had her hands clasped. She was looking up at him with her large eyes and Edward not only obtained an advantageous respite, but looking down at her from above, he began to lose the oppressive feeling that he was mere prey, and he regained his self-assurance. He stepped back, away from her, so that he could survey the whole of her, and once again commanded, "Pray!"

When she remained silent, he yelled: "Aloud!"

And the skinny, naked, kneeling woman began to recite: "Our Father, who art in heaven, hallowed be Thy name, Thy kingdom come. . . ."

As she uttered the words of the prayer, she glanced up at him as if he were God Himself. He watched her with growing pleasure. In front of him was kneeling the directress, being humiliated by a subordinate; in front of him a naked revolutionary was being humiliated by prayer; in front of him a praying lady was being humiliated by her nakedness.

This threefold image of degradation intoxicated him and something unexpected suddenly happened: his body revoked its passive resistance. Edward was excited!

As the directress said, "And lead us not into temptation," he quickly threw off all his clothes. When she said, "Amen," he violently lifted her off the floor and dragged her onto the couch.

9

That was on Thursday, and on Saturday Edward went with Alice to the country to visit his brother, who welcomed them warmly and lent them the key to the nearby cottage.

The two lovers spent the whole afternoon wandering through the woods and meadows. They kissed and Edward's contented hands found that the imaginary line, level with her navel which separated the sphere of innocence from that of fornication, didn't count any more. At first he wanted to verify the so long awaited event verbally, but he became frightened of doing so and understood that he had to keep silent.

His judgment was quite correct, it seemed. Alice's unexpected turnabout had occurred independently of his many weeks of persuasion, independently of his argumentation, independently of any *logical* consideration whatsoever. In fact, it was based exclusively upon the news of Edward's martyrdom, consequently upon *a mistake*, and it had been deduced quite *illogically* even from this mistake. Why should Edward's sufferings for his fidelity to his beliefs have as a result Alice's infidelity to God's law? If Edward had not betrayed God before the fact-finding commission, why should she now betray Him before Edward?

In such a situation any reflection expressed aloud could reveal to Alice the inconsistency of her attitude. So Edward prudently kept silent, which went unnoticed, because Alice herself kept chattering. She was gay, and nothing indicated that this turnabout in her soul had been dramatic or painful.

When it got dark they went back to the cottage, turned on the lights, made the bed, and kissed, whereupon Alice asked Edward to turn off the lights. However, the light of the stars continued to show through the window, so Edward had to close the shutters as well upon Alice's request. Then, in total darkness, Alice undressed and gave herself to him.

Edward had been looking forward to this moment for so many weeks, but surprisingly enough, now, when it was actually taking place, he didn't have the feeling that it would be as significant as the length of time he had been waiting for it suggested; it seemed to him so easy and self-evident that during the act of intercourse he was almost not concentrating. Rather, he was vainly trying to drive away the thoughts that were running through his head of those long, futile weeks when Alice had tormented him with her coldness. It all came back to him: the suffering at the school, of which she had been the cause, and, instead of gratitude for her giving of herself to him, he began to feel a certain vindictiveness and anger. It irritated him how easily and remorselessly she was now betraying her God of No Fornication, whom she had once so fanatically worshiped. It irritated him that nothing was able to throw her off balance, no desire, no event, no upset. It irritated him how she experienced everything without inner conflict—self-confidently and easily. And when this irritation threatened to overcome him with its power, he strove to make love to her passionately and furiously so as to force from her some sort of sound, moan, word, or pathetic cry, but he didn't succeed. The girl was quiet and in spite of all his exertions in their love-making, it ended silently and undramatically.

Then she snuggled up against his chest and quickly fell asleep, while Edward lay awake for a long time and realized that he felt no joy at all. He made an effort to imagine Alice (not her physical appearance but, if possible, her being in its entirety) and it occurred to him that he saw her *blurred*.

Let's stop at this word: Alice, as Edward had seen her until this time, was, with all her naiveté, a stable and distinct being. The beautiful simplicity of her looks seemed to accord with the unaffected simplicity of her faith, and her simple fate seemed to be a substantiation of her attitude. Until this time Edward had seen her as solid and coherent; he could laugh at her, he could curse her, he could besiege her with his guile, but he (involuntarily) had to respect her.

Now, however, the unpremeditated snare of false news caused a split in the coherence of her being and it seemed to Edward that her convictions were in fact only something *extraneous* to her fate, and her fate only something extraneous to her body. He saw her as an accidental conjunction of a body, thoughts, and a life's course; an inorganic conjunction, arbitrary and unstable. He visualized Alice (she was breathing deeply on his shoulder) and he saw her body separately from her thoughts. He liked this body but the thoughts struck him as ridiculous, and together they did not form a whole being. He saw her as an ink line spreading on blotting paper, without contours, without shape.

He really liked this body. When Alice got up in the morning, he forced her to remain naked, and, although just yesterday she had stubbornly insisted on closed shutters, for even the dim light of the stars had bothered her, she now altogether forgot her shame. Edward was scrutinizing her (she gaily pranced about, looking for a package of tea and cookies for breakfast), and Alice, when she glanced at him after a moment, noticed that he was lost in thought. She asked him what was the matter. Edward replied that after breakfast he had to go and see his brother.

His brother inquired how he was getting on at the school. Edward replied that on the whole it was fine, and his brother said, "That Chehachkova is a pig, but I forgave her long ago. I forgave her, for she did not know what she was doing. She wanted to harm me, but instead she helped me find a beautiful life. As a farmer I earn more, and contact with Nature protects me from the skepticism to which city-dwellers are prone."

"That woman, as a matter of fact, brought me some happiness too," said Edward, lost in thought, and he told his brother how he had fallen in love with Alice, how he had feigned a belief in God, how they had judged him, how Chehachkova had wanted to re-educate him, and how Alice had finally given herself to him thinking he was a martyr. The only thing he didn't tell was how he had forced the directress to recite the Lord's Prayer, because he saw disapproval in his brother's eyes. He stopped talking and his brother said:

"I may have a great many faults, but one I don't have: I've never dissimulated and I've said to everyone's face what I thought."

Edward liked his brother and his disapproval hurt, so he made an effort to justify himself and they began to argue. In the end Edward said:

"I know, brother, that you are a straightforward man, and that you pride yourself on it. But put one question to yourself: *why* in fact should one tell the truth? What obliges us to do it? And why do we consider telling the truth a virtue? Imagine that you meet a madman, who claims that he is a fish and that we are all fish. Are you going to argue with him? Are you going to undress in front of him and show him that you don't have fins? Are you going to say to his face what you think? Well, tell me!"

His brother was silent and Edward went on: "If you told him the whole truth and nothing but the truth, only what you really thought, you would enter into a serious conversation with a madman and you yourself would become mad. And it is the same way with the world that surrounds us. If I obstinately told a man the truth to his face, it would mean that I was taking him seriously. And to take something so unimportant seriously means to become less than serious oneself. I, you see, *must* lie, if I don't want to take madmen seriously and become one of them myself."

10

It was Sunday afternoon and the two lovers left for town. They were alone in a compartment (the girl was already gaily chattering away again), and Edward remembered how some time ago he had looked forward to finding in Alice, whom he'd chosen voluntarily, the seriousness of life, which his duties would never provide for him. And with regret he realized (the train idyllically clattered against the joints between the rails) that the love affair he'd experienced with Alice was worthless, made up of chance and errors, without any importance or sense whatsoever. He heard Alice's words, he saw her gestures (she squeezed his hand), and it occurred to him that these were signs devoid of meaning, currency without funds, weights made of paper, and that he couldn't grant them significance any more than God could the prayer of the naked directress. And all of a sudden it seemed to him that, in fact, all the people whom he'd met in his new place of work were only ink lines spreading on blotting paper, beings with interchangeable attitudes, beings without firm substance. But what was worse, what was far worse (it struck him next) was that he himself was only a shadow of all these shadowy people. After all, he had been exhausting his own brain only to adjust to them and imitate them. Yet even if he was inwardly laughing, and thus making an effort to mock them secretly (and so exonerate his accommodation), it didn't alter the case. For even malicious imitation remains imitation, and the shadow that mocks remains a shadow, subordinate, derivative, and wretched, and nothing more.

It was ignominious, horribly ignominious. The train idyllically clattered against the joints between the rails (the girl chattered away) and Edward said:

"Alice, are you happy?"

"Sure," said Alice.

"I'm miserable," said Edward.

"What, are you crazy?" said Alice.

"We shouldn't have done it. It shouldn't have happened."

"What's gotten into you? After all, you're the one who wanted to do it!"

"Yes, I wanted to," said Edward, "but that was my greatest mistake, for which God will never forgive me. It was a sin, Alice."

"Come on, what's happened to you?" said the girl calmly. "You yourself always used to say that God wants love most of all!"

When Edward heard Alice, after the fact, coolly appropriating the theological sophistries with which he had so unsuccessfully taken the field a while ago, fury seized him:

"I used to say that to test you. Now I've found out how well you are able to be faithful to God! But a person who is able to betray God is able to betray man a hundred times more easily."

Alice found more ready answers, but it would have been better for her if she hadn't, because they only provoked his vindictive rage. Edward went on and on talking (in the end he used the words "disgust" and "physical aversion") until finally he did obtain from this placid and gentle face sobs, tears, and moans.

"Goodbye," he told her at the station and left her in tears. Only at home several hours later, when this curious anger had subsided, did it occur to him what he had done. He imagined her body, which had pranced stark naked in front of him that morning, and when he realized that this beautiful body was lost to him because he himself, of his own free will, had driven it away, he inwardly called himself an idiot and had a mind to slap his own face.

But what had happened, had happened, and it was no longer possible to right anything.

Though we must truthfully say that even if the idea of the beautiful, rejected body caused Edward a certain amount of grief, he coped with this loss fairly soon. If once the need for physical love had tormented him and reduced him to a state of longing, it was the short-lived need of a recent arrival. Edward no longer suffered from this need. Once a week he visited the directress (habit had relieved his body of its initial anxieties), and he resolved to continue to visit her, until his position at the school was clarified. Besides this, with increasing success he chased all sorts of other women and girls. As a consequence of both, he began to appreciate far more the times when he was alone, and became fond of solitary walks, which he sometimes combined (come, let us turn our attention to this for the last time) with a visit to a church.

No, don't be apprehensive, Edward did not begin to believe in God. Our story does not intend to be crowned with the effect of so ostentatious a paradox. But Edward, even if he was almost certain that God did not exist, after all felt happy and nostalgic entertaining the thought of Him.

God is essence itself, whereas Edward had never found (and since the incidents with the directress and with Alice, a number of years had passed) anything essential in his love affairs, or in his teaching, or in his thoughts. He was too bright to concede that he saw the essential in the unessential, but he was too weak not to long secretly for the essential.

Ah, ladies and gentlemen, a man lives a sad life when he cannot take anything or anyone seriously.

And that is why Edward longed for God, for God alone is relieved of the distracting obligation of *appearing* and can merely *be*. For He solely constitutes (He Himself, alone and nonexistent) the essential opposite of this unessential (but so much more existent) world.

And so Edward occasionally sits in church and looks thoughtfully at the cupola. Let us take leave of him at just such a time. It is afternoon, the church is quiet and empty. Edward is sitting in a pew tormented with sorrow, because God does not exist. But just at this moment his sorrow is so great that suddenly from its depth emerges the genuine *living* face of God. Look! Yes. Edward is smiling! He is smiling, and his smile is happy . . .

Please, keep him in your memory with this smile.

FOR THE BEST IN PAPERBACKS, LOOK FOR THE

In every corner of the world, on every subject under the sun, Penguin represents quality and variety – the very best in publishing today.

For complete information about books available from Penguin – including Pelicans, Puffins, Peregrines and Penguin Classics – and how to order them, write to us at the appropriate address below. Please note that for copyright reasons the selection of books varies from country to country.

In the United Kingdom: Please write to *Dept E.P., Penguin Books Ltd, Harmondsworth, Middlesex, UB7 0DA*

In the United States: Please write to *Dept BA, Penguin, 299 Murray Hill Parkway, East Rutherford, New Jersey 07073*

In Canada: Please write to *Penguin Books Canada Ltd, 2801 John Street, Markham, Ontario L3R 1B4*

In Australia: Please write to the *Marketing Department, Penguin Books Australia Ltd, P.O. Box 257, Ringwood, Victoria 3134*

In New Zealand: Please write to the *Marketing Department, Penguin Books (NZ) Ltd, Private Bag, Takapuna, Auckland 9*

In India: Please write to *Penguin Overseas Ltd, 706 Eros Apartments, 56 Nehru Place, New Delhi, 110019*

In Holland: Please write to *Penguin Books Nederland B.V., Postbus 195, NL–1380AD Weesp, Netherlands*

In Germany: Please write to *Penguin Books Ltd, Friedrichstrasse 10–12, D–6000 Frankfurt Main 1, Federal Republic of Germany*

In Spain: Please write to *Longman Penguin España, Calle San Nicolas 15, E–28013 Madrid, Spain*

In France: Please write to *Penguin Books Ltd, 39 Rue de Montmorency, F-75003, Paris, France*

In Japan: Please write to *Longman Penguin Japan Co Ltd, Yamaguchi Building, 2–12–9 Kanda Jimbocho, Chiyoda-Ku, Tokyo 101, Japan*

A SELECTION OF FICTION AND NON-FICTION

The Rebel Angels   Robertson Davies

A glittering extravaganza of wit, scatology, saturnalia, mysticism and erudite vaudeville. 'He's the kind of writer who makes you want to nag your friends until they read him so that they can share the pleasure' – *Observer*. 'His novels will be recognized with the very best works of this century' – J. K. Galbraith in *The New York Times Book Review*

Still Life   A. S. Byatt

In this sequel to her much praised *The Virgin in the Garden*, A. S. Byatt illuminates the inevitable conflicts between ambition and domesticity, confinement and self-fulfilment while providing an incisive observation of cultural life in England during the 1950s. 'Affords enormous and continuous pleasure' – Anita Brookner in the *Standard*

Heartbreak Hotel   Gabrielle Burton

'If *Heartbreak Hotel* doesn't make you laugh, perhaps you are no longer breathing. Check all vital signs of life, and read this book!' – Rita Mae Brown. 'A novel to take us into the next century, heads high and flags flying' – Fay Weldon

August in July   Carlo Gébler

On the eve of the Royal Wedding, as the nation prepares for celebration, August Slemic's world prepares to fall apart. 'There is no question but that he must now be considered a novelist of major importance' – *Daily Telegraph*. 'A meticulous study, done with great sympathy . . . a thoroughly honest and loving book' – *Financial Times*

The News from Ireland   William Trevor

'An ability to enchant as much as chill has made Trevor unquestionably one of our greatest short-story writers' – *The Times*. 'A masterly collection' – *Daily Telegraph*. 'Extremely impressive . . . of his stature as a writer there can be no question' – *New Statesman*

A SELECTION OF FICTION AND NON-FICTION

A Confederacy of Dunces John Kennedy Toole

In this Pulitzer-Prize-winning novel, in the bulky figure of Ignatius J. Reilly, an immortal comic character is born. 'I succumbed, stunned and seduced . . . it is a masterwork of comedy' – *The New York Times*

The Labyrinth of Solitude Octavio Paz

Nine remarkable essays by Mexico's finest living poet: 'A profound and original book . . . with Lowry's *Under the Volcano* and Eisenstein's *Que Viva Mexico!*, *The Labyrinth of Solitude* completes the trinity of master-works about the spirit of modern Mexico' – *Sunday Times*

Falconer John Cheever

Ezekiel Farragut, fratricide with a heroin habit, comes to Falconer Correctional Facility. His freedom is enclosed, his view curtailed by iron bars. But he is a man, none the less, and the vice, misery and degradation of prison change a man . . .

The Memory of War and Children in Exile: (Poems 1968–83) James Fenton

'James Fenton is a poet I find myself again and again wanting to praise' – *Listener*. 'His assemblages bring with them tragedy, comedy, love of the world's variety, and the sadness of its moral blight' – *Observer*

The Bloody Chamber Angela Carter

In tales that glitter and haunt – strange nuggets from a writer whose wayward pen spills forth stylish, erotic, nightmarish jewels of prose – the old fairy stories live and breathe again, subtly altered, subtly changed.

Cannibalism and the Common Law A. W. Brian Simpson

In 1884 Tod Dudley and Edwin Stephens were sentenced to death for killing their shipmate in order to eat him. A. W. Brian Simpson unfolds the story of this macabre case in 'a marvellous rangy, atmospheric, complicated book . . . an irresistible blend of sensation and scholarship' – Jonathan Raban in the *Sunday Times*

Cat's Grin François Maspero

'Reflects in some measure the experience of every French person . . . evacuees, peasants, Resistance fighters, *collabos* . . . Maspero's painfully truthful book helps to ensure that it never seems commonplace' – *Literary Review*

The Moronic Inferno Martin Amis

'This is really good reading and sharp, crackling writing. Amis has a beguiling mixture of confidence and courtesy, and most of his literary judgements – often twinned with interviews – seem sturdy, even when caustic, without being bitchy for the hell of it' – *Guardian*

In Custody Anita Desai

Deven, a lecturer in a small town in Northern India, is resigned to a life of mediocrity and empty dreams. When asked to interview the greatest poet of Delhi, Deven discovers a new kind of dignity, both for himself and his dreams.

Parallel Lives Phyllis Rose

In this study of five famous Victorian marriages, including that of John Ruskin and Effie Gray, Phyllis Rose probes our inherited myths and assumptions to make us look again at what we expect from our marriages.

Lamb Bernard MacLaverty

In the Borstal run by Brother Benedict, boys are taught a little of God and a lot of fear. Michael Lamb, one of the brothers, runs away and takes a small boy with him. As the outside world closes in around them, Michael is forced to an uncompromising solution.

A CHOICE OF PENGUIN FICTION

Stanley and the Women Kingsley Amis

Just when Stanley Duke thinks it safe to sink into middle age, his son goes insane – and Stanley finds himself beset on all sides by women, each of whom seems to have an intimate acquaintance with madness. 'Very good, very powerful . . . beautifully written' – Anthony Burgess in the *Observer*

The Girls of Slender Means Muriel Spark

A world and a war are winding up with a bang, and in what is left of London, all the nice people are poor – and about to discover how different the new world will be. 'Britain's finest post-war novelist' – *The Times*

Him with His Foot in His Mouth Saul Bellow

A collection of first-class short stories. 'If there is a better living writer of fiction, I'd very much like to know who he or she is' – *The Times*

Mother's Helper Maureen Freely

A superbly biting and breathtakingly fluent attack on certain libertarian views, blending laughter, delight, rage and amazement, this is a novel you won't forget. 'A winner' – *The Times Literary Supplement*

Decline and Fall Evelyn Waugh

A comic yet curiously touching account of an innocent plunged into the sham, brittle world of high society. Evelyn Waugh's first novel brought him immediate public acclaim and is still a classic of its kind.

Stars and Bars William Boyd

Well-dressed, quite handsome, unfailingly polite and charming, who would guess that Henderson Dores, the innocent Englishman abroad in wicked America, has a guilty secret? 'Without doubt his best book so far . . . made me laugh out loud' – *The Times*

A CHOICE OF PENGUIN FICTION

The Ghost Writer   Philip Roth

Philip Roth's celebrated novel about a young writer who meets and falls in love with Anne Frank in New England – or so he thinks. 'Brilliant, witty and extremely elegant' – *Guardian*

Small World   David Lodge

Shortlisted for the 1984 Booker Prize, *Small World* brings back Philip Swallow and Maurice Zapp for a jet-propelled journey into hilarity. 'The most brilliant and also the funniest novel that he has written' – *London Review of Books*

Moon Tiger   Penelope Lively

Winner of the 1987 Booker Prize, *Moon Tiger* is Penelope Lively's 'most ambitious book to date' – *The Times* 'A complex tapestry of great subtlety . . . Penelope Lively writes so well, savouring the words as she goes' – *Daily Telegraph* 'A very clever book: it is evocative, thought-provoking and hangs curiously on the edges of the mind long after it is finished' – *Literary Review*

Absolute Beginners   Colin MacInnes

The first 'teenage' novel, the classic of youth and disenchantment, *Absolute Beginners* is part of MacInnes's famous London trilogy – and now a brilliant film. 'MacInnes caught it first – and best' – *Harpers and Queen*

July's People   Nadine Gordimer

Set in South Africa, this novel gives us an unforgettable look at the terrifying, tacit understandings and misunderstandings between blacks and whites. 'This is the best novel that Miss Gordimer has ever written' – Alan Paton in the *Saturday Review*

The Ice Age   Margaret Drabble

'A continuously readable, continuously surprising book . . . here is a novelist who is not only popular and successful but formidably growing towards real stature' – *Observer*

A CHOICE OF PENGUIN FICTION

The Power and the Glory   Graham Greene

During an anti-clerical purge in one of the southern states of Mexico, the last priest is hunted like a hare. Too humble for martyrdom, too human for heroism, he is nevertheless impelled towards his squalid Calvary. 'There is no better story-teller in English today' – V. S. Pritchett

The Enigma of Arrival   V. S. Naipaul

'For sheer abundance of talent, there can hardly be a writer alive who surpasses V. S. Naipaul. Whatever we may want in a novelist is to be found in his books . . .' – Irving Howe in *The New York Times Book Review*. 'Naipaul is always brilliant' – Anthony Burgess in the *Observer*

Earthly Powers   Anthony Burgess

Anthony Burgess's magnificent masterpiece, an enthralling, epic narrative spanning six decades and spotlighting some of the most vivid events and characters of our times. 'Enormous imagination and vitality . . . a huge book in every way' – Bernard Levin in the *Sunday Times*

The Penitent   Isaac Bashevis Singer

From the Nobel Prize-winning author comes a powerful story of a man who has material wealth but feels spiritually impoverished. 'Singer . . . restates with dignity the spiritual aspirations and the cultural complexities of a lifetime, and it must be said that in doing so he gives the Evil One no quarter and precious little advantage' – Anita Brookner in the *Sunday Times*

Paradise Postponed   John Mortimer

'Hats off to John Mortimer. He's done it again' – *Spectator*. A rumbustious, hilarious novel from the creator of Rumpole, *Paradise Postponed* examines British life since the war to discover why Paradise has always been postponed.

The Balkan Trilogy and Levant Trilogy   Olivia Manning

'The finest fictional record of the war produced by a British writer. Her gallery of personages is huge, her scene painting superb, her pathos controlled, her humour quiet and civilized' – *Sunday Times*

Maia   Richard Adams

The heroic romance of love and war in an ancient empire from one of our greatest storytellers. 'Enormous and powerful' – *Financial Times*

The Warning Bell   Lynne Reid Banks

A wonderfully involving, truthful novel about the choices a woman must make in her life – and the price she must pay for ignoring the counsel of her own heart. 'Lynne Reid Banks knows how to get to her reader: this novel grips like Super Glue' – *Observer*

Doctor Slaughter   Paul Theroux

Provocative and menacing – a brilliant dissection of lust, ambition and betrayal in 'civilized' London. 'Witty, chilly, exuberant, graphic' – *The Times Literary Supplement*

Wise Virgin   A. N. Wilson

Giles Fox's work on the Pottle manuscript, a little-known thirteenth-century tract on virginity, leads him to some innovative research on the subject that takes even his breath away. 'A most elegant and chilling comedy' – *Observer* Books of the Year

Gone to Soldiers   Marge Piercy

Until now, the passions, brutality and devastation of the Second World War have only been written about by men. Here for the first time, one of America's major writers brings a woman's depth and intensity to the panorama of world war. 'A victory' – *Newsweek*

Trade Wind   M. M. Kaye

An enthralling blend of history, adventure and romance from the author of the bestselling *The Far Pavilions*

The Farewell Party

A telephone call announcing an unwanted pregnancy sends Klima, jazz trumpeter from Prague, back to the fertility spa where he had spent a night with a pretty nurse named Ruzena. As Klima tries to persuade Ruzena to have an abortion, as Ruzena wavers between compliance and refusal, others are drawn into the conflict . . . And Kundera's novel opens up a brilliant exposé of the illusions and ambiguities by which we live.

'Kundera, himself an internal exile in post-Dubček Czechoslovakia . . . remains faithful to his subtle, wily, devious talent for fiction of "erotic possibilities" . . . *The Farewell Party* is the kind of "polical novel" a cunning, resourceful, gifted writer writes when it is no longer possible to write political novels' – *The New York Times Book Review*

The Joke

When Ludvik sends his girlfriend Marketa a postcard – 'Optimism is the opium of the people . . . Long live Trotsky' – she is not amused. Nor are the authorities. So Ludvik is sent to exercise his unappreciated sense of humour in a labour camp.

Joke follows joke, until Kundera's satirical love-story reaches its magnificent climax and fate, quite unexpectedly, steals the last laugh . . .

The Book of Laughter and Forgetting

'No question about it. The most important novel published in Britain this year was Milan Kundera's *The Book of Laughter and Forgetting*, a whirling dance of a book by a Czech novelist who is fully the equal of the great satirist Japoslav Hašek, creator of *The Good Soldier Švejk*. Kundera is a self-confessed hedonist in a world beset by politics, and his marvellous novel mingles a hedonist's love of eroticism, fantasy and fun with knife-sharp political satire (it recounts, for example, the case of a Communist leader who is so thoroughly erased from history that nothing is left of him but his hat). A masterpiece, full of angels, terror, ostriches and love' – Salman Rushdie in the *Sunday Times*